I0536842

Wait!

An Oxley College Novel
#2

STACEY NASH

Wait!

Copyright © Stacey Nash 2015
First published in Australia 2015 by Stacey Nash

All rights reserved.

The right of Stacey Nash to be identified as the author of this work has been asserted by her under the *Copyright Amendment (Moral Rights) Act 2000.*

This book is a work of fiction. Characters, events, and incidents either are products of the author's imagination or are used fictitiously. Any resemblance to event or actual persons, living or dead, is entirely coincidental.

This book or any portion thereof may not be reproduced or transmitted in any form by any means, electronic or mechanical, including photocopying, recording, or by any information storage system without the express written permission of the author except for the use of brief quotations in a book review.

Edited by **Lauren McKellar**
Cover Art by **KILA Designs**
Interior Design by **Max Effect**

By Stacey Nash

Forget Me Not (*Collective Series, #1*)
Remember Me (*Collective Series, #2*)
Coming Soon!
Never Forgotten (*Collective Series, #3*)

Shh! (*Oxley College Saga, #1*)
Wait! (*Oxley College Saga, #2*)
Coming Soon!
Stop? (*Oxley College Saga, #3*)

Dedication

TO MY PARENTS,

who taught me what it means

to be loved.

O-Week

Chapter 1
Jordan

"**DUDE. YOU** going to get your arse out of that car and help me, or what?"

The way Logan sat frozen in the damn Corolla staring at the back wall of Oxley College, you'd think he was the one moving in. Those days were long gone for him now though—almost three months since he'd graduated and four years since he'd lived right here, at the same dorm he'd nagged me to choose. Not that I really had any choice. I wasn't in a position to pick. Pizza boys sure as hell don't earn enough to cover the boarding fees, so when he nudged me to apply for a residential scholarship I did, thinking it would be a long shot.

"Yeah," my brother replied, slamming the door which immediately popped back open. His old car was dodgy as all shit. "Block D, right?"

I fished the key out of my pocket and checked the tag for the tenth time. "Yep."

With a single finger, which was all he could pry off the box of my stuff in his hands, Logan pointed toward a top floor window. "Great view of the car park."

Repositioning the quilt tossed over my shoulder, I jostled the suitcase Liv had insisted I borrow into my free hand and scooped up the clothes airer she'd said I couldn't live without. "Whatever, man. You gonna lock this piece of crap?"

"Respect the Corolla. This old girl has reliably driven you around for years. She's good as new." Logan walked toward the path that led out of the car park.

"Wishful thinking, bro."

He led the way into what I guessed was the back courtyard. I'd never set foot inside Oxley before, but with all the talk from him and Liv, I felt as if I'd lived there with them. Armidale was a country town, but UNE was a decent sized university with several residential dorms. According to my brother and his girl, Oxley was the pick of them all. The other half a dozen seemed much the same to me, only this one had co-ed blocks. Not many did.

Logan turned to the left and bounded down a few steps then around to the left again and into the front courtyard. Apparently Oxley had two main areas in which to hang out, both courtyards, aptly named Front and Back. We passed one door and he swung into the second that had a placard right by it announcing the entrance as 'D.' Logan stuck his head into an open doorway on the left like he owned the place and shouted, "Anyone home?"

"Logan Hays!" A dude that looked like he'd enjoyed a few too many upsized burger combos emerged from inside and slapped my brother on the shoulder.

"Dono. You still here? It's been what ..."

"Five years."

"Man, you gotta be close to done."

"Perfection takes time." The guy grinned at me. "This Jordan?"

"Yup. Make sure you watch out for him for me." Logan said.

"Geez, Loges. I can look after myself."

Dono nodded at my brother, but his grin remained fixed on me. "There's a welcome pack on your desk. I'm having a meet and greet down here at five, right before tonight's function. Make sure you're here."

"Sure," I said.

Logan climbed the steep staircase before Dono was back in his room.

"Pick up that quilt or it'll be covered in filth by the time we get to the top," Logan ordered over his shoulder. Sure enough the blue fabric scraped across the brown tiles.

"Quit it," I growled, but scooped it up anyway, double layering the thing over my shoulder. We trudged up two flights of stairs, past what seemed to be one floor of dorm rooms and all the way to the top, where the dark tiles ended in a hand-railed landing and a wedged open door. I drew a deep breath, pausing before I entered. College life would be different. Meeting new people was always ... well, it was what it was. They'd ask questions and expect answers. Delve into all that personal crap that was none of their goddamn business. I was only really here in the dorms to give Logan and Liv some space, and to shut them up. I could have just as easily lived in our apartment while I studied.

3

Music blared through the hall as we entered and damn, someone had good taste. The bass of Quiet Renegade practically rattled the walls and I found myself smiling as I mouthed the words I knew well. They weren't all that popular a band, but rather more of a unique genre Logan had introduced me to a few years ago.

Meanwhile, he'd stopped in front of the second door on the left. He grinned at me with that dumbass half a smile he usually reserved for Liv. "This is it, little bro."

I fished the key from my pocket and jammed it into the lock, then used my shoulder to shove the door open. The musty smell that hit me wasn't nasty or unpleasant … more like the room had been closed up for far too long. Logan drew an audible breath and exhaled, as if it were the best smell in the world. The guy was weird as they came.

"You're gonna love it here," he told me, dumping his armload onto the tiny single bed that rested against the wall. No way would I fit in that. Not after the double I'd had at home for the past three years.

I emptied my stuff onto the wooden bench and turned around. "So you keep telling me."

"Get the hell out," a girl screamed in excitement. Logan and I exchanged a curious glance, and I poked my head into the hall. Not that it was any use. There was only one open door and no one there anyway.

Logan shouldered past me. "I'll go grab the last load of stuff. You stay here and meet the natives." Once in the hall he gave me a knowing look before disappearing through the door that led to the stairwell.

As indifferent as I felt about being at Oxley, curiosity

had me by the balls. That open door was a lure I couldn't ignore. Screw unpacking; it could wait for later. I sauntered right up to the room in question and propped my arm on the doorjamb, ready to meet my screeching neighbour. But blow me down, if the room wasn't empty. Of people, at least. Whoever lived there had a wicked setup. Twin speakers were perched on either side of the desk and that was where Quiet Renegade boomed from. Posters of the band plastered the cement-rendered walls and a kickass-sized bottle of vodka sat centre stage on the wooden desk. A small TV was jammed into the corner and despite the earlier screeching, this sure didn't look like a chick's room. Well, other than the vodka.

Unsure if I should stand there and wait, I lingered a moment. There didn't seem to be anyone around though, so I returned to my room. There wasn't a lot to unpack, and by the time Logan returned I'd just about finished. He dropped a grocery bag on the desk. "From Liv."

"Geez." I peeked inside. "A sandwich press? And ... are they muffins? That woman's out of control."

"Watch it," Logan warned.

I shot him a grin since I hadn't meant it as an insult and peeled open the container of baked goods. Logan shook his head to say he didn't want one. That didn't stop me though. Those things were like heaven in a paper wrapper. Logan parked his rear on the bed and watched me eat like the freak he'd become this past week.

"Go home," I told him around a mouthful. "There's nothing for you to do."

Logan continued staring at me, and holy hell, was the sissy tearing up? He scrubbed a hand along his jeans.

"Make sure you swing by, all right? I'm gonna miss seeing your ugly mug every morning."

"Dude. I'm like five minutes away. Grow a pair already."

"Just say you'll do it."

"Fine, I'll do it."

It's not like I wouldn't. I'd miss his face too, not that I'd ever admit it. He'd probably cry for real then and I didn't need that shit.

Logan dragged his arse up off the bed and clapped me on the shoulder. I snuck my arm under his and pulled him in for a hug. "See you on Tuesday."

"Tuesday?"

"Yep. Liv's cooking dinner."

Logan smiled as if I'd given him the last slice of Meat Lover's pizza. "All right. Then ... I guess this is it."

"Get out already!" I shooed his overprotective arse toward the door and once he was out, pulled it closed behind him. Dropping onto the bed, I spun the delicate silver ring around my pinkie finger. No way was I gonna cry, but there was a stupid lump in my throat that would have made talking difficult.

Chapter 2
Hex

ADMIRING MY nails, which were longer than they'd ever been, I poured myself a liberal splash of vodka and mixed it with lemonade. Liquid courage, that's what this was, and I'd only need one more then I'd be right to head downstairs to the party that was happening tonight. I didn't bother with the stupid meet-and-greet the senior guy said I must to attend. Mum had only just left by the time five rolled around and I'd wanted to catch a quick nap since we'd had an early start.

From my window, I could see people filling the courtyard. The music blared loudly, dead opposite to the voices, I assumed. Everyone looked a little awkward, standing around, cradling plastic cups as if they were scared of each other. It wasn't hard to pick out the seniors. They all rocked massive smiles and worked the crowd.

I tipped my head back and downed the drink in a single gulp. Well, only one way to make this crap downstairs bearable. *Eeesh*. The drink practically stole my breath. I must have made it a bit strong.

A quick look in the mirror and everything was in place—my hair looked pretty decent, shorts weren't riding up my butt, and all the essentials were tucked away beneath my tank top. Everyone had said it was going to be freaking freezing here in Armidale, but so far it was like living in a sauna. The air felt thick and hot, and that sun had one heck of a bite. Good thing it was sinking now, so my shoulders wouldn't burn. Again. They already stung from the rays they'd seen while we lugged my stuff in from the car this afternoon.

Right. I drew in a deep breath, and squared my shoulders. This would be a piece of cake. I tucked my room key into my bra and snuck one last look out the window at the courtyard below. People. Easy-peasy.

Before I could over-think the whole thing, I yanked open the thick wooden door and stumbled as it caught my heel on the way out. Good thing my Docs were solid. Those fashionable strappy sandals everyone wore this summer wouldn't have saved my bony ankle from certain destruction.

All the doors in the hall stood closed, marking my dorm floor as dead empty. I'd heard voices earlier this afternoon, but whoever it was must be down there already. The resident senior had said there were three first years on this floor. It was a pity there was no way of telling which rooms were occupied. The other rooms would fill up later in the week when the senior students returned— right now only the resident seniors were here—so I'd find out who lived where soon enough.

Good God, I was still stalling—standing here, staring at closed doors like a freaking lunatic. Before I could conjure any more time-wasting thoughts, I stepped out of the hall and into the stairwell.

Music from the courtyard echoed all the way up the structure, bouncing off the concrete walls and tiled stairs as if they were made for this very purpose. The music wasn't too bad. Not top forty, but not golden oldies either. Good party tunes.

As I emerged into the throng of it, I plastered on the friendliest smile I could muster. It turned out I didn't need to seek out someone to make me look less alone, because my block senior, Jason Donagan, marched up to me with a mock scowl. "Where were you?"

I shrugged. "Sorry."

"Well, you missed out on meeting the other freshers in our block." He waggled a finger in a fake scold.

"Oops."

"Looks like you need a drink."

"Ahh, yeah. That'd be great, thanks."

He disappeared into the crowd, which wasn't as thin as it had looked from my window. People were scattered around in small groups, looking awkward. Some girl caught my attention from over by a wooden picnic table. Dark hair that almost reached her waist swished as she swayed to the music, seemingly without notice, since her focus and smile were both set on me. Maybe she'd be a good one to start with. Before I could make a move, another girl bounced in front of me, grabbing my arm as if we were best buds. "I'm-Amber-and-you-have-awesome-hair."

9

It took me a second to make out what she was saying, she spoke so fast. I fingered the blue tips of my shoulder-length brown hair. The colour had been freshly applied this morning. "Thanks."

With her arm hooked through mine, she piloted me toward the largest group of people, which held the dark haired girl. She gave me a massive smile; her and Amber must already be friends.

"Hey everyone," Amber cooed, "meet my new friend ..."

"Hex," I answered.

"Hex," she mimicked. "Where are you from?"

"Umm ..." It wasn't a trick question, so why was I stumbling? "North."

"Ahh, a coastie."

"Not quite, it's more inland—"

The other girl extended a slender hand. "McKenzie. Second year applied science. I'm on the social committee, so I could crash o-week."

Jason reappeared and passed me one of the plastic cups everyone else seemed to have. I shot him a grateful smile and swallowed its contents in two gulps.

Jason whooped. "Looks like you've been here before, Hex."

The evening wore on much the same, meeting new face after new face. With so many names I'd be lucky to remember two or three come morning. Amber remained glued to my side, and after only an hour in her company I was certain we'd wind up good friends. The girl sure was fun and seemed to draw in a crowd with her bubbly voice.

The drinks flowed steadily, but there wasn't so much that people got plastered. The music lulled and a song I knew well blared to life. I grabbed Amber's hand and pulled her up onto one of the long wooden picnic tables in a corner of the courtyard. She squealed the second she realised what I was up to, and in three seconds flat had her hands above her head, her eyes closed, as she shimmied her body like a pro. I'd definitely found a new friend. Someone wolf whistled below us, but I drowned them all out with my singing.

When the music ended a chant filled the air.

He-ex. He-ex. He-ex.

I grinned as I took a plastic cup some guy held up to me. Amber joined in the chant and it was obvious they wanted me to drink. I yelled, "Bottom's up," and tipped the entire contents of the cup into my mouth. Amber's name came next and she followed my lead, giving the people what they wanted.

My legs felt the effects of my earlier drinks, but it was all good. Until Amber decided it was time to climb down. She stumbled to the side, and we both grabbed hold of each other at the same moment, me saving her from falling. She laughed as if it were the funniest thing ever. A laugh that was the most contagious I'd ever come across. I burst into a fit of giggles as we both stood there, clutching each other by the arms.

Another cup of beer appeared in front of me. The hand holding it, attached to a random guy I hadn't met. I accepted the drink with thanks, a giggling Amber still clinging to my side.

It took a good few minutes before we finally pulled ourselves together. Sucking back a lungful of hysterical laughter-stopping air, I stepped down off the table and

11

right into the personal space of a six-foot-odd hunk of solid muscle. My drink splashed out of the cup, its cool liquid trickling down my arm. Blue eyes regarded me with a deadly seriousness that shouldn't be seen in a face that handsome.

I held his stare for a long minute.

There was no way I would back down to a guy. His jaw clenched and my god, it was as chiselled as any A-grade movie star's. A peppering of jet-black stubble gave him a rugged edge, or maybe that came from his shaggy hair. But boy, he needed to give it up already. He continued to stare as if he were waiting for me to apologise. God only knew how I'd offended him. A quick check proved my feet weren't stomping his toes, nor had my drink landed on his shirt. He wore low-slung jeans and a plain grey T-shirt, both of which fitted his toned body perfectly.

I raised my right eyebrow.

That made both of his dip.

I held out my free hand and he took it. "I'm Hex."

"Hex?" His nose screwed up.

"Yes, Hex."

"Weird name."

"No weirder than your attitude."

"You should slow down."

"Excuse me?"

He dipped his head toward my almost-empty plastic cup. "With the drink. You should slow down."

"And you should piss off."

Who did this guy think he was? Probably some member of the anti-fun brigade, and that was too bad, because damn, his whole look was amazing.

A laugh burst from him so suddenly, I flinched, and realised our hands were still clasped. "Jordan," he said, as if he'd remembered he hadn't given me his name.

"Well, the pleasure was all yours, Jordan." I retracted my hand. "Don't party too hard, now."

Chapter 3
Jordan

NOTHER NIGHT, another party. This place bloody well knew how to throw a welcoming, and I wasn't complaining: warm weather, cold beer, decent company. Overall, I'd met a bunch of decent people and chalked up the past few nights as a win. The first two days were just the freshmen and resident seniors, but the rest of college started showing up late yesterday and continued rolling in today.

With the fading sunlight came another beer fest. Apparently, getting trashed together formed instant friendships. And that's what orientation, or O-week, as the older students called it, was all about. Getting to know the people we'd be living with for the next twelve months. We still had another two days of bonding time before classes started on Monday, but according to Logan Sunday night was supposed to be a quiet one.

And there she was again.

The life of every party rolled into one blue-haired, compact little body. The girl could sure pull off boots with short shorts and make it look damn sexy. Not to mention that hair ... on other girls crap like that looked try-hard, but on Hex it belonged. When the boys had pointed her out that first night, sculling her drink from atop the table, I'd groaned. Too bad once I got face to face with her all that weird shit had spewed out, instead of a smooth line. What the hell was I thinking, telling her to stop drinking? Geez, I didn't know the girl and I was acting all ... *Logan.* Although I was pretty damn sure even he wouldn't stoop to that. We both knew all too well that partying too hard could kill. No wonder she'd walked away. Dumbass: served me right for taking a stupid dare. What was with that? I hadn't done anything like it in years, but the second Nate had challenged me to talk to her I'd shot up. Maybe I was looking for an excuse.

I took a sip of beer from the plastic cup I'd been nursing. Hex scanned the crowd, every few seconds her attention flicking back to the dude at her side who was no doubt laying it on thick. It was damn obvious she wasn't interested. Poor sucker.

"Hey." Something whacked the side of my head. "Sis, you with me?"

"What the hell?" I swung my attention back to Nate, with whom I had spent most of the past few days.

"This is Luca." He indicated a guy standing to his left. With his thick thighs, wide shoulders, and solid form, he was built to play rugby prop. I'd bet my bottom dollar he had a Kiwi heritage too. "Second year. Lives on my floor."

"Hi." Luca extended a hand, which I shook.

15

My phone vibrated in my pocket. A quick look revealed it was a text from Penny, my co-worker, my friend, and my little bit extra. "Won't be a sec."

"Sure," Nate said. I took a step back and opened the message.

Meet at the usual tonight?

I typed back.

Love to, but can't.

How about later?

Oxley's parties have been going late.

I wasn't quite sure why I'd put her off. We'd been issuing booty calls to each other for the past six months. It wasn't a bad set-up, and it suited us both to the ground. Penny liked to keep it casual because of her ridiculously protective family, and no-strings-attached hook-ups suited me fine. It kept my focus in the right places: school and work.

Luca bumped into my shoulder. "Whoa ... who is she?"

I didn't need to follow his line of sight to know he was talking about Hex. She'd caught everyone's attention this week. And it wasn't because she was gorgeous, or even because she looked sexy as hell. It was the vibe she threw off. Confidence; the girl was comfortable in her own skin, and she didn't give a crap what anyone thought. Her name was enough proof of that. It couldn't possibly be her real one.

16

"Good luck tapping some of that, man," Nate said. "Sis here tried on our first night and she shot him down like he was rabid."

"Damn. Too bad, Sis." Luca swung his focus back to me, slipping in the stupid nickname that I'd picked up on the first night. He probably didn't even know what it meant.

"I never really tried." I let my attention wander her way. "If I had she'd have wound up in my bed."

Nate laughed. "Keep telling yourself that, mate."

While we'd been talking, a blonde chick who Nate and I had met last night sauntered up and waggled her fingers in greeting. I dropped an arm over her shoulder to prove my point and she snuggled into my side.

"How's it going?" I asked.

She looked up at me, all fluttering lashes and cute smile. "Who would have wound up in your bed?"

"My own sweet arse. Those beds are too small for sleepovers."

She giggled.

Dono's voice boomed across the courtyard and everyone shut up to listen. "The buses have arrived. Make your way to the car park and we'll see all you losers in town for one hell of a night."

I removed my arm from Blondie's shoulders. "Catch you later, Jordan," she said with a flirty smile. Be damned if I could remember her name.

"Sure ..." I answered.

She cast a look over me then sauntered off. I rose an eyebrow at Nate, surely having shown him my prowess with chicks. Luca chuckled.

"Not the same, Sister. The challenge was the blue-haired babe." Nate swallowed the rest of his drink and crushed the cup.

"Quit it with that name already." It wasn't like people would call me a 'sister' when I was a nurse, anyway. Although I wasn't sure the technical term was brother, either.

He smirked. "Never."

Tonight the crowd was thicker than it had been any other night. I had started recognising a few faces, and now it felt as if I were back to swimming in a sea of strangers. The entire vibe of the place had shifted too, no longer wary and slightly uncomfortable. Instead, it buzzed with noise and excitement, and way too much touchy-feely crap. Every second chick hugged anyone who dared walk past her. And despite the display I'd just put on, that wasn't my scene.

The bottle neck to get out of the courtyard was insane, so I hung back and let the crowd dissipate.

"Let's go," Nate said and I gulped the last of my beer.

By the time we reached the bus almost everyone had already filed on. The three vehicles looked crowded, lined up one behind the other. It was standing room only when we climbed on board, and loud chatter filled the confined space. It died down the moment the bus moved, only to be replaced with singing. It was more of a chant than a song and before long everyone joined in. Luca's deep baritone came from behind me, and even the first years, who had no idea of the lyrics, sang along. Clearly, it was an Oxley tradition. Not knowing the words, I enjoyed the atmosphere for the ten minutes it took to reach town.

Our bus pulled up out front of the Central Hotel where

dim light shone through the already crowded windows, party music thrummed from inside, and people leaned against the railing of the second-floor balcony. Everyone on the bus stood and began surging forward to get out.

Once inside, the place was packed. And again, it was standing room only. Getting anywhere near the bar looked impossible due to the sea of people waiting for service. That didn't stop us queuing up though. Luca stayed with us, and it seemed he was one for small-talk. By the time we'd been served by a sweaty bartender, we'd covered pretty much all I was comfortable with: majors, girlfriend status, blocks of residence, taste in music. We shouldered into a tiny space, and I spotted Blondie from earlier.

"You like rugby?" Luca asked.

The girl's gaze connected with mine, and she must have taken that brief eye contact to mean I was interested, because in an instant she flew to my side, and tugged on my hand.

"Let's dance," she shouted in my ear to be heard over the ruckus. Not something I really wanted to do, but why not? It wasn't like I'd rather go where this conversation was headed. Footy was something I'd prefer to keep in my past. I skulled the rest of my beer—better that than coming back to a warm drink.

People crowded the dance floor, their bodies writhing so close to one another that there was barely room to move. Although it wasn't really my thing, somehow the girl dragged me right into the thick of it. I'd probably had too much to drink; the room sure had a pleasant buzz. She shimmied up against me, and damn, if I let this girl keep going, we'd wind up in her bed. I placed my hands on her shoulders to keep a little distance until I could get a read on her.

People bumped up against me from all sides. We made it through one more song then Blondie pointed toward the toilets. Nodding that I understood, I watched her bop her way through the crowd. That was my cue to head back to the boys.

I turned to the side and used my shoulder to push a path through the writhing bodies. As I manoeuvred past a group of girls, the crowd surged in, throwing me against a soft body. I looked down to apologise and hazel eyes met mine.

"Hex." Her name crossed my lips before I'd had time to think.

Her mouth curled up. "Jordan. Have you come to tell me it's time for bed?"

What the hell? There was no way she could have heard my claim to the boys that I could get her in my bed. Her smirk only grew more defined with my confusion.

"Not tonight," I hedged.

"Too bad." She resumed dancing, her body so close her breasts brushed against my chest. A surge of heat dragged me under, begging me to pull her closer. My hand hovered over her shoulder while she looked up at me through dark lashes, her eyes full of something entirely too daring. Then like the flick of a switch her look morphed to something else; a challenge? "Too bad," she repeated, this time her voice husky, sexy.

Those eyes held my stare and hot damn this girl sure was good.

Her lips parted.

Someone's hand curled around my waist, drawing my attention back to the fact I still stood in the middle of a crowded dance floor. It dropped away as I spun around, and Blondie looked up at me. I motioned toward the bar then turned back around, but Hex was gone. Two steps away, her attention had shifted elsewhere, back to the girl she danced with.

Blow it. I took two huge steps forward, grabbed her shoulder and she spun as I bent my head. She was so close her shaky exhale brushed my mouth. Her eyes widened, those sinful lips parted again, and she didn't move. Not even to breathe. I dropped my voice to a deeper tone. "When I want you in my bed, you'll know it."

Retreating into my own space, I walked back to the bar.

Chapter 4
Hex

GROANING, I rolled over and squinted into the darkness, trying to figure out where the infernal noise was coming from. The buzz continued and through the haze of sleep, I realised it was my phone vibrating against the desk while screeching out "Stronger", a song about courage. I somehow managed to swing myself around in the bed and reach over to the desk without getting upright. I swiped my thumb over the answer icon and moaned, "Yeah?"

Inhuman wailing filled the other end of the line.

"It's four a.m.," I complained.

I held the phone to my ear and lay back down, closing my eyes. Just when I almost dozed back to sleep, the crying petered off into sniffling sobs. "It was my fault."

"No, it wasn't. He's an arsehole."

"Oh, Gregory." Not sniffling anymore; wailing again. "Greg, Greg, Greg."

I sighed. Obviously I'd said the wrong thing. This time.

"If I had been more attentive ... given him a better sex life ... oh, Greg." I cringed, although I couldn't make out the rest of her words through the blubber.

"Shh," I coaxed. "It's all right. It's going to be okay."

I rolled onto my back and closed my eyes with the phone still at my ear. My head throbbed like a jackhammer. Was it only half an hour ago that I'd come to bed? Maybe—who freaking knew? It had been one heck of a night, and that Jordan guy ... I closed my eyes, and crooked my arm over them to block out the dusky light that peaked through the edge of the curtains. He was the least of my worries right about now.

"If only—"

"Forget about the 'if onlys'. They're not going to change a thing."

At that she started crying again, this time whimpering sobs. And I felt for her, I really did. The man was an asswipe and she needed to move on ... but life wasn't that simple, and I got it.

It would have been nice to curl up against her until we both fell asleep.

"Shh," I cooed for the second time. "Why don't you climb in bed, pull the covers up, and dream about that sexy cop from *NCIS*?"

There was no answer, only rustling that sounded like maybe she'd followed my suggestion. Good. It wouldn't be much longer and we'd both be asleep. I began humming down the line; that same song that was my ringtone. It was pretty much our mantra.

When life kicks you down, bite back the frown.

23

Just keep it together and all will eventually get better.
Nothing ... nothing ... nothing is worth letting you drown.

I'm not sure when her crying stopped or when I fell asleep, but eventually both happened.

MY HEAD pounded me into wakefulness. At least, I guessed that was what woke me. The sun peeking around the edges of the thin curtains shone bright. I went to move, but my stomach protested, sloshing around as if it were full of curdled milk. I rolled onto my side and my cheek smashed against something hard. My phone. *Huh, not a dream after all.* I scooped it out from under my face and studied the screen. The call had somehow ended, thankfully.

Last night the seniors had raved about brunch— available to self-cook between ten and two on weekends—it sounded mighty fine to me. Greasy food was exactly what my roiling tummy needed to settle it down. Hopefully, I hadn't slept through the meal like yesterday. And wow, *midday already.*

Sparing a glance at my nails, I was relieved to see they actually looked half decent. None of the layers had been peeled back, nor had they been chewed to the quick. It was an awful habit that stress seemed to make worse.

I gathered up fresh clothes—jean shorts, baggy cotton button down shirt, fresh underwear—and made my way to the bathroom, where I steamed it up washing my hair and ran a razor over my legs. Sleep deprivation was a

24

bitch, but thankfully, the water made me feel a little more human.

I stepped into my clothes, shimmied the shorts up to my waist, and buckled up. Standing in front of the mirror, I ran my hands through my damp hair, fluffing out the ends. Red rimmed, my eyes still looked as if I hadn't slept in a week, but nothing could be done about that. The burger I'd craved since I first woke should help, somewhat.

By the smell permeating the air as I drew closer to the dining hall, I hoped to god I hadn't missed brunch. It smelled delicious. At one p.m., I was pushing my luck, but dear Jesus, could the smell be any more mouth-watering? I trudged up the stairs and into a room teeming with people. It seemed like I wasn't the only one who'd slept in. Last night had been something; all that dancing and drinking and so many new people. The first few nights were awesome, but last night the older students sure showed us a good time. This college thing was a billion times better than I'd expected when I went to enrol.

I spotted a group that held a few familiar faces at one of the long tables near the centre of the room. Amber caught my attention from her spot in the middle and beckoned me over. Her other hand was wrapped around a bacon, egg, and who-knew-what-else burger that had my mouth watering.

"Good morning," she announced, far too bubbly for someone who'd stayed up most of the night.

I gave her a flat stare and Amber chuckled. "Feeling a little seedy, my friend?"

"I need food."

She pointed toward a huge cook-top at the edge of the room. "Make your own."

There was no need to tell me twice. Swiping a couple of eggs from the servery, I toddled off toward the spot where a few other late-comers were frying up a storm. I squeezed into a free space and cracked the eggs onto the hot plate.

"How you feeling today, Hex?" the guy beside me asked. I gave him a once-over out of my periphery. Couple of days' growth, tanned arms, wide shoulders ... *hot*. The type of hotness that drips off guys who've got the whole package.

"Dandy," I replied, "and you?"

He chuckled. "Not bad. Not bad. Sure was a great night."

"The best yet," I answered.

Sunny-side up, and still nice and runny, my eggs were done, so I flipped them onto a plate with a couple of pieces of toast and returned to my friends. The guy sitting to Amber's left looked familiar. Perhaps we'd met them last night.

"Who was that guy?" Amber asked.

I shrugged. "Probably someone I met last night."

I slouched into my chair and tried to pick up on the conversation. Failing miserably, I asked my friend, "What's happening today?"

"Nothing. Classes start tomorrow, so the party's over."

And reality came hurtling back. I was here to study, to figure out a viable career path, even though I didn't particularly want to. "Oh ..."

Amber must have noticed the disappointment in my

voice, because her eyes suddenly lit up and she said, "Doesn't mean we can't hang out though. What are you up to?"

"I might boost my vitamin D intake. There's a quiet, grassy spot out back—"

"Count me in."

After finishing off the lunch of champions, I headed up to my room and switched on my laptop. There was only one thing to take care of before I could lie out. Once it purred to life, I opened up internet banking and sure enough my monthly allowance was sitting pretty. I really only needed to keep $200 for the month, maybe $300, so I set the transfer to Bronwyn Penton—$2,700. It was a little less than I'd passed off each month last year, but it should be enough.

Now that was done, it was time for some sunshine, so I grabbed supplies for a sleepy afternoon: a drink, towel, my well-loved copy of *Little Women*, and a decent slathering of sun cream.

I headed downstairs and spread my beach towel out on the grass, lying down and crooking an arm over my eyes. Not that the sun was bright. The long shadows cast by the dorm had crept across the green lawn. What a great spot; nestled behind the main building, it was far quieter than the courtyard, even though a few people still wandered past. Two different sets of music came from opposite parts of the building, bouncing off the walls inside the courtyard, competing with each other. I was set for a relaxing afternoon, lazing about. That didn't stop my mind from fixating on tomorrow though. It was a little daunting ... my high school results hadn't been that great, but Mum had practically pushed me out the door, insisting I needed the college experience. Then there was the agreement with my father that had slammed me smack-bang in an Arts degree. A taste of everything, until I figured out what I liked, I doubted I'd be good at any of the subjects. I wasn't entirely sure I was ready for O-week to end.

"Oh my God ..." Amber plopped down beside me. "Have you met Nate Baxter yet?"

"Don't think so," I answered.

"Good. I'm calling dibs."

I peeled my arm off my face to look her in the eye. "You're calling dibs on a guy you've known for what ... three days, max?"

"Absolutely."

I repositioned my arm without responding. She was crazy.

She picked up my water bottle. I made a grab for it, but didn't quite reach before she wrapped her lips around the nozzle and downed a decent-sized gulp. Amber placed the bottle back on the grass and scrunched up her nose. "Don't you wanna share cooties?"

"You are not the one with cooties."

She laughed. "You're right. God knows what trash you've let lick the inside of your mouth."

I winked. "No trash, honey. Only the best for me."

What she didn't know was that I was all talk. I hadn't kissed a guy in quite some time.

Amber was barely there two minutes before the guy who'd spoken to me at brunch ambled by with the bloke who'd sat beside Amber. Standing over us and blocking the little sunlight that was left, they mostly chatted to

Amber. I wasn't too keen on buying into the conversation anyway; my mind lingered on my early-morning phone call. Maybe I'd made the wrong decision by coming here. It was even harder to hear someone hurt than what it was to see. Because when someone you love hurts, then you hurt, too.

Wearing a billowing summer dress, McKenzie strolled in from the car park carrying what looked to be a box of wine. Not the type that came with bottles inside it, but rather a bladder inside a cardboard box.

"What're you doing?" I shouted.

"We're having a quiet drink," said one of the guys "you two girls want to join us?"

"Hell yeah." I scooped up my bottle.

"Stay there," McKenzie said. "I'll come back."

When she re-emerged from the courtyard, McKenzie had not only the same cask, but a handful of wine glasses with a white Central Hotel logo that made them look suspiciously like they'd been swiped from the pub we were at last night.

She dropped the wine into the middle of the circle we'd formed. Guy One pounced on the glasses with huge hands. Filling them, he handed one to Amber then one to me. I would've preferred to stick to my drink bottle, but meh, whatever. The wine wasn't too bad. A little sweet, but hey … it was generous of McKenzie to share. I wasn't complaining.

Soft conversation came from my right. The second guy, the one from brunch, had settled in next to Amber and leaned toward her so far that his leg rested atop hers while they murmured. I wasn't the only one who noticed,

29

either. McKenzie's focus got stuck on the kissing knees, and her brows pinched. Uh oh. I cleared my throat, but Guy Number One filled what was becoming awkward silence for the rest of us while his mate flirted with Amber. "Have you girls ever played I Never?"

Now that was something I could get down with; a game. "No," I answered, "tell me more."

"Well ..." Now he had Amber's attention too. The other dude still sat so close to her he could probably pass on an STD, but now he wasn't practically licking Amber's ear McKenzie seemed more at ease. "I say something I've never done before and everyone who has done it takes a drink."

Sounded like a sure way to get trashed, or maybe it was a great way to get to know new people. "Alright," I said, "I'm in."

"Me too." Amber repositioned herself, crossing her legs out in front. Hopefully, she'd picked up on the tension radiating from McKenzie's direction. Last thing we needed was to make enemies out of brand new friends when we weren't even a week into this whole college experience.

"I'll start," Guy Two said. "I've never kissed a dude."

I peeked around and McKenzie took a sip then smiled at me. Right ... I'd done that. I followed her lead and downed half my glass. Easy.

He gestured to McKenzie.

"I've never kissed a girl." Of course both the guys in the group swigged their drinks right away, while watching us girls. I couldn't resist. I raised my glass to my lips and pulled a steady sip.

Cat calls filled the air.

30

I lowered my glass, and there he was—Jordan—walking along the path in all his half-dressed hotness. Yep, he wasn't wearing a shirt … only a pair of board shorts and holy Jesus … my mouth dried up. Like, completely devoid of any moisture. His pants hung just under his hipbones and he had that sweet *V* of muscles that you only saw on underwear models or Olympic swimmers. His whole torso—curved shoulders, divine chest, tattooed left pec—was covered in a sheen of sweat, as if maybe he'd been running, or working out, or god, I didn't care.

And he was watching me as if he'd heard what I'd admitted to in the game. His intense gaze felt as if he could see right through the lie. He wouldn't ruin my bluff. Damn him, if I wasn't going to actually have some fun here.

"Hey, Jordan." Shouting, I beckoned him over and patted the ground beside me. "Sit your sweet rear down here for a bit."

Smiling, he shook his head, which sent a mop of damp, dark waves tumbling over his eyes. He pushed them right back off, and holy mother of sinners, shirts should be banned for muscular guys. Seeing his exposed biceps raised like that was almost too much. A thick vein ran along it, as if to highlight the toned muscles. Despite the negative response, Jordan stared at us for several seconds then actually surprised me by heading over and sitting his impressive rear end right where I'd told him to. I immediately wished I'd told him to sit opposite me, next to McKenzie, because now I couldn't check him out without fully turning my head his way. Hindsight was a cow.

"Luca." Jordan nodded to Guy One, who issued a return nod as Jordan placed a balled-up beach towel by his side.

31

Well, that explained the sexy had-been-wet look.

"I've never had sex on the beach," McKenzie said. And I paid no attention to who downed their drinks and who didn't. I was too busy re-filling my glass to share with our newest player. I wanted to get a better look at that tat. Or maybe just the perfect chest it called home, but passing him his drink didn't allow the angle I needed.

"Hex," Guy Number Two said, "sex on the beach."

"Sure," I responded. "Best cocktail ever."

Someone scoffed and I couldn't help the smile that tugged at my mouth, because yeah, I knew that wasn't what he meant. I handed the glass off to Jordan and took a swig of my drink bottle, emptying it. While I refilled from the cask, he was uncharacteristically quiet while he looked around the group like he was lost, as if maybe he didn't know anyone other than Luca.

I gestured around. "Everyone, this is Jordan. Jordan, everyone."

A chorus of hellos followed. "Amber and McKenzie introduced themselves and it turned out Guy Two was called Max, which I probably should have remembered.

"You go next," Amber said. "Just say something that you've never done and anyone who has done it has to drink."

"Alright," Jordan said, "I've never regretted not kissing a girl who practically begged for it." He raised the glass to his lips and my God, did he actually say that he regretted not kissing me? This game wasn't about drinking. No way, it was all about flirting, and boy was I down with that, even if the other night I'd talked about bed, not kisses.

Guy one—who I now knew as Luca—let out a raucous

32

roar.

"No regrets here," Max whispered a little too loudly, and his fingers traced tiny circles on Amber's knee.

"My turn," I announced. "I've never begged a guy to kiss me."

Take that, Mr Smooth. This time I didn't drink and he was staring at me. I could feel it, and I liked it far more than I should have. There was something about this guy that screamed *challenge.* And a challenge was something I couldn't back down from. No matter how long it took, I'd get him to kiss me, no begging or asking, or anything. He'd like it too. No regrets.

"I've never seen a ghost," McKenzie said, breaking the moment.

Jordan focused on the ring circling his littlest finger, touching it almost reverently.

"Lame!" Luca cried, but McKenzie actually drank. "Stop trying to scare the freshers. There're no ghosts here."

"There's an Oxley ghost?" Amber asked. "Where?"

"There's more than one," McKenzie declared in a spooky voice. "There was this girl who killed herself back in the eighties. Her spirit haunts ..."

"Don't say it. Don't say it!" Amber squealed. "I don't want to know."

Luca slapped Max's hand in the air.

I gulped. So much for flirty. This game had taken a dive. Her turn in questions was picked up when Max declared, "I've never seen a dead body."

Jordan jumped to his feet so quickly his foot clipped Luca's knee and sent the contents of his glass right into Amber's lap. She squealed at the sudden dampness and

33

while everyone laughed, Max whipped off his shirt and tried to mop it up. I burst out laughing at that, 'cause poor Amber was cornered. Yanking my towel out from underneath us, I tossed it at my friend so she could clean up without the hassle. By the time I looked at the spot to my right, Jordan was gone. Off like a shot, he power-walked down the road, away from Oxley and out of sight. Like he was the one who'd seen the stupid ghost in whatever block he lived in.

"That was weird," McKenzie said. I couldn't agree more.

Chapter 5
Jordan

MY PHONE read eighty-thirty a.m. I should've been up an hour ago, but I'd decided to forgo breakfast in exchange for more sleep. It was a pretty good deal until I remembered that my tertiary education began at nine-thirty. I hauled my arse out of bed, in desperate need of coffee. That little kitchen at the end of the corridor was sure to have all the necessary equipment, so I dragged myself down the hall. The kitchen was on a right angle to the bathroom. With the two doors sharing a common jamb it meant the steam seeping out under the closed door warmed my toes. Looked like I'd be skipping a shower as well, unless whoever was in there was almost done. Getting used to this communal bathroom thing was taking a bit of work, but it should be pretty simple once I figured out people's routines. Surely it couldn't be harder than sharing with Liv. That chick took all bloody day to get ready for a trip to the supermarket.

Of the nine people living on this floor, I'd only met two. A surfie-looking dude, who'd been high every time I'd spoken to him and third year chick, who seemed nice enough.

A quick scan of the wardrobe-sized kitchen turned up a kettle and fully stocked pots of tea, coffee, and sugar. A toaster too. Sweet; maybe I should bring my sandwich press out here and add it to the supplies. Probably be better than shoved into the corner of my desk, unused. I grabbed a mug off the bench that sported blue dots on its pink surface. It was either that or the 'I hate morning people' mug and well ... the morning hater could kick it.

No sooner had I topped off the brew with a splash of milk I'd found in the bar fridge than the bathroom door flew open. Steam billowed into the hall, as if someone had lit liquid ice and holy hell, today was my day.

Coffee and a view.

I let out a low whistle and Hex spun around, frowning. Wet hair piled over her shoulder made the coloured ends look longer, the blue tips almost reaching her left breast. I deliberately let my gaze roam over that sweet body, knowing she watched my every move. Once again, she wore jean shorts. Today's shirt was a tee as opposed to yesterday's button-up, and the way it stretched across her body had me leaning against the doorframe as I raised the coffee to my lips and took an agonisingly slow sip. "Well, hot damn. You just used my shower."

Her eyes widened, then narrowed quicker than if someone had torn open the roof and let the direct sunlight splash into her sleepy-looking gaze. "Get out of town. You

36

don't live on this floor, Jordan."

"Sorry to disappoint you, doll, but I do."

Her wet hair had dripped all over, rendering that white shirt almost see-through in the right places. I was tempted to tell her just to see the response.

"And you are not drinking out of my mug!"

"I'm not?" I took another sip from my new favourite mug, trying to force my lips not to curve.

"You are!" she screeched.

The few times we'd interacted she'd been in control of the conversation, with me the one floundering. There was no way I'd expected a reaction like this and I loved it.

She stood there for a few seconds, gaping at me while I enjoyed the view. Then as if she'd come to her senses, she smiled and leaned against the wall. "You got classes today?"

I nodded, realising I knew next to nothing about her. "I've never asked what you're studying."

"Bit of this, bit of that ..."

"What kind of answer is that?"

"An honest one. What about you?"

"Nursing."

She raised an eyebrow, which was a damn sight better than the ribbing I copped from the boys. Then she looked me over, slowly. Finally, she smiled. "Huh. Nice. Where are you from?"

"What is this, get to know you, Twenty Questions?"

She shrugged. The truth was it was more words than we'd ever exchanged, yesterday's dumb game included. But I didn't want to tell her where I was from or talk would turn to family, and Logan was my only family I felt

37

comfortable talking about.

The dripping ends of her hair had plastered against the white-opaque fabric. The damp arc was now so big her lacy white bra was visible beneath. I gulped.

That shirt was getting mighty distracting. The temptation to toy with her grew too great, so I asked, "Heading to classes soon?"

She shoved a hand in her tight pocket.

"You probably should dry your shirt first." I inclined my head toward her chest.

Hex looked down, and it took a few seconds before realisation dawned and her arms shot across her chest. Her face flushed. She spun and bolted into what had to be her room. Well, I'd be damned. If she was that easy to torment then this was sure going to be a fun year.

I DRAGGED my arm through the water then followed it with the other one. Since I didn't play ball anymore, swimming was one of the few things that let my mind rest. Maybe it was the release of pent-up energy that helped. I slammed into the pool's edge, and hauled myself out of the water. Fifty minutes in the lanes and I felt pretty fresh. I speared a hand through my hair to flick the moisture off, and grabbed my towel from the stands.

Out of the water, my mind took up right where it left off. Everyone called campus 'up top' since the school was perched on a hill. That was probably the most useful piece of information I'd learned in my entire first day, other than the location of the Science faculty, but I'd already known that from open week. The whole day was a bit of a bludge, really.

It turned out in class, I was in the minority. Not that I cared—being one of only a handful of males would be interesting. And speaking of interesting, I hadn't been able to shake this morning's image of Hex from my mind all day. The girl was bad news and not only because she seemed like a party animal. The way she'd niggled at my thoughts for the past six hours was a distraction from study I didn't need. I had four long years ahead, and I couldn't afford to lose focus. That meant there would be no permanent fixtures.

Regardless, there was something about Hex that worried me. Not that I could put my finger on what it was; she was just different.

"Hey, you!" A voice sounded from behind me. Liv ducked around in front, before I had time to turn. "How's the water?"

"Wet." I grinned at my brother's girlfriend. I hadn't been sure if she was working today. She had taken on a job at the sports centre last year, and despite returning to studies this semester, she planned to do both. She only had another two years before she graduated thanks to all the advanced credit from her previous law subjects.

Liv swatted me with the back of her hand. "Funny." Her eyes softened. "How about Oxley—is everything going well?"

"Loving it."

"I was worried about you last night ..."

"Yeah, well. It was nothing." My showing up unannounced wasn't something we needed to talk about. "It's all good." The steely look meant she didn't believe me, but I wasn't about to give her time to push further. "I better get going if I'm gonna make dinner."

"Honey, you already missed it. Oxley runs dinner from five-thirty until seven." She shook her head.

"Damn. I did?"

She gave me a slow nod, with a downturned lip.

"Damn it. It was on when I left, but I thought ..."

"Nope. Logan's picking me up in ten, if you want to come over—"

"I'm good."

"We'd love to have you."

"It's all right, Liv. I'll order in."

She looked at me for far too long then gave a quick nod, as if to herself. "Right. Then, I'll see you Tuesday."

"Yep, tomorrow."

She swooped in for a hug, and geez, I wasn't sure how this girl had wormed her way into our lives, but it wasn't a bad thing. I couldn't lean on her and Logan forever though. I'd done that for long enough.

I knotted the towel around my waist over my boardies, and toed on my flip-flops. No point showering here; the walk back to Oxley would only take ten minutes.

Those ten went fast. Daylight was long gone by the time I walked through the gates and a few people sat around in the back courtyard. Sure seemed like it was the place to be. I scooted around to the right, making my way into Front.

"Sis!" The shout sounded like Nate.

"You talkin' to me?" I spun around, knowing full well

he was.

A grin spread across his face. "Got someone who wants to meet you."

"She'd better be hot."

Nate laughed. "You'd be surprised."

He eyed off my tattoo and I waited for the question everyone always asked.

"Cool tatt. What's it stand for?"

I fingered the ring on my pinkie. "Not much. Got it almost two years ago."

"Your parents must be cool. I had to wait until I didn't need parental consent to get this baby." He lifted his sleeve to show off a Celtic armband.

I offered a smile. What I didn't say was when your sister's dead and your brother's your guardian, things are different.

I followed him into Back, to the table where I'd seen the bunch of people gathered. They were all blokes; not sure how I missed that before. There were a few faces I recognised: Luca and my resident senior, Dono. Nate gestured toward a short stocky bloke sporting a backwards Brisbane Bronco's cap.

"Cade, Sis. Consider yourselves introduced."

Cade extended a hand and we shook. "Name's Jordan," I said.

"Dono here tells me you're not half bad with a football."

I eyed up the senior, wondering how the heck he knew I once played rugby. "Yeah, I can play."

"You don't look like a prop," Cade said. "Half-back?"

This guy must captain Oxley's team. "Yeah, that or the wing."

"You can run then?"

I loosened the towel around my waist and twisted it into a roll which I slung over my shoulders. "Yeah."

Cade tipped his chin. "You're on the team."

"Didn't say I wanted to play, bro."

Cade's mouth turned up. "You'll play. Love of the game doesn't just disappear."

He wasn't wrong, but that didn't mean I wanted to join in. When I first moved to Armidale a few years ago, I'd not only played for school, but also town. The inter-state school's comp had wanted me again, and Logan thought I was a fool for not accepting. But footy wasn't my life. It hadn't been in four years.

Cade's focus dipped over my shoulder and when it didn't return after a few moments, I looked that way. Hex and her friend Amber strutted by with another cask of that nasty shit they were drinking yesterday. They swung off into the other courtyard.

"I'll think about it," I told Cade and turned to leave.

"Your name's on the list, Sis."

Damn that stupid nickname. Just because I was studying Nursing ... I still wasn't sure if it was short for Sister or sissy. Either way, it was a dig. Maybe a footy reputation would throw off the pansy image, but whatever.

I didn't bother to respond as I strode away. The front courtyard was empty of people, so it was easy to head right for my block and jog up the stairs.

Planting my hand on the frame, I swung myself into the hall. Hex's light shone out her open door, and Amber's short arse walked right toward me. She tossed me a smile that made her seem sweeter than I suspected she was and scooted past, whispering, "Love to chat, but I gotta use the ladies."

I swivelled into Hex's doorway and leaned against the jamb, my fingers working the edge of the towel that still hung around my neck. The sweet sound set-up took prime position on the desk, gigantic speakers off to each side, and a small TV in the corner. A huge-arse bottle of vodka sat on the top shelf. This was the room I'd seen that first day. It suited her.

Standing by her desk with the cask balanced on the edge of the bench, she had the two coffee mugs from our kitchen propped under the tap as she filled them.

"You're drinking."

"Just a quiet one," Hex said without turning to face me. "You want to join us?"

She actually wanted me to stay. I wasn't sure I wanted to, but a response slipped out anyway. "Only for a bit. I should be ... I dunno ... studying, or some shit like that."

She laughed. "Boring."

Spending half an hour with her wouldn't hurt. It wasn't like I had anything better to do. Hex's gaze dropped, her blue eyes hooded with thick lashes as she looked well below my face. Knowing she was checking me out wasn't a bad feeling. And I sure as hell wasn't about to go cover up while she was enjoying the show, even if I did feel like man candy, or whatever the hell girls called guys they liked to eye-ball.

Her attention came to a halt at my chest, and her head cocked to one side. "Cool tattoo."

"Thanks." I readjusted the towel around my neck.

43

"Have you been swimming?"

"Umm, yeah. Blowing off some of the first day steam."

Hex's lip quirked and I realised what I'd said. "Chilling ... you know, relieving tension. How do you manage it?"

This time she laughed, and raised a provocative eyebrow. "Wouldn't you like to know?"

"Ah, yeah. Actually I would." I threw her a look of my own and tossed in a wink for good measure.

Hex leaned across her desk and shoved the window open, then scream-sang, "When life kicks you down, bite back the frown. Just keep it together."

Amber reappeared and plopped herself on the bed. "What the heck was that?"

"Hex, being ... Hex." I couldn't suppress the grin that crazy girl brought on.

Hex reached across, flicked on the music and shuffled back onto the desk, her attention once again on my body. I shifted my arm on the jamb above head height and rested my temple against it to make my abs pop.

"I'd offer you a drink, but all my cups are in use."

"No matter. I'm here for the company anyway."

The massive bottle of vodka sat to her left, on the bookcase. It looked like one of those sizes they hung upside-down at pub bars. It was almost three-quarters gone when five days ago it had been full. That had to be at least a litre, probably more, gone. Sure we'd partied pretty hard the past week, but all the grog was free, and each time I'd seen her she'd had Oxley plonk in her hand. So where did all that hard liquor go?

My gaze slid over her small frame. There was no way ...

Hex brought the pink mug to her lips.

"How were your classes?" I asked.

She shrugged. "All right."

"Mine were awesome." Amber crossed her feet and shuffled back against the wall. "I'm definitely in the right course; teaching's going to be great. Did you know we can do prac this year?"

"That's great," Hex mumbled into the mug.

"What about you?" Amber directed the question at her friend, whose gaze had slid back to me. "I can't remember what you're doing ... Arts, right?"

"Something like that."

In a complete turnaround to earlier, Hex clearly wasn't all that keen to have company, so after watching the girls finish off their drinks and pour seconds, I made my way back to my room and flopped onto the bed. That vodka—it reminded me of worse times.

My legs ached as I walked up the drive, the steep incline stretching already exhausted muscles. It felt damn good though, the way the game exhausted every part of me. At least it did until his screaming met my ears.

"What the hell, you little bitch?"

A thud so huge the windows rattled, welcomed me home. The tang of cigarette smoke filled my nose. I should've turned around, walked back down the drive and taken coach up on his offer of a bed, but there was no way I could leave her.

"Get your arse back here and clean up."

I shoved open the door. The squeak of rusty hinges didn't draw his attention. This time.

"Good-for-nothing drunk skank."

45

He sat in his recliner, surrounded by a sea of empty beer cans. Kayla crouched on the floor, scooping them into a plastic bag. She didn't raise her head, just hid behind her dark hair. The tang of alcohol filled the room; beer no doubt had spilled on the carpet.

"You beat 'em all in training, kid?"

He'd seen me.

"We'll win the finals."

"If that coach can make your lazy arse work, you will."

Kayla slunk out of the room.

"I pulled fifty push-ups tonight without breaking a sweat."

He grunted. His attention shifted to the game on the TV; a grand final from before I was even born. That night, asking about training, was one of the few times he gave a shit about anyone other than himself.

The Party's Over

Chapter 6
Hex

ALTHOUGH THE place was packed, I didn't see anyone I knew at the university bar. I claimed one of the few free tables by the huge glass doors that led onto what looked like a terrace. If the ashtrays and people puffing away out there were any indication, it doubled as a smoker's corner. I wasn't all that hungry, but the smell of hot food permeating the air rapidly changed my stomach's state. That delicious greasy smell of deep fried food was most prominent. Underlying it lingered a scent more pungent; maybe a curry.

Amber had said she might be there around lunch, so while I waited, I fished out my phone, and flicked though my social media, but after scrolling down and back up again I couldn't tell what any of my friends back home were up to. Probably because my wandering mind remained firmly in the class I'd just left.

Drama wasn't hard as much as awkward. I felt stupid

standing up there, acting out a scene as if I were another person. An angry person ... it didn't sit right when I still felt like me. It was a dumb subject choice, but since I didn't have a career path chosen, my father had said I had to try subjects from different faculties to keep my options open. Science, Drama, Economics, and English Lit. The only one that looked like it was going to be interesting was English. My high school teacher, Ms Helva, had been right. It was my cup of tea. The reading list alone had me excited. There was a real mixture of classics, commercial fiction, and even children's books. It was only week one and we'd already started with *Pride & Prejudice*. I could almost handle three years of it. Pity I had no idea what to do with an Arts degree that didn't yet have a set major. Guess I'd figure that out when I got to it.

Chatter already filled The Bar, so I'm not sure what made me raise my head and look toward the door at that exact moment. The moment Jordan strolled in looking like hotness personified. The sight wasn't quite as fine as when he'd lazed in my room shirtless, but it wasn't far off. Perfectly messy, his dark hair hung just shy of his eyes. He looked as if he hadn't shaved in a few days, despite the fact I'd heard him in the bathroom this morning. That dark scruff seemed to be his normal look though. And the shirt he wore was a firm enough fit that if I strained my vision right I could see the muscles underneath. Or maybe that was just my vivid memory.

He never even looked my way as he stormed through and headed straight to the stairs that led up to god-only-knew where. Actually ... he looked kind of pissed. Which was new on him. In the week we'd known each other I'd seen laid-back, commanding, freaked out, and not happy, but never angry.

I scooped up my bag and made for those same stairs that I hadn't even realised were there, let alone that this place had a second floor. As I climbed them, the voices below faded, and were replaced with the whir of an espresso machine. I sucked in a greedy breath and yep ... sweet, sweet coffee. Jordan had led me to a secret cafe. My foot hit the top stair and he stood by a tiny version of the counter downstairs. I glided up beside him and took an overly obvious breath. "Looks like you found Heaven."

Jordan turned to me, his face pinched in a frown that matched his clearly sour mood. "Hey, Hex."

I raised a brow.

"What?" he snapped.

I raised the other one.

"Can I help you?" A waitress had appeared at the counter. Her dark hair was pulled back into a messy bun, and she looked no older than us, and bored. Serving was clearly another task in her never-ending day. She shifted her weight, the light glinting off a gem in her nose.

"Long black," Jordan said, his tone clipped.

She looked at me expectantly.

"I'm not staying." I glanced toward Jordan. "Pretty sure I'm not welcome."

"Sorry," he sighed, then readjusted his plain grey T-shirt. "Order something, Hex. Hang with me for a bit."

I gritted my teeth and stomped down an *I'd love to*. "Convince me."

Jordan gave me one hell of a closed-lipped sexy smile. "Please."

"Please?" *He really wanted me to stay?*

"Or I could scoop up your hot little arse and carry you back to college, so we can hang out in private." He winked, but I was more interested in making sure he was okay.

"Tempting as that sounds, I think I'll settle for a latte." The waitress acknowledged my order with a nod.

"Where's your sense of adventure?" Jordan teased and that was a really good question. It seemed I was more flirt than follow-through.

The waitress moved to the coffee machine which buzzed as it made our drinks.

"I have plenty of adventure." I tapped him on the chest and all words fled my mind at the firmness which met my finger. "You, Mr Boring, are the one who always skips out on the fun."

At that Jordan's eyes darkened to a deep navy, challenging me as he reached out and trailed the back of his hand across my cheek. His fingers came to rest under my chin and good god, I shivered more than if I'd stepped out into the dead of winter. Only this shiver was different. It left me tingling and covered in goose bumps that were way too pleasant. I swallowed.

"Nine dollars."

Jordan's gaze was still locked with mine and I'd registered that the waitress spoke, but I couldn't look away from the intensity in his eyes. Eyes that I swore repeated the words from that game of I've never: *a girl that's begging me to kiss her.*

Damn it. I wasn't begging, nor would I ever. I shook my head to clear it of the haze.

"Ahem. That's nine dollars, people." The waitress

sounded testy.

I dug into my bag, but by the time I'd found my purse Jordan already had both cups in his hand and his back to the counter. He walked over to a low table surrounded by a couple of arm chairs, slid the cups onto the wooden surface and plopped into the chair that had its back to me. I took the seat opposite and Jordan shot me one of his challenging stares. "Who skips out on the fun?"

Oh, right. I'd called him Mr Boring. Smiling, I slipped five bucks out of my purse and placed it on the table.

"I don't want your money," Jordan said.

"Take it."

"No."

"Jordan ..."

"Hex?" He smirked.

I left the cash on the table. I'd make him take it later. I was not letting this guy buy me a drink. But then why was I here, if it wasn't to flirt with the gorgeous man across the table?

Damn him. This was about more than that. I'd been worried earlier because he'd looked as if he wanted to a punch a wall.

"Everything all right with you?" I asked. "You looked pretty pissed before."

His scowl returned in a nanosecond. "It's nothing."

"Bullshit."

Jordan looked me in the eye and I held my ground. "It's not nothing. You stormed in here like someone had called your mother crazy, then you snapped my head off for saying hello. So don't tell me it's nothing."

"I said it's nothing."

"Stop being such a boy, Jordan. Tell me what the problem is."

"Fine." He shifted to the edge of the chair, his back straight and hands planted on his knees. "Every arse in this tiny country town thinks like a fossil, even the goddamn academic staff. It's so fucking backward and the older people are the worst. It doesn't matter who does what—if a chick's a goddamn mechanic or a guy's a kindergarten teacher. Who cares, so long as each person has the necessary skill set; that's all that matters, right? They're just jobs."

He sprung up and took two long strides to the banister, slammed his hands on the rail and leaned against the wood, glaring at the pool tables on the ground floor. "The professor thought I'd joined the wrong class, Hex. The wrong fucking class, just because I'm a bloke. I'm over it."

Pushing my drink aside, I rose and joined him in looking over the balcony. "Come again? Is this about your major?"

The vein in his right arm popped right below the line of his sleeve. It was always prominent, but now I couldn't stop staring at it. Maybe because I wasn't quite sure what to say, but boy did I get it. People assumed I slept around because I liked flirting, when in reality, the only guy who had ever had his hands on my body was Josh Farnell, and that was well over a year ago. We were together for almost two years, but he split when I stopped hanging at parties to stay with Mum.

"Hey, Sis!" some guy called from the tables below. He pointed right at us.

Jaw set, Jordan turned around without acknowledging

our fellow Oxley resident. He took five strides back to the lounge and slumped into it. "That shit just proves it."

"What shit?"

"Sis," he growled, as if I should know what he meant. I didn't, so I sat there and waited. "It's a dig at my degree."

"Sissy?"

"Or Sister."

I picked up my latte and took a sip. It was only as I was putting it back down that I noticed the napkin stuck to the bottom of the mug. I peeled it off and something inside me itched to make Jordan smile; to get him to stop glowering into his coffee. I scrunched the paper into a ball then tossed it at his head, which incidentally swung up at the precise moment my projectile hit. *Bam, forehead shot.* God, I was good. Without breaking his surly look, Jordan snatched a coaster off our coffee table and Frisbeed it into my chest.

Now he smiled. It wasn't huge and it didn't touch his eyes, but it was there.

I flung the wadded napkin back at him.

He flung it at me.

I smiled, too.

A sudden commotion came from below. Jordan sprung to his feet and peered over the side of the banister, checking out the loud noise; yahooing, cheering, and clapping. I manoeuvred around the coffee table to take a look and the same bunch of footy guys still milled around the pool table. The one who'd called out to Jordan earlier held the crowd's attention, as if he were some kind of hero. I didn't know him, but I had seen him around Oxley. Always loud and obnoxious, he was a bit of a douche.

Jordan's smile morphed back into a scowl, and we couldn't have that. Turning around, I swept up all the coasters, their thick cardboard damp between my fingers. Pulling my arm back I let one fly like a boomerang. It sailed through the air and landed square on the green velvet of the pool table. *Damn, too far.* I pulled back on power as I flung a second one, which was a better shot. It clipped Footy Dude on the shoulder. It can't have been too hard though, because he raised his hand to the spot, but didn't look around.

I chuckled. Jordan looked at me, wide-eyed.

A third coaster found its way into my hand. It felt damp and heavier than the first two. While Jordan was still looking at me as if I were a lunatic, I hoicked it too, and BAM. It hit Douche Canoe in the ear. Perfect shot. He spun around and I dropped to the floor, tugging Jordan down beside me.

"You can't do that shit." He laughed.

"Sure I can." I popped up and the guy had his back to us again, so I flung the last coaster. It soared through the air, and my aim was spot on. It hit him smack in the back of his head.

Giggling, we both dropped below the banister wall. And god this was childish, but hell it was fun. Jordan's arm felt warm against mine and with a huge grin, he looked as if he'd enjoyed watching that idiot get his comeuppance. That smile was so deep I could crawl inside it and live happily ever after. And that laugh, low and throaty ...

"How old are you two?" The surly waitress peered down at us.

"Old enough," Jordan responded, crawling into his seat.

56

"Do it again and you're out." She turned on her heel and stalked away, leaving Jordan and I grinning at each other like a pair of kids who'd pranked the teacher.

Chapter 7
Jordan

ALTHOUGH THE week had gotten off to a slow start, we were now in full swing. My days were chock-full with lectures, and unlike a lot of people, I hadn't been able to work my schedule to have a full day off or even half of one. Instead it was Monday to Friday with at least four classes a day including tutes, sometimes more. Not that I minded, I'd intentionally crammed as many classes in as I could. But in hindsight, if I had a day off I could've swindled an extra shift at work.

"You about done?" Penny called from up front of the shop.

It was Thursday night, so I was where I'd been every Thursday for the past three years: Mozzarellas Pizza. It wasn't a bad gig. Not only did I score freebies, Carlos was a great boss. I'd progressed up the ranks somewhat and was now a shift supervisor, which is why Penny and I were the last out. It was also why we had the car, or maybe that was because she was Carlos's niece.

"Almost," I called back. "Just gotta do the floors."

"Hurry your arse up!"

I pulled out the hose and flicked it on, washing all the night's crap into the drain where the centre of the floor dipped. When the water splashed back clear, I turned the high-pressure hose off and grabbed a dustpan to scoop up all the chunks. A lot of crap could accumulate over the period of a workday. I tossed the gunk into the bin, rinsed off my hands and pulled back on the hose, watching it retract into the spool at one hundred clicks an hour. I whirled around, ready to get the hell out of there and back to Oxley—it had been a long night—but Penny was right up in my space. She laid her hand on my arm and gave me a look I knew well. "Want to have some fun?"

"Not tonight."

"Jordie..." She pouted, and moved so close her breasts pressed against my arm. Her slender fingers closed around my chin and tugged it around, bringing us eye to eye. Deep brown, her eyes were so different to Hex's. They didn't have the same spark of fun. Penny lowered her lashes and puckered her lips in a way that reminded me just how talented those babies were. She had my mouth watering and my whole body paying attention as she leaned in and grazed their softness against my mouth. I was hopeless as she slid her tongue against my lower lip, invading me with her minty taste. As if it had its own mind, my mouth opened and she wasted no time. Her kiss was desperate, needy, and expressed exactly what she wanted to do when we got somewhere without her uncle's CCTV.

Her uncle's CCTV. He played footage of the time he was offsite while he did paperwork the next day.

I pulled away, my arms still hanging by my sides, and took a step back. I tried to speak, but had to clear my throat first.

Penny gave me a sultry smile.

Kissing me in the middle of the shop was insane. Me allowing it was even crazier. There was no way Carlos could find out about our arrangement. He was so damn overprotective of his niece and I couldn't risk losing my job. With no parental support, I needed the money to live. Sure I was on a scholarship, but that didn't include textbooks, or public transport, or all the shit I needed to survive.

We ducked out the back entrance and she set the alarm behind us then locked the door. Mozzarellas' white Ford Focus was the only car in the empty parking lot, even though dance music boomed from the pub with which we shared this space. School was in and that meant the town filled with college kids, who either walked, rode the bus, or caught a cab. No one bothered driving to the drinking holes. The pumping music drew my gaze to Central Hotel's top crowded balcony, and I wondered if Hex was up there.

Penny's hand slid into mine, tugging my attention away from the pub. She hit the key lock and the Focus's indicators flashed. Reclaiming my hand, I opened the passenger door and climbed in before she could make another move on me. It'd be good to get back to Oxley. Who knew—maybe Hex would be about since it was only eleven.

Penny walked around the front of the car more slowly than a model on a catwalk. I wasn't oblivious to her sexy strut or the fact her tits almost escaped her skin-tight Mozzarellas polo shirt. Her intentions were obvious; tonight she wanted some loving. Keen as she was, that wouldn't happen. Lately, it felt somehow off. Her display on premises, when we'd always been so careful, was insane.

As we drove back to college, Penny's hand found its way to my knee. I slid mine underneath and lifted her fingers, placing them back on the wheel and once again told her, "Not tonight."

I wasn't sure why I knocked her back ... no-strings-attached hook-ups usually required no thought. I guess I just wasn't in the mood.

"Sure," she said, "I get it. Now you're a college stud, I'm small game."

Already having said no, I sighed as she pulled into Oxley's car park and shifted the gears into park. "It's not like that."

"Fine," she snapped, focusing on the road in front. "Good night, Jordan."

She was pissed, but whatever. I wasn't about to invite her in just because she'd spend the next week sulking if I didn't. Pity sex wasn't good for anyone.

I climbed out of the work car. The neon pizza box on the roof didn't flash off then back on in her usual goodbye as she pulled away. She'd get over it. I heaved a frustrated sigh and turned toward Oxley. It wasn't like I'd told her never again.

The place rocked loud music as I walked into the front

courtyard. It wasn't a function as such, but a shit ton of people had congregated here anyhow. I walked around the footpath and before I'd even made it a quarter of the way to my block, a bunch of partiers called my name. I gave them a wave and kept walking.

"Jordan!"

I stopped to seek her out.

"What the hell are you wearing?" Hex called.

"Work uniform," I shouted back. Her butt was firmly planted on the top of the wooden picnic table and it looked as if she wasn't moving from her perch.

"Come, be sociable!"

"Gimme five." I threw a smile her way, continued walking around the courtyard and ducked up the stairs to our block. Even with a room facing out of college, the music reverberated through clearly, as did the raised voices which sang along.

This sure was different than coming home from work to Logan and Liv mauling each other on our couch. I grabbed a couple of beers from the emergency six-pack I'd put in the fridge earlier this week and headed back downstairs. When I emerged into the courtyard someone cheered and it was picked up by everyone, followed with a "Here's to Jordan." During O-week I'd quickly learned that song meant you had to down your drink fast, so I popped the top of my beer. Everyone was in various states of drunk fuckery, but it was Hex who snagged my attention. Her hair had changed colours, the perfectly ragged ends were now bright purple, and she wore a loose, almost see-through, long-sleeved shirt. Still seated on the wooden table, she grinned at me.

62

"To new friends." I raised the bottle to my lips and drank.

My phone vibrated in my pocket, but my attention remained on the chorus of cheers breaking out as I slammed the empty bottle onto the table.

Cade swaggered around to me in a way that made me think he was half tanked. I hoped to god he wasn't about to bang on about footy again. I hadn't stopped thinking about his offer since he'd made it and as much as I enjoyed being on the field I didn't want to get back into that whole scene. He twisted his Brisbane Broncos cap around backward. "Mate, was that a fucking Mozzarellas uniform?"

"Yeah."

"You'd better bring home some free fucking pizza next time. You can't work at the best pizza dive in town and not share."

I'd been around blokes like him before; it wasn't worth the effort to say no. That didn't mean I'd do what he ordered though. "Sure, next time."

"How'd you score a job there?"

"I've been there forever."

He swayed dangerously close then planted a hand on my shoulder for support. "Forever?"

"Since I was sixteen."

"Mate, you're a local? No wonder Dono wants you on the team. You know the fields, and probably the competition too. Did ya play local comp, or only schools? And state ... you played in the school state comp a few years ago, yeah? Wait ... what the hell are you doing living in this shithole dorm if you're a townie?"

"Man, hold up." The guy had verbal diarrhoea. His face looked pretty ruddy and by the smell of the glass in his hand he'd had a few bourbons. "I'm a local and I played town comp as well as schools."

"We need you." He emphasised his words with a punch to my shoulder. "Come on, Sis. Make Oxley proud."

I looked around for an out. For Hex. But she wasn't sitting on the table anymore. "Rugby's not really my thing these days."

"What the hell, man? You can't go from state to not playing. You should be angling for pro."

I wasn't going anywhere near pro. I'd put those dreams behind me long ago, because they weren't mine. I raised my second beer toward Nate, who'd stepped out of block B, and there she was, dancing with Amber. Hex had her hands raised in her favourite dance move and the way her and Amber were moving should be censored, it was so damn sexy. A couple of other girls jumped up and joined in, but those two ... they owned the entire courtyard.

"Sis," Nate called across the crowd, pointing my way.

I shot him a finger back and Hex moved, storming across the courtyard. She pounced on my mate like a growling tiger. All up in his face, she pointed a finger right at his chest. "Show some goddamn respect for people that could save your life one day."

Ah, shit. I hauled myself over there.

"Whoa." Nate held his hands up. Amber appeared between them, yelling, "What the hell, Hex? You're acting like a crazy woman."

"I'm not freaking cra-she." Hex flicked her gaze back to Nate. "Say you're sorry."

64

Nate spluttered and I just about joined him. What was her problem?

"Sorry for what? You're the one who just went psycho." Amber asked.

"Hey!" I frowned at Amber. "Not on."

"That ridiculou-sh nick-name."

Great, she was slurring.

"Sis?" Nate looked as if something unpleasant had crawled up his arse.

"Hell, Hex. Like it matters." I snuck an apologetic glance to my friend.

Hex's lips thinned, her arms crossed tight over her chest, her tiny feet planted wide on the grass.

"Sorry," Nate snapped.

"Sh-like you mean it, arseh-hole." Hex jabbed him in the chest again and I snatched her hand, enclosing it in mine, but she reefed it away only to take a swing. Nate stepped out of the firing line, which sent her toppling to the side.

"What's your problem?" Amber said, but Hex never spared either of us a sideways glance. Her eyes remained firmly fixed on Nate, and even with her head craned right back she looked pissed off. I had to admit part of me was amused because she looked so goddamn cute all angry like that, but the rest of me screamed danger, 'cause holy hell, she was a tornado.

"I'm ... ah ... sorry?" Nate hedged, looking my way.

This was getting out of hand. I pulled Hex into my side, before she needed a goddamn gag.

"That'sh better," she slurred.

This girl was totally tanked, again. I should have run a

mile in the opposite direction, but instead I felt a crazy urge to get her out of here safely.

"It's not a big deal," I said, for everyone's benefit. "Come on, Hex. I'm starving. Let's have toasties."

She squinted at me as if she were trying to figure something out, but I didn't give her time, just tugged on the hand I still restrained in an effort to stop her from poking the ever-loving crap out of Nate.

"Hey ..." she said as we entered the stairwell. "You tricked me." She reefed her hand out of mine and stopped at the bottom of the stairs, hands on hips. "You're trying to make me go to bed again."

"Did not. I'm going to make you a toastie just like I promised, and it's gonna be the best fucking toastie you ever had."

"With cheese?"

"With cheese."

"Promise?"

"Promise."

She grabbed hold of the handrail and hauled herself up a few stairs, then swayed back. I placed my hand on her back to keep her steady.

"Geez, girl. You'll fall down."

She giggled at that, and pulled herself up a couple more stairs. My heart jumped into my throat as she swayed again. This was dangerous.

"The stairs won't stay still," she said, still giggling.

I slung my arm around her shoulders and the other under her legs, lifting her off the ground. She coiled an arm around my middle and snuggled into my chest. "You smell good."

"You're drunk."

"And you're gonna make a toastie. Yum!"

By the time we reached the top of the stairs her eyes had closed and her cheek rested against my chest. She looked so peaceful that it was hard to believe the outburst a few minutes ago had come from the same sweet mouth, but I'd seen this type of behaviour before, so I believed it all right.

I shouldered open the door to our hall. The door to her room stood closed, and my keys were in my pocket, so what the frig was I going to do with her? I walked down the hall and stood outside her door, watching her. I could put her in my room, but then she might think I'd taken advantage of her when she woke in the morning. She'd have to have a key somewhere ... although I could find Dono and ask him to unlock her room with his master key. Now that was a good plan.

"Jordan."

The softness in her voice took me by surprise and I looked down, meeting her tired eyes. "Yeah?"

"I'm sleepy."

"I know."

"In there." She jutted her chin toward her chest then her breathing deepened to a soft snore. Shit. I stood in front of her door, staring down at her sleeping face: the soft features, the arched brows, the way her cheekbones angled under her eyes ... God, she was beautiful in a way other girls weren't. Pity she liked to party so hard. A girl like that wasn't someone I needed to get involved with.

"Hex, you gotta wake up."

She didn't stir.

"Hex."

She flinched. "What? What the hell? Put me down." She just about fell arse-over-tit as she struggled to get out of my arms. "Not cool, Jordan."

"Whoa, calm down."

Holy hell, this was like whiplash. One second she was all peaceful and sweet, the next she'd morphed back into fighting mode. I set her on her feet and moved toward the kitchen before she went ape-shit about toasties, too. I wasn't quite fast enough though. She stormed down the hall and peered into the kitchen as I retrieved the butter and cheese from the fridge.

"Toasties!" she squealed, flicked the sandwich press on.

"Yep."

I made quick work of slapping them together before she could switch to angry-drunk again. Placing them into the hot press, I turned to her. "What was that shit with Nate about?"

"It's a hurtful nickname and it's not true." She stuck out her bottom lip. Her hand darted out, wrapping around my bicep, which she squeezed. "See? Not sissy."

I chuckled, and Hex spun around so fast her hand planted on the wall outside the tiny kitchen to stop her falling over. Then she tramped down the hall, fingers down her top. That girl would to do herself harm if she wasn't careful. She fumbled with the lock and went inside.

Silence ensued while I watched the press, waiting to hear the sizzle of melted cheese. When it finally came, I flipped the sandwiches out onto a couple of plates someone had knocked off from the dining hall. Unplugging the press, I left it open to cool. Yeah, I'd be thanking Liv for this later. Midnight snacks were perfect for sobering up. Balancing both plates, I walked toward Hex's room. The door stood open and light flooded the room, but everything was dead silent. Probably because she lay on the bed, asleep again, with her hand curled around her phone. Thank god. We'd become friends and seeing her like this ... it was too close to home.

I slid the plates onto her desk and shook my head as I watched her. If it were possible to see someone fall into a deeper sleep, it happened. While I watched, her breathing not only evened out, it grew louder and she became so still it was creepy. She couldn't sleep like that though, or she'd wake up in a drunken sweat, even though the summer heat was waning. I snuck across the room and unlaced her boots, sliding them off over her feet.

Hex groaned. "My father's an asshole."

She rolled onto her side, and scooched right up against the wall with her face angled so I couldn't see it anymore.

Aren't they all?

I pulled the covers over her then dragged my attention away from her peacefully sleeping form. This girl sure was something else. She acted cool, played hard, and partied even harder. But what was she hiding—a bad relationship with her father? Or worse?

I stepped out into the hallway and eased her door closed. She needed a friend, one who wasn't going to ignore all the shit that hid underneath her tough exterior. No matter what Hex needed, I promised myself right then and there that I'd be there for her.

As I walked into my own room, I remembered the

69

earlier incoming message. I pulled the phone from my pocket and almost choked. It'd been more than a year since I'd last seen my mother's name on my screen.

How are my boys?

I slid it back in my pocket without answering. She only made contact when she wanted something.

My eyes shot open, my heart pounding like a bloody jackhammer, trying to tear my chest apart. My bedroom window rattled with a sharp knock. Suppressing a sigh, I hauled myself out of bed. Saving Kayla's arse in the middle of the night was getting mighty old. We should just switch bedrooms, so she had the one furthest from our parents'.

I yanked the curtains back and the face peering through my window wasn't my sister's, but rather her best friend's. Cheeks puffy, nose red, and eyes wide, Becky looked spooked. Placing my hand on the window to brace against its usual opening squeal, I slid the darn thing open. "What's wrong?"

Becky shook her head. "She's too drunk. There's something wrong and I ... I ... I don't know what to do."

"Where is she?" I pulled my jeans on over my boxers and tugged a shirt over my head, then shoved my feet into my joggers.

"At the park. There was a party and ..."

Tuning her out, I vaulted through the open window and started jogging. It was only a few blocks away, but I couldn't get there fast enough. Becky kept pace beside me.

We came around the corner, and I spotted a single form

lying face down near the swings. Alone. I spun on Becky. "What the hell? You left her by herself?"

"I … I …" She began blubbering. "I was trying to get her home."

My knees smashed into the woodchips, and I snatched Kayla's wrist into my hand. It felt like ice. Shit. Her pulse beat rapidly against my fingers. Way too fast. I rolled her over and Kayla's eyes were closed, her lips off colour. Under the street light, they had an almost blue tint around the edges. I grabbed her hand to hoist her into my arms.

"Call a taxi," I ordered Becky.

"But we're underage. We could get in trouble."

"I don't care. She needs a doctor."

"Andrew Hinton said maybe she was paralytic. I don't even know what that means."

"It means if we don't get help she's in trouble, so call someone with a goddamn car." I turned my attention back to my sister. Rubbing her cold hands in mine, I spoke softly. "I'm here, Kays. I'm here."

Chapter 8
Hex

WE WERE four weeks into term and I sucked at this. I'd hated Science at high school, so I don't know what possessed me to take it now. Probably my father's non-gentle prods. I may not have 'spoken' to the man in four years, but that didn't mean he didn't email me—instructions, requests for exam results, what I needed to do to maintain his 'support'. Our correspondence was always clinical and I had no problem with that. I had nothing to say to the man anyway.

The lecturer's notes blurred into an indecipherable mess on the board out front of the class and although she talked about chemicals, mixing, and peptides, the little symbols didn't mean a thing to me. It may as well have been another language; I had no idea how I'd ever manage to understand it. But I had to ... at least enough to pass the subject. We couldn't afford for me not to. Even though I hated Science, we needed the study allowance my father provided.

I must have daydreamed through the entire lecture, because suddenly the professor dismissed us. I jumped up from my desk and began the trek across campus. Halfway to the cafeteria my phone buzzed with an incoming call.

I pulled it out of my jeans pocket and swiped the screen on, sighing when I saw Aunt Susan's name. Science had finished and I didn't have another lecture for two hours, so I hit accept. "Hi."

"Darling. How are you?" My aunt and I had always been close. At least, we had been before.

"Life's good."

"Are you enjoying university?"

"Classes are interesting, college is cosy, and the boys are hot. What more could a girl want?" *Lies, almost all of them.*

"That's my girl." She chuckled. "How's the money holding out? Do you have enough?"

I should have guessed *he* was behind her call. I stared at the cement path as I started walking from the Arts building up toward the cafeteria to grab lunch. "Is that why you called?"

"He needs to know you're taken care of."

"Well, you can report back that his money's being well spent and next time he can get off his rear and call himself. No wait … my mistake, he wouldn't want—"

She sighed down the line. "If you won't answer his calls, he can't know if you need anything."

I kicked the brickwork lining the fountain. "If you rang to talk about your brother you can hang up now."

A long moment of silence stretched down the line

73

while I imagined the stern look on her face melting into a more resigned one, like it always did when we spoke about *him*.

Finally, she said, "Tell me about the boys."

"Well..." I sat on the fountains' edge, which looked different somehow. "It was a figure of speech. Everyone here is really lovely. I've made some great friends, and for the best part the guys aren't bad on the eye, but I'm not looking for a boyfriend." To be honest, I wasn't even looking for a casual fling. Romance of any kind wasn't on my radar; I'd seen firsthand how badly it could end. While I told Susan about college life—sans boys—I stared at the running water, trying to figure out what about the water feature had changed.

"Ah, but that's when the right boy will come along."

I sighed. "I don't need a guy in my life to be happy."

"Of course you don't, sweetheart." She didn't sound as if she meant it. "I've heard some things about your mother ..."

I was tempted to hit *end call*, but we hadn't talked in a while and I really did miss my aunt. "She's doing just fine. She doesn't need a man either. Neither of us do."

"Oh honey, I wasn't saying—"

"Look, Aunt Susan. I've got to go. Class ..." Up toward The Bar's entrance, Jordan walked right toward me, his focus set on me, as if he were trying to puzzle something out. Walking fast too, he was almost in front of me in only a few seconds. "Class is about to start."

"Don't be a stranger," Aunt Susan said. "I love you."

"Love you too. Bye." I hit *end call* as Jordan stopped.

"You've got class?"

Running my fingers through my freshly redyed blue tips, it was as if all words had been vacuumed from my brain.

"'Cause I was going to grab a coffee."

"I lied. I'd love to." It was out before I'd had time to think it through.

Jordan tipped his chin back and laughed. "Who'd you lie to? Your mum or dad?"

"Neither." I walked away, toward The Bar.

Jordan caught up within a few steps and together we made our way to the tiny cafe upstairs. I'd been here with Amber on Saturday night and the upstairs bar had served drinks, so it turned out it was a cocktail lounge come coffee bar. We placed our orders, and as I slumped into the comfy couch my phone buzzed with an incoming message.

I spared a peek at the object and *his* name illuminated the screen. Like hell I was going to answer that. Picking at my thumbnail, I said to Jordan, "What happened to you on the weekend?" I hadn't seen him since that night he put me to bed a good week and a half ago. "I didn't see you out in town."

"You didn't look."

"I looked all over the Central and you weren't there."

"That's kind of sweet, but you know, there's more than one bar in town."

"And you weren't at any of them."

"I don't need to go out drinking every night to have fun." He slouched back in his chair, running a hand through his unruly mop of dark hair. Was that a dig at me? It wasn't like I drank every night. And damn him. I didn't

75

need to drink to have fun. Fun was something that just happened. It was more a state of mind than whether you'd been drinking or not. Clearly he didn't know the difference.

"Have some fun for once, Jordan. I dare you."

He drummed his fingers against the chair arm and gave me a look, as if he thought I was insane. "You dare me?"

"I dare you. Do something stupid."

His fingers slid around the coaster, and I shook my head, but it was too late. It flew through the air and clipped my chin in imitation of the last time we'd sat in this same spot.

"Lame. You can do better," I taunted.

"Okay, Ms Darer ..." He held my stare. "Challenge accepted."

"Green. The water was green." I finally figured the difference in the fountain out. I pointed the other hand toward the window that overlooked the water feature marking the centre of our student hub. "I dare you to go one better than that."

Jordan pushed himself out of the lounge and walked over to the window. "You want better than the fountain running blood?" He swung around to look at me, then returned to his chair and leaned in, whispering, "Done." Then he resumed his casual, I-don't-give-a-rat's slouch. "But you've got to be out of bed early."

"Whatever, Mr Boring." I doubted he had it in him, but Jordan looked pretty smug as he slid his coffee off the table and took a sip.

A SHARP rap on my door jarred me awake. I groaned and pulled the covers over my head. Honestly, I never dreamed he was serious about the morning thing.

"Hex." Even through the thick timber, he sounded exultant to be awake at such an ungodly hour.

"Go away, Jordan. It's still dark."

"No it's not. The sun's rising. Hurry up."

I growled as I hauled myself out of bed and pulled on my sweat pants and a Quiet Renegade tee. Taming my hair into a messy bun was almost as hard. If this was his idea of fun, he had a lot to learn.

Jordan knocked again and I yanked the door open. "I'm coming."

His twinkling eyes met mine the second the door was no longer between us. He chuckled, as if this whole thing were amusing. Then his gaze slipped down my body, spending entirely too long on my chest. Which honestly, wouldn't be much to look at in this thin T-shirt. Ah crap ... no bra. I slammed the door closed and fixed my wardrobe mishap then opened it again. A smug smile was still stretched across Jordan's lips.

"You think this sight is funny, huh? Well, you don't look much better yourself, stud muffin."

"Stud muffin? Your name calling keeps getting better."

"Shut up." I shuffled out into the corridor and pulled my door closed. Jordan backed up out of the way, the backpack slung over one shoulder bouncing against his hip while he continued grinning. "Get your morning

77

attitude the hell away from me."

He laughed again and by god, I was about ready to slap him like a five-year-old. He took a few long steps into the kitchen and waited until I joined him, then shoved my pink coffee mug toward me, and maybe I wouldn't have to attack his pretty face after all. Anyone who premade coffee was a godsend. We stood in the tiny kitchen, sipping at our coffee until it was all gone. He didn't speak a word, as if he finally got how to do mornings. They really weren't my strength; neither was anytime before noon. I needed some warming up, and this morning was no different. Still half-asleep, I placed my cup on the sink and Jordan tilted his head toward the door. I sighed, and nodded, even though crawling back into bed topped my wish list.

As soon as we slipped into the stairwell I said, "Your idea of fun is seriously warped."

Jordan laughed again. "You're the one who made that stupid dare."

We emerged into the courtyard and the sky looked amazing. Sure, I'd seen the sunrise before, but that had only been after staying up all night. This? Well, this was an entirely different experience. A kind of milky grey, it looked as if the night were fading. Bordering the morning sky, the four walls surrounding the courtyard blocked the horizon from view.

A fat bar had been drawn over the gates into Oxley, but Jordan pulled out his entry card and swiped. The latch clicked free. He hefted the huge iron gate forward then waved his hand in a grand flourish for me to go first. Not rolling my eyes proved difficult.

Wait!

The gate closed behind us and it struck me that I'd never heard Oxley this quiet before. With absolutely no noise, except the sound of some ridiculous bird that thought this was a grand time to tweet his love of daybreak. If that was what you called this moment in time. It felt more like the opposite of twilight. Once outside the confines of our dorm, I could see a smudge of white on the horizon. Weird. I'd thought sunrises were normally orange or pink or purple—anything but black or white, really.

Jordan headed to Elm Avenue and the coffee must have finally kicked in because it was impossible to stay cranky with the beauty of the light falling through the green leaves. Orange and yellow splayed out from the east like fingers reaching for the top of the sky.

"Pretty, isn't it?" Jordan bumped my shoulder with his as we walked the path that led up the hill. By now I was panting a little, which wasn't a pretty sound, so I nodded and kept walking.

Once the ground evened out and we'd hit campus, I asked him, "What type of fun is this supposed to be?"

He shoulder bumped me again. "You'll see."

Without a soul in sight, the place felt as deserted as Oxley had been. Even walking around up here after a late night at The Bar wasn't this quiet. This morning campus held an almost peaceful quality that made me want to lie on the lush grass and stare at the brightening of the sky. Or maybe that was merely the ache to go back to sleep.

I followed him past the library right to the fountain that only yesterday had run green. Still a little discoloured, it was nowhere near the bright hue it had been.

"Original," I said eyeing the backpack Jordan pulled off his shoulder.

He tapped his nose, a huge smile on his face. If I wasn't mistaken he was actually enjoying this, and that made me smile to myself. He tugged a plastic bottle out of his bag, and the guy was a good prankster. I laughed as he uncapped the lid and poured the contents into the water which immediately frothed up.

"Challenge met," Jordan declared, shoving the detergent back in his bag. Then he retrieved a much smaller bottle and emptied it into the now foaming water. It instantly turned the same blue as my hair: Turquoise.

It looked like an exploding washing machine that had gotten into the blue food dye.

Jordan zipped up his bag and stood back, admiring his handiwork, his arms crossed and smirk satisfied. A few seconds passed then he laughed, and not with his usual small chuckle. This was a smooth noise, deep, like the rumble of a cascade.

I had a new favourite sound.

"See? Fun," I said. He glanced my way and raised a fist in the air for a bump. I knocked mine against it.

The bubbles grew more foam-like as the minutes passed and it may have been a tiny act of vandalism, but really it was harmless and every single person who walked by today would smile. Bringing laughter to the student population couldn't be a crime. It wasn't like there were any fish or wildlife in the water to harm, and hey, the foam would clean the brickwork. Thoroughly.

My gaze kept connecting with Jordan's while we both stood there, grinning like idiots. The sun had moved fully above the horizon, but there was still peacefulness about the day. Crazily, I no longer wanted to go back to bed. I walked over to the grass I'd wanted to fall against earlier. It must have only been about six a.m., so we had plenty of time to kick back. Flopping under one of the massive oak trees, I crossed my hands under my head, gazing up at the pale blue, cloudless morning sky.

Jordan didn't sit down, but rather looked around nervously.

"What's up?" I asked.

"You think that's wise?"

"If they were going to catch us on camera it's already happened."

I could practically hear the cogs turning in his mind. His shoulders slumped and he fell to the ground beside me, lying close enough that his body heat warmed my side. Yeah, that did strange things to my tummy.

I punched him in the arm. "Nice dare."

"Next dare's yours, crazy girl."

"Hey ... the name-calling is my thing. Don't be a copycat."

Jordan rolled onto his side, facing me. His fingers pushed a stray clump of hair off my forehead. "I dare you to ..." He scrunched his mouth to the side.

"Kiss me."

Holy cow, where the hell did that come from?

Jordan grinned. "Are you begging me, Hex?"

"In your dreams." I shot up so fast my head slammed into his chin. Jordan groaned and rolled onto his back. How the hell did I recover from that? I needed to say something. Jumping to my feet, I shoved my hands into my pockets and the silence stretched between us, growing more awkward by the second.

I started walking away, my steps growing faster. This was mortifying. It wasn't like I didn't want to kiss him, I was just ... it was all a joke. I'd ruin everything, like I always did. I needed to go back to bed and curl up in ball, not waking until I'd had enough sleep to act normal.

Jordan shot past me and skidding to a stop along the gravel, turned to face my way. I couldn't meet his eyes, so I focused on the ground and tucked my shoulder to walk past him.

"Hex." He grabbed my arm. "Don't be ridiculous."

I stopped, but didn't look back. "I didn't mean it."

The distance between us closed a little as his hand on my arm dragged me close, but I stepped back, my arm pulling taut between us, and Jordan's expression fled through emotions so quickly, I didn't have time to guess at how he was feeling. This time he let me go, and didn't even call my name as I strode, like the total coward I was, all the way back to Oxley.

Chapter 9
Jordan

RIDAY AFTERNOON rolled around and music pumped out of her room again. It made me wonder when the hell Hex studied, which was what I was trying to do. I had an assessment on basic health observations due next Tuesday and although Human Bio came easy, today, concentrating was hard. What the hell was she was doing in that room? Maybe dancing to the music in that sexy rhythmic way she had ... I shook my head to drive out the image, because that was a sure-fire way to get no study done at all. The memory of yesterday morning lingered so freshly—she kept popping into my head. We'd almost kissed after the fountain fiasco and I was damn sure I hadn't imagined her freaking out about that. It wasn't like I'd intended to kiss her ... it had just kind of happened. Doing all the stupid stuff made me feel so alive. It had been like being a kid with Kayla again—and that was it. My sister and I had always done stupid shit together and I hadn't been dumb like that in years. That was the only explanation for feeling attracted to someone who embodied what I hated the most— excessive drinking. Hex's personality was so addictive it had me confused.

I slammed my pen down on the desk and peered out the window. Not that I could see much other than the car park. And the common room, but no movement came from there. It could be deceiving though; behind the thick curtains people would be playing pool like always. At least I knew Hex wasn't down there, not with the Quiet Renegade concert belting out of her room. The girl had stellar taste in music.

My phone rang. That would be Logan, since he hadn't returned the text I'd sent yesterday. I reached for it. "Ye-ello."

"Can you get your arse in by five? Kaleb called in sick and we're busier than a brothel with a buy-one-get-one-free sale." It was Carlos.

I peeked at the clock. Four forty-five. "If you want me there in fifteen minutes, you better send one of the drivers my way."

"Sure thing, kid." The line went dead.

The study could wait until later. I slammed my text book shut, and reefed my shirt over my head, exchanging it for the red Mozzarellas polo. Next I slipped off my jeans, switching them out for black work pants, then shoved my phone and keys in my pocket, locking the door on my way out. An extra shift would be handy; god knew I needed the money.

As I walked past Hex's room, I couldn't resist peeking

inside. With her back to the door, she was dancing, almost exactly as I'd imagined. The way she moved made me itch to grab her hips, and move my body in time with hers. A moan vibrated deep in my throat.

She spun around, checking out my uniform. "You'll be living at that place soon."

"And give up watching you move like that?" I dragged myself away before I missed my ride or did something stupid. Like follow through on our empty flirting.

By the time I reached the front car park, the Mozzarellas Focus was already idling right near the footbridge.

"Hey Zahin." I climbed in the little car. "We got any deliveries?"

"Boss said to get you in first. Deliveries can wait ten minutes."

"Huh. The place must really be slammed." And sure enough when we pulled into the parking lot, it was. The shopfront overflowed with people and it was only five p.m. It'd be crazy later. I pushed through the employee entrance and after a quick survey of the kitchen went straight to work at the ovens. Topped bases lined the long bench behind the oven, a backlog that would need to go through pronto.

Into the rear of the oven, out the other side then box it up. The steaming pizza cases disappeared after that, snatched up by the front-end staff. I lost count of how many went through, and not once did I stop to think about anything but churning them out. Sometime later Penny whisked by, looking different. Her arm brushed mine on the way past otherwise I wouldn't have seen her. We'd been so busy I hadn't even noticed her up front.

The orders kept rolling in.

Hissed whispers sounded somewhere behind me. I turned around, but the two juniors both worked with their heads down. Three pizzas later it started up again, this time escalating to growled exchanges. I spun around in time to catch one scowling at the other and that was my cue to move off the ovens. Switching places with the scowler, I slipped in beside the guy with whom he'd been topping bases. "You guys cool?"

Joe grunted and dropped a whole handful of ham smack in the centre of the pizza. Reaching past him, I spread it out to the edges. But didn't push the questioning any further. By the way they were both glaring at each other, maybe keeping them apart was best for now. We were almost out of ham, so I told the kid I'd be back in a sec and ducked into the cool room. The door closed behind me only to reopen less than two seconds later.

"Jordie." Penny pulled the door closed as she sashayed into the walk-in fridge. Unusually, her blonde hair hung about her shoulders, and her lips looked somehow plumper than normal. Her fingers closed around my collar and she tugged me to her. Right to her, so her chest felt like fire against me due to the arctic air. My body respond-ed to her immediately. Her lips wasted no time finding mine, their warmth warding off the numbness that had set into my fingers. Her hands seared heat against my chest, and my muscles tightened. As if I didn't need it to keep warm any longer, all the blood drained right to where I didn't want it to be. At least, not while I was in the boss's cool room and he sat as his desk just outside it. I kissed her back, letting our tongues tangle in a way that was

86

almost languid. Penny tasted like she always had: mint overridden by stale cigarettes. My hands wandered to her hips and I wondered what Hex would taste like. How her lips would feel against mine. If kissing her would be as slow, as lazy as this.

Penny ended the kiss and stepped back out of the cool room without so much as a backward glance.

Shaking away the haze in my mind, I snatched a bag of ham from the metal shelf and got back to work.

Penny came out back a few times, but each visit was with a purpose that didn't include conversation. It wasn't until ten p.m. that things finally started to slow down.

"You right to shut shop?" Carlos asked. "Kaleb was on lock-up before he called in sick and you know how I don't like anyone closing alone. It's not safe." He shuffled his weight, glanced toward the front of the shop and shook his head. "I'd stay if I could, but Marcy ..."

"She'll have your balls. Get out of here." I flicked the towel I was holding at my boss, but he didn't crack a smile. In fact, he'd been giving me weird looks all night, as if maybe he had seen the cool room fiasco. Good thing that room wasn't home to any cameras.

Carlos's scowl deepened. "Don't dis the family, boy."

Geez, he said that himself all the time. We always joked about Marcy. "What was with tonight's busyness any-way?"

"Kitchen's out at Evan's Hall."

"Shit. Yeah?"

He filled his pockets with his keys, phone, and other junk off his desk. "Some electrical issue."

"The entire dorm?"

87

"No idea. I only care about food, kid, not bedrooms."

Carlos slipped out the front, no doubt to wish Penny a good night. After he'd left, orders continued trickling in and by the time we closed, there were still two others with us. We'd asked them to stay back even though we were supposed to minimise wage costs and all that, but we'd been slammed tonight, so surely the takings could cover an extra hour or two for a few juniors.

"Night." I nodded to the rest of our crew and climbed into the car where Penny waited. She'd been strangely quiet since our encounter in the cool room. She didn't start the engine, merely sat there, staring out the front windshield. Whatever game she was playing, I wasn't about to buy into it, and as much as I'd let that kiss happen, I didn't want to take things further tonight.

Penny shook her head, her blonde hair bouncing off her chin.

"What's up?" I asked.

She started the car, still staring ahead. It was clear she wasn't going to talk, so I flicked the radio to the only other channel in town, not the boring-arsed news station it had been set to. Dance music rocked the airwaves, probably because it was near midnight on a Friday.

Despite the day and hour, we didn't see much movement on the drive home. Not too many people out walking, like there sometimes were on Friday and Saturday nights. Piss-poor students would do anything to save a buck, and that included walking between the dorms and town after a few drinks. Not tonight though. It was probably too early.

Penny pulled into Oxley's car park, and as I reached for

the handle she finally spoke. "Who is she?"

I sighed. "Who's who?

"Don't play dumb with me, Jordan. You've met a girl, and the least you can do is tell me who's trumped my position as your booty call."

"It's not like that—"

"I'm not an idiot."

"Look." I turned to face her. "This has always been casual, and I thought we were on the same page."

"Yeah ... casual." She looked out her window, blocking her face with her hair.

"Penny, come on. There is no one."

Her head bent, but her thumbs pinched the bridge of her nose. I was an asshole.

"Penny—"

"Shh." She finally faced me and her smile didn't hold its usual warmth.

She leaned across the seats and brushed a soft, lingering kiss across my lips.

I should have mourned the end of easy sex, but as I climbed out of the car, I felt free.

Neither of us said goodbye.

There wasn't much movement in the courtyard, or maybe it was like the streets—either too early or too late. Light shone through Hex's curtains, so she at least was home and not out. She must have had a quiet night.

I made it all the way to my block without seeing another soul and even up on my floor, where all the doors were closed. I slipped off my ring, grabbed my stuff and headed to the shower to wash off the inch-thick layer of pizza grease.

While the water pounded against my aching back, the door squealed, as was the norm when it opened. Someone must still be awake, anyway. My thoughts drifted to the shit that had gone down tonight. We'd always been upfront with each other ... or at least I had. We'd even agreed to call things off if one of us grew too attached. Is that what had just happened? Did our hook-ups mean more to Penny than I'd thought?

Feeling more than a little agitated, I turned the water off and scrubbed a towel over my head. Why'd chicks make things difficult? Pulling on a pair of shorts, I gathered my gear and stepped out into the bathroom. Once I hit the hall, voices wafted in and out. All the doors were still closed, but the closer I got to Hex's the more obvious it was. That was where the sound came from ... and it wasn't only her and Amber. A low-pitched voice followed giggling. I raised my fist and rapped on the wooden surface. The door opened.

"Oh, it's you." Amber blocked my entrance. I looked right past her, scanning the room. Hex sat on the desk, her criss-crossed legs up on it, while she picked at a packet of hot chips.

"Si—Jordan! Busy shift, bro?" All six foot of Nate was sprawled over Hex's bed, as if he didn't give a rat's it was her personal space. The spot she laid in each night. The place she dreamed sexy dreams. *He should be on the floor.* "Yeah."

Amber moved from the doorway and grabbed a box of food off the desk—some sort of chicken, by the smell of it—and dropped onto the end of the bed, pushing Nate's legs aside. He barely shifted.

I dumped my shower gear by the door, walked across the room, brazen as Nate, and plopped myself on the bench right next to Hex. I dropped my arm over her shoulder and plucked a chip from her stash. She was so close, her scent got right up in my nose and hot damn, the girl smelled better than frying bacon. She had her own smell that was almost like blueberries; sweet, fruity, and all girl. I inhaled deeply and took another chip. "Where'd the food come from?"

"Town." Hex pointed a chip at Nate. "... and it is not a real thing."

"It's as real as that chicken leg." Nate smirked. "Or maybe two of them and a wing."

"I hate to say it, Hex, but he's right." Amber nibbled on her piece of chicken.

Hex threw the chip back into its box. "You idiots are making this garbage up. No way is that a thing."

"You guys walked all the way to town for hot food?" I pinched another chip, making sure I stayed close. "What the hell are you lot talking about anyway?"

Hex leaned into me. "Amber drove us."

"Sex." Nate winked at me. "And not the vanilla kind—"

"Stop," Amber squealed. "We do not need to hear any details."

Before I could stamp his pick-up efforts in the bud, Hex said, "I hate to break it to you, Nate, but that stuff only happens in porn."

The girl had spunk, I'd give her that. Amber reached across and held her hand up which Hex high fived.

Chuckling, Nate said, "Well, we could try it and—"

"Get out of here!" Hex wriggled out from under my arm

and pointed toward the door, which only made Nate laugh even louder. Dragging himself off the bed, he bowed at the waist and came up winking. "It is getting late. Ladies, Sis, good evening."

Hex rounded on him, her finger right up in his face. "I told you, dick-face, drop that dumb nickname."

"Language, sweet Hex." Nate disappeared through the door.

Amber jumped up from the bed, snapping the fast food container shut so forcefully the box crumpled. "I better get to bed too."

"Yeah right," Hex mumbled, but it was too late for her friend to hear. Amber had already chased Nate down the hall.

I stole another chip and Hex passed off the rest of her late-night snack to me.

"Damn, these things are good," I said by way of thanks.

"Keep them." She patted the back of my hand. I flipped it over, snatching her fingers before she could pull away. She studied our joined hands while I studied her face, her expression that gave away no secrets.

I rubbed my thumb across her palm, still waiting for a clue as to what she was thinking. "Have some fun with me tomorrow."

Hex's eyes flicked up to mine and the silence stretched so long a sweat broke out along my neck. Or maybe it was my imagination making the hair prickle. I'd probably taken the flirting a step too far; it had kind of happened without conscious thought. If her hand didn't feel so damn good in mine, I would've pulled it back. But she wasn't flinching, so neither did I. I ran my thumb over the soft centre of her palm again and Hex closed her eyes. Her tongue slid over her bottom lip and her teeth caught the pink flesh. I was too far gone, so I pulled out the big guns without a second thought. "I dare you."

With that I dropped her hand, and casually popped another chip into my mouth. When I was two steps out of her room, I threw over my shoulder, "Fun dreams." Then I pulled the door closed.

Chapter 10
Hex

I **DOZED ON** and off all morning, thanks to the circus parading outside my door. I swear every kid in this place was hanging out in my block when they should've been sleeping like normal people. It was Saturday, after all. At eleven I decided it was futile and couldn't ignore my growling stomach any longer, so I dragged myself out of bed and down to the dining hall for weekend brunch. After making my usual egg special, I spotted Amber at a table. More interestingly, Amber and Nate. He watched her twirl a strand of hair around her finger while she spoke. That girl sure had been giving her feminine magic a workout, and it seemed to be paying off. Whatever she was talking about, Nate hung on her every word. I took a seat opposite them, which was next to the girl we'd played I Never with, McKenzie.

As I closed my mouth around a forkful of egg, Jordan slid into the seat next to me. He was like a moth to light lately; he seemed to zoom in without any sign he was nearby. "What are we doing today?"

"I assumed you had something planned."

"We?" Amber questioned. Someone nudged my foot under the table. By the raised brow, I'd say it was her.

"Yup, we," Jordan said. "Hex here promised a Saturday full of adventure."

Amber's eyes widened. A chunk of egg wedged in my throat; I spluttered.

"Not that type of adventure." I kicked Amber back.

Nate's mouth curled.

"You guys want something fun to do?" McKenzie piped up. "What about Blue Hole? We had all that rain last month, and it's supposed to be hot today."

Jordan clicked his fingers then pointed at her. "Yes!"

"What on earth is Blue Hole?" Amber asked.

"An awesome swimming spot." Jordan pulled out his phone and started texting. "We'll need transport."

"Hold the phone, I can drive," Amber said, a huge grin in place.

"Sweet. What type of car have you got? It's not a good road."

McKenzie frowned. "My Datsun gets out there fine."

Jordan placed his phone on the table, text abandoned. "Probably shakes the shit out of it though."

"It survives."

Jordan and Nate exchanged one of those guy looks, like they thought girls knew nothing about cars.

"A four-wheel drive," Amber said.

"Hey." I stopped the conversation right there. "What if I don't want to go to a stinking swimming hole?"

95

"You want to go." Amber nudged me under the table again, then rolled her eyes toward Nate. "What about you, Nate?"

"Sounds better than spending the day here."

Jordan's arm slunk over my shoulders and he squeezed. I should be flattered he wanted to spend the day hanging out with me, but I couldn't help wondering what his agenda was. Was he okay with being friends? Or was he angling for a hook-up? Because I wasn't sure I could go there and not get attached. Not with him—he was too caring, too fun, too Jordan. And if I did get attached then my heart would surely burn.

"Meet back out here in thirty," McKenzie said. "That'll be plenty of time for you losers to get organised."

Half an hour later, with my swimsuit hidden under a baggy tee / jean shorts combo I trudged down to the courtyard. Jordan and Nate were already there wearing normal clothes, towels in tow, and so was McKenzie. She didn't have a towel with her, but rather a towel holder, or two of them: Max and Luca, who we'd hung out with a few times before, both footy guys.

"I invited the boys to join us," she said by way of explanation. "We'll have to take two cars."

While everyone sorted out the details, I looked toward the other courtyard. Finally, Amber appeared, dressed more like she intended to head to the beach than some murky swimming hole in the middle of the bush. She looked fantastic in a pair flip-flops, and a pale yellow sarong knotted over her boobs.

Someone wolf whistled, and Amber fluffed out her chestnut-coloured hair.

"Let's go." McKenzie grabbed Max's hand, walking away before anyone could answer. He turned over his shoulder, his gaze roaming over Amber.

We all set out toward the parking lot, meeting up with her along the way. Max somehow pried his hand out of McKenzie's grasp and fell into step beside my friend.

"Luca!" McKenzie called. The big guy's conversation with Nate immediately stopped as he rushed to catch up, swinging the pink bag he carried and tapping her in the rear. They peeled off toward a rusty blue Datsun. Luca was a really nice guy and sometimes it seemed like McKenzie didn't realise he clearly liked her. She yanked open the passenger door then shouted, "Come on, Max!"

I turned in time to catch him wink at Amber. "See you there, pretty girl."

Jordan and I exchanged a glance. This whole day could go horribly wrong with the whole Nate-Amber-Max-McKenzie thing.

We arrived at Amber's RAV4 and the guys exchanged one of *those* looks again. Jordan slapped the hood. "That is not a four-wheel drive. It's a—"

"Just because it's purple doesn't mean it can't do rough." Amber hit the key-lock then jumped in. I claimed the front seat and she shot me a death glare which I returned. I wasn't about to get carsick riding up back so the guy she wanted to nail could take shotgun. It might be mean, but she'd thank me when her car didn't smell of puke.

The trip out of town went quickly, and although everyone talked, I found myself lost in my own thoughts. I had an English Lit essay on *Pride and Prejudice* due at the end of next week and hadn't even looked at it yet. I wasn't really stressed about that, or the Science paper I was sure to fail. It was the call from Aunt Susan over a week ago that still played on my mind. When I came here to study I knew there would be no one at home to diffuse the gossip. Even though Mum had pushed me out the door, forcing a 'better life' on me, she wasn't equipped to cope. Hopefully she was holding up okay. If people minded their own business things would be fine. But Susan having 'heard' about her was a sure sign every nosey parker in town had his or her thumb in our business.

Jordan's finger prodded my shoulder. "You read, right?"

"Read what?"

"Books. Geez, girl, pay attention to the conversation. I saw that *Pride* book on your desk and that other tattered thing—"

"*Jane Eyre* and *Pride and Prejudice,* or do you mean *Little Women*?"

"I dunno, all of them. Maybe?"

Amber looked across at me. "I was saying true love is romantic, but Nate reckons its all bullshit that's only in old books and movies."

I turned in my seat to look at him, noticing his tormenting smirk. "It's in the newer ones too."

"No." Amber slapped her hand against the wheel. "Don't tell me you agree with him."

"Well—"

She darted a look my way. "You've read *Pride and Prejudice*, met Mr Darcy, and don't believe love like that is real? What wrong with you?"

I laughed; he'd sure riled her up. "You've got to remember those books are set last century. Things aren't the same as they were then. Women aren't expected to marry for money or standing anymore, and no one cares if you marry outside of your class. So, what they viewed as true love might be entirely different if you apply it to today's standards. Not that any of those books aren't romantic, but exploring the notion that people are destined for each other was a crazy thing back then. True love, no matter which century it's in ..." I could feel Jordan watching me intently from the back seat and the connection was too much, so I closed my eyes then reopened them, focusing on the scenery whizzing past my side window. "... is a romantic notion."

The light heartedness had seeped out of the conversation, replaced with words I thought were true.

"That's for sure." Amber sighed.

"But that's all it is," I said, "a notion."

Amber studied the road ahead, her brows drawn. "Are you saying you think there's no such thing as true love?"

"Absolutely."

"Why not?" Jordan asked.

"People are inherently selfish. No one puts someone else's needs above their own all the time, and when they do it's generally for a reason that benefits them. True love—literary true love—it just doesn't exist in real life."

Even if I wish it did. The car started vibrating. Violent bumps, as if it were trying to throw us all out. So much dust billowed around us that McKenzie's car up front had grown near invisible through the swirling cloud. The taste of dirt polluted the air.

99

Jordan leaned between the front seats, no doubt to be heard above the ruckus. "You might wanna slow down or you'll murder the transmission. The road's corrugated the rest of the way in."

"The transmission?" Amber said. Yeah, I had no idea either.

"Just take it easy," he warned.

Amber slowed down. Although the bumps were still violent it was a little easier on the rear, and my teeth too. I wasn't in constant fear of rattling them right out of my head. When we finally pulled up at a dirt strip that doubled as the car park, there was no water in sight, despite having crossed over a creek a little way back. Only a bunch of picnic tables, and one of those information signs that had its own tiny roof. Jordan shot out of the car and Nate followed, bounding out like a puppy let off its leash. They went straight to the information board, while Amber and I exchanged a look before we climbed out too. McKenzie and co. piled out of her car as well.

"Come on, kids," Jordan shouted over his shoulder. "Let's do this."

"We're swimming," I yelled back. "What's the hurry?"

Jordan tossed his towel at Nate and turned around with such a predatory look on his face that I wanted to swallow my words.

"You wanna see a hurry, Hex? Huh ... you wanna?" He stalked toward me and I gulped, ducking behind Amber. But she was poor cover. Strong arms scooped me up off the ground and hoisted me into the air all while my traitorous friend laughed. Jordan held me like a small child, cradled against his rock-hard chest. I kicked and flailed, trying to get away, because god knew what he had planned. I'd bet my bottle of vodka it wasn't going to be pleasant.

"Put me down!" I demanded.

He didn't. He marched through the bush, and down a path I could see disappearing behind us. Jordan laughed. Not his nice deep chuckle that I loved, but an evil, I'm-going-to-get-you laugh. I'd bet that vodka again that he was a youngest sibling, because this had *tormenting little brother* written all over it. I should know; I'd had one. Once.

A branch scraped my arm. I did the only thing I thought might work. I looked up into his face, made puppy-dog eyes, and dropped my voice to a whimper. "Please."

He stopped, and loosened his grip, letting me slide an inch. Surely he was going to put me down, but he caught me before my toes reached the ground and when I saw what was in front of us, his wicked plan grew obvious. Jordan strode toward the huge body of water out front, flicking his flip-flops off near the edge. I knew the moment his feet entered, because the muscles along his shoulders tensed. Holy crap, it must have been freezing. I dropped my cheek against his firm chest and whimpered, "No."

Jordan kept advancing.

Following behind us, my friends cheered him on.

"Traitors!" I bellowed.

A chuckle rippled through Jordan's chest, then the world tilted to the left and his solid arm slid up my back until everything—including the trees on the other side of the tiny lake—flipped upside down. My head pointed toward the water with my hair brushing its surface.

I screamed.

He was going to dunk me.

The water loomed closer and closer.

"You're an arse!" I squealed.

He lowered me to the shimmering surface. "Jordan whatever-the-hell-your-last-name-is DO NOT plunge me into that water or we will NEVER be friends again."

"Do it!" Nate bellowed from the shore.

Jordan spun me around so quick my stomach lurched. I clamped my legs around his waist and threw my arms about his neck, holding on for dear life. Smirking, he started toward the shore, and the way his abs moved against me had my legs clenching tighter to maintain the tiny amount of space between us. No way was I going to feel this ... this attraction for him.

"Now those are fighting words." The smirk on his face was far too amused. "And my last name's Hays."

"Well, Jordan Hays, you almost blew our entire friendship."

He threw his head back and laughed. "Just hurrying it up, Hex."

"I'll hurry you, right out of my circle of friends."

"You wouldn't dare."

"Oh, I would."

We reached the edge of the water and I released my death grip on Jordan, sliding to the ground.

Everyone else had moved down by the pond, too. Paying us no attention, McKenzie and Amber had lost their outer layers, and the boys had all stripped down to boardies.

Nate shook his head. "Should've dunked her, you

pansy."

Ignoring them, I peeled off my tee and stepped out of my jean shorts, then began applying sunscreen. My skin wasn't that fair, but if I didn't lather it on I'd burn for sure.

When they'd said Blue Hole I'd imaged a round pond, the colour of tropical water. Kind of idyllic, I guess. But this was way different. The water didn't ripple, but rather looked like smooth glass, and the colour was somehow more greeny-brown than blue. The only similarity to what I'd envisioned was a couple of huge rocks sitting out in the water like mini icebergs.

I snuck a peek at Jordan and my cheeks turned to fire. His attention was not only on me, but the look on his face made it obvious that he liked what he saw. I threw the tube of sun protection to the ground and ran to the water as if I hadn't noticed.

I hit the water at full-speed and didn't stop, running into the icy depths until the water reached my thighs, then I jumped out and swam into the deeper water, freestyle. I wasn't the strongest swimmer, but I reached my destination quick enough: the rocks. I climbed up onto the biggest one, and rested back on my elbows, letting the sun warm my shivering body.

The sound of my friends' conversation and splashing filled the otherwise peaceful afternoon. I closed my eyes, enjoying the warmth of the day. It was so peaceful out there, even with Amber's squealing and McKenzie's giggles.

The tiny splashes of someone swimming my way broke my solitude. Without looking I knew it was Jordan. His presence felt somehow different to anyone else's. Making good use of his arm bulging with glorious biceps, he vaulted himself out of the water, and up onto another rock, so close I could have touched him.

I got snagged on his tattoo; I'd never really been in the right position to see the details that were obviously there. Long and thin, it spanned across his entire left pec just above his dark nipple. It wasn't intricate or bold, but looked like a fallen figure eight. I'd seen the symbol somewhere before, but couldn't quite place it. His state of shirtlessness was as impressive as it had been the few times I'd managed to catch him half-naked before. Not only did he actually have pecs rather than a flat chest, but those abs looked as if they belonged on Superman. My heart picked up pace.

Oh boy ... not good.

I slid along the smooth rock and down into the water, landing with a splash. The freezing water stole my breath. Warm as the weather was today, the sun mustn't have scratched past the surface, especially down around my toes. I sucked in a sharp breath and ducked my entire head under. When I came up, running my hands over my hair, I shook the water off.

"Liv hates it out here, but you love this, don't you?" Jordan said.

"Never said I loved it." I splashed water up onto his rock, and it hit that perfect chest in a massive wave. "Who's Liv?"

"A friend."

That shouldn't have bothered me near as much as it did. Not so much I turned around and swam farther out into the water. A guy like him probably had a string of

104

girls they brought to places like this. Forcing myself to focus on each stroke, I realised I'd never really bathed anywhere like this before and it sure was different. The water had a slight dirty tang and although it was clear, it was nothing like swimming in a pool or the ocean.

After a while my stupid inner compass brought me right back to the Man of Steel, sunning himself on the rocks. He looked so peaceful I couldn't resist ruining it. With as much stealth as someone has propelling themself through water, I came at his spot from behind, snuck right up until I was close enough to see his chest rise and fall, then screamed. "WAKE UP!"

Jordan flinched so hard, he toppled to the side, almost sliding right off his perch. Lucky for him though, he managed to stay out of the water. Chuckling, I hauled myself back onto the spot I'd claimed earlier and shaded my eyes from the sun with an arm across my face.

He lay back down, propping himself up on his elbows. "You remind me of my sister."

Disappointment swamped me. "Yeah?"

"Yeah." The smile he gave was somehow wrong. Wrong in a way that made me reach out and brush my foot against his.

"Yeah ..."

This mood wasn't fun. I slid back into the water and slapped my palms against the surface, splashing water right into his face. His expression immediately turned mischievous and I knew I was in for trouble. I spun to swim away, but Jordan jumped into the water and grabbed my foot. Just as I got horizontal, he reeled me back in. My body crashed against his and his arms closed around me. My heart kicked up its rhythm, which matched the delicious shiver spilling through my entire body. For the second time today Jordan was too close, and I enjoyed it way too much.

"It's a good thing," he said. "Kayla was all kinds of fun. She did these crazy things all the time ... like the day you tossed those coasters at Cade. She was the type of girl that made everyone around her laugh. And you, you make me miss her a little less."

I let myself relax in his embrace. Jordan's hold loosened, so I flipped myself around. My back pressed against the warm rock, so our bodies touched from shoulder to pinkie toe along their entire length. I hadn't missed that one word which made me want to let him know that I cared. "What happened?"

"We lost her."

I wasn't sure how to respond to that. Losing someone you love is pure heartache. There are no words that work to effectively show empathy to news that someone has felt that pain.

"She died four years ago." The way he said it wasn't sorrowful or the way you'd expect. It was just matter of fact.

"Oh Jordan, I'm so sorry. I know that's a dumb thing to say, but I feel your pain."

This time he was the one to break the mood by splashing water into my face. He pushed off and swam far enough to be out of reach. He stopped to tread water, his hair, completely wet, hung in dark ringlets across his forehead. His lip tipped up in the same cheeky smile from earlier. "Race you to the other side."

Maybe Amber wasn't the only one working magic.

Against my better judgement, I was falling for Jordan Hays.

Chapter 11
Jordan

I THREW MYSELF into the couch and flicked on the TV. Liv was banging around the bathroom getting ready for work, while Logan snored. Apparently the rest of town being closed for Good Friday didn't stop the sports centre doing business, nor the trendy little cafe where my brother had worked since his college days. Turned out there weren't any jobs for psychologists in this small town, so he was biding his time until Liv graduated.

I kicked my feet up onto the coffee table and caught Liv's scowl as she sauntered into the room, clicking an earring into place.

"There's some fish defrosting on the bench. Make sure it goes in the fridge as soon as it's thawed and if you feel like baking, we need something sweet, maybe a cake."

She glided toward the door. Even in joggers and sports shorts that chick pulled off elegant. She paused on her way out, gym bag slung over her right shoulder. "Savvy and Dane should arrive mid afternoon, at a guess."

"Got it." I flicked through the channels. Home shopping, a Moses movie, parliament stuff, cartoons, and not much else.

"Don't wear out the remote."

I grunted as the door snapped closed behind her. It looked like I was in for another boring-as-bat-shit day. I scooped my phone off the same table that held my feet and scrolled down to Hex's name, then typed out a quick text.

Why did the chicken cross the road?

I stared at the screen for a good two minutes. She didn't answer. She was probably still in bed as well. It was only nine a.m., after all.

I hadn't stopped thinking about her since our day out at Blue Hole. I had no idea how he'd managed it, but Nate wound up riding shot-gun on the way home, which put Hex in the back with me. I watched her sleep the whole trip. Knowing it was creepy didn't stop me. Not for a second. Especially with the knowledge we were coming up to Easter, which meant I wouldn't see her for three weeks.

Three long weeks.

We'd all exchanged numbers that day when I realised. Like almost everyone else, Hex had gone home for the break. As did I. The entire town felt deserted with the mass exodus of students. Their departure meant I couldn't even pick up extra shifts at work, because it was nowhere near as busy as it was during term time.

My phone pinged with an incoming text.

Jordan Hays. Is life that boring without me that you've resorted to dumb jokes?

How's home?

Home is home. How's things?

Quiet.

Same here. Mum's still sleeping, I'm baking a cake.

Most parents would be up and at work by now. Maybe Hex's mum was a shift worker.

I need a cake. Wanna bring it over?

It's a three hour drive and I have no car. Besides, it has nineteen candles.

A birthday cake?

The coffee machine whirred to life, my clue Logan was awake. Leaning back on the couch, I tipped my head to better see into the kitchen. Coffee in hand, Logan turned my way. His hair was too long for his usual messy-style, and ditto on the facial hair. With dark patches under his eyes, he looked like shit. Had done since I'd been back on break—not that we'd seen a lot of each other. He always seemed busy. He dipped his chin. "Morning."

Before I could respond, his phone rang. Logan snatched it up off the bench, took one look at the screen and groaned. That didn't stop him picking up though. He held the device to his ear. "Yes?"

Whoever was on the other end certainly had a lot to say. Logan had time to look around the room, set his coffee down, roll his eyes back, and finally lean on the bench, pinching the bridge of his nose.

"My answer hasn't changed. It's still no."

I frowned as I watched his face set in a look only one person ever brought on. *Our mother.*

"Look, I don't have that kind of money. It's about time you grew up and took responsibility for the problems you created for yourself."

There was another brief pause in which Logan tipped his chin back and slapped a frustrated palm against his forehead.

"Do it. I don't care."

He pinched his nose again and caught my gaze.

"Who was that?"

"Just work." He tossed the phone on the counter and disappeared toward the bathroom, forgotten coffee still steaming.

Why the hell did he lie? If that was our mother, then it sounded like she was being a pain in the arse. She obviously wanted money from him. Maybe I should mention the text I'd received, but then what was the point if he was keeping things from me anyway?

I scooped my phone back up and there was another text from Hex.

The very same. Happy birthday to me.

Damn. She was making her own birthday cake.

What are you doing for your birthday?

Her response was immediate.

Eating a triple swirl cake. Then pigging out on Easter eggs.

For real? Surely you're doing something special?

For real. I'm planning an epic cake fest. That's pretty special.

Are your folks at work?

I wished mine were. It was such a normal thing to do, but nothing about my family was normal, or simple. As soon as I hit send, I remembered she'd said her mum was asleep.

Something like that.

"Logan," I called. "Was that our delightful mother on the phone?"

He appeared in the door, towel around his waist. "I said it was work. I'm getting ready to go there now."

"Well, she texted me a few weeks back, so be ready. She wants something."

My brother nodded once before turning back to the bathroom. He'd never lied before, so why did he feel the need now?

THE FOCUS hit a dip in the road, and I threw my hand over the pizza box balanced on my lap to hold it steady. Penny hadn't spoken much for the entire shift. Even now, she kept her attention on the road ahead, concentrating as if she were driving the Indy 500. Silence seemed to be the way of things lately. Penny didn't talk, Logan didn't talk, and Liv only talked fluff. Even Hex had stopped texting when I'd started asking questions about her lack of birthday celebrations. I couldn't get her to admit it, but I strongly suspected she spent the entire day alone.

I was more than two weeks late, but I hoped my gift made her smile.

We pulled into Oxley's car park and after thanking Penny, I climbed out of the car. It was the Saturday before classes returned, but the dorm wasn't yet half full. Everyone must be returning last minute. Hex was there though. Even though I hadn't had time to even say G'day, I'd seen her arriving as I left for work.

I walked through the courtyard and up into block D without seeing another soul, despite a number of light-filled windows. At ten p.m. it wasn't that late.

The coastie kid who lived at the very end of our hall raised his hand when I emerged from the stairs. "Hey," I said. "Did you have a good Easter?"

He responded with lopsided smile I assumed meant he spent it sitting on the beach, high as a kite. "Yup."

I lifted a fist to Hex's door, but it swung open before I could knock.

"Jordan!" She threw her arms around me in a bone-crunching hug that had me juggling the box behind her back to keep from dropping it.

Her hair smelled of blueberries and sunshine, and my shoulders dropped as all the tension seeped out of my tense muscles. "Welcome home."

She gave another squeeze, then Hex's arms dropped as she took a step back and inside. I offered the box and her entire face beamed. "You brought pizza?"

"Just leftovers ..." I shrugged her excitement off. "I wasn't letting it go to waste."

She took the warm box and placed it on her immaculate desk. Her entire room was all perfectly set out, as if she'd only just finished setting it back up. The fact we had to pack away our rooms for breaks was a pain in arse, but Oxley needed them for distance education students who visited while we were off. She flicked open the box and let out a loud laugh.

Yep, totally worth the ribbing from the new junior, Kev.

Hex flew across the room and into my arms again. If this was the kind of reception bringing her pizza caused then I'd be sneaking one home every shift. She pulled back too quickly with a wide grin.

"Best birthday present ever."

"It's only a pizza."

"You wrote my name on it. With pepperoni."

I smiled. I'd tried to make the base into a cool shape,

114

but the only thing that looked half-decent was the heart Kev had made for a joke. I wasn't about to give her that, so I'd settled for a normal base with Happy Birthday, Hex spelled out in toppings. Not the most inventive, but still kinda cool.

Removing a slice for herself, she passed me the box. I wasn't that fond of the stuff, probably because I'd worked with it for years, but I took a slice anyway and held it up as if to cheers. "Happy birthday."

She dropped onto the corner of her bed, so I took a seat in the desk chair.

In between bites, she said, "How was your break?"

"Long." I wanted to tell her about Logan, but how did I say my brother's acting weird without sounding like a whiny kid? I shook the thought away. That didn't matter right now. All that mattered was that I'd made this beautiful girl smile. Even if I shouldn't like that idea as much as I did.

Chapter 12
Hex

EDNESDAY NIGHTS were the pits. All my English classes were on Monday and Tuesday. Wednesday was a mix of Drama, Economics, and Science, but Thursday ... it was all Science. I had lab and a tutorial, where we were expected to contribute to discussion and since returning from Easter break the professor had a habit of calling on me. Not that I cared if the whole class knew I was bullshitting when I pulled a fake answer out of the air, but the professor could fail me. So to minimize the chances of a repeat from the first week back, I spent Wednesday night trying to make sense of this week's topic.

Spinning around on my chair, I glanced at my open door. To say I was looking for a distraction would be an understatement. I knew Jordan wasn't in, because I'd seen him leave when I'd sat down an hour ago. Dressed in board shorts and carrying a towel, he must have been heading to the pool at the sports centre. We hadn't spent a lot of time together in the past week, because he had a heavy workload with assignments. Still, we'd seen each other in passing almost every day.

I swung back around to my desk and picked up my water, taking a liberal sip and once again tried to focus on the prescribed readings.

The squeal of water running through the pipes stopped. I hadn't even realised someone was in the shower until the noise was no longer present. Frick, my focus was shot. I needed to look at the book, not think about the shower.

The little circles and lines that made up different molecules didn't mean a lot to me, but I could learn stuff by rote, so even though I didn't understand the symbols I recognised a water molecule from that of say, blood.

"Working hard?"

I flinched at the sound of Jordan's voice, not realising he was back. Putting the swivel on my chair to good use, I spun around and holy wow. He wore nothing but a towel wrapped around his narrow waist. That tattoo grabbed my attention again. Its rough lines were almost jagged where it spanned across his perfect pectoral muscle. And his shirtless perfection was exactly why I studied with my door open.

"I was working ..."

"I'll let you get back to it then."

Like that was going to happen.

Jordan sounded a little off tonight. His voice was tight, words clipped. I watched him disappear from my doorway. Maybe he needed to loosen up a little. There

117

were a few beers in the kitchen, which Jordan had been fussing to fit in there the other day, so maybe it was his. Leaving my books exactly as they were, I pushed up out of the chair and went to the kitchen, grabbing two bottles from the mini fridge. The girl from the room next door, shuffled past as I strode down the hall, passing me a friendly smile.

Jordan hadn't bothered to close his door either. He stood in the middle of the room rubbing a towel over his wet hair. A white T-shirt covered his muscled chest, but I knew exactly what lay beneath. Now we were into autumn, the weather had been growing cooler, but it wasn't freezing yet. Gulping back the urge to tell him to strip that darn shirt off, I made myself at home by dropping both bottles on his desk, then leaning a hip against the wooden surface.

"Wanna hang?"

Jordan eyeballed the beers then shifted his gaze to mine. "Sure, but I don't need the beer."

"I found it in the fridge. Yours?"

I'd been right. He was off tonight. Well, a little fun should help that. He nodded, so I cracked the cap of one beer and handed it to the guy with abs of steel. Despite saying no, he took it anyway. Leaving the other bottle in place, I retreated to my room for my vodka. Pouring a liberal splash, I topped it with lemonade from the fridge then returned to Jordan's room. "Have you been swimming?"

"Yep," he said. "It helps clear my head after a long day."

"I could use some head clearing."

He took a swig of his drink. "Why's that?"

I shrugged. "Science sucks."

"Hmm." He leaned against the inside of his door.

"What about you?"

He drank again. The way he was going, he'd be onto the second one in no time. "Family shit."

I waited for more of an explanation, but Jordan swallowed another mouthful of beer, seemingly not wanting to talk.

"Cheers." I held up my glass and he clinked his bottle against it.

We fell into a silence that was somewhat awkward. The last thing I wanted was for this to get weird; then I'd have to head back to the books and leave a clearly sad Jordan alone. Naturally, I pulled out the fun card. "I dare you to skull that drink."

Jordan brought the beer to his mouth and tipped his head back, downing the entire thing. Whatever had gotten under his skin, it sure had stripped away his usual restrained self. He slammed the empty down and picked up the full one, twisting off the cap. "I dare you to short sheet Dono's bed."

"What are you, twelve? That's so lame. I dare you ..." I tapped a finger against my thigh. This would have to be good. "To call in a fake pizza order for Cade Matthews."

Beer sprayed out of Jordan's mouth. "Do you have any idea what a pain the arse that is for the shop? Not to mention a waste of food." He swiped the back of his hand across his mouth. "I dare you to sneak into Nate's room and steal his favourite shirt. You know, the one with the music-farting dog, and hoist it up the flagpole."

My eyes widened. "That, my friend, is a good one.

We're doing it."

Jordan's smile made an appearance for the first time tonight.

I downed the rest of my drink in as few gulps as possible and jumped up, grabbing Jordan's hand to pull him out of the door. Laughing, he reached back to lock up, fumbling with the keys and an almost empty bottle in his one free hand.

I dropped his hand and made for the fridge, grabbing a fresh beer from his six-pack, which I shoved toward him. He dropped the empty in the kitchen bin. "It's only nine p.m.; Nate should be around."

We snuck down the stairs, and when we reached the bottom, I peeked out of the door and into the courtyard. A few people sat at the picnic table, none of them our target. The heat of Jordan's body warmed my back as he leaned around the corner. "And he's home."

Sure enough, Nate's window glowed with the light from within. I pulled myself back into the stairwell, my shoulders brushing against Jordan's chest as I retreated. "Okay, I'll distract him while you get the shirt."

"No way. This is your dare, I'll distract him by pointing out McKenzie and Luca over there, who ... I'll figure it out. You grab it from in his cupboard while I've got him out of the room."

I totally grinned like a little kid, then darted out of our block, across the courtyard and into the door that led up to block B and Nate's room. Jordan's footsteps pounded the concrete behind me and halfway up the stairs, I skidded to a stop, drawing in a composing breath. his eyes met mine and I burst into laughter again.

"Stop it or he'll be on to us," Jordan warned. He moved around me, disappearing onto the first floor. I took another deep breath and a third. Smoothing down my flyaway hair, I stepped into the corridor, to where Jordan stood in front of Nate's closed door.

"What? Not home?" I knocked on the door, my gaze roaming over the almost-blank white board. The only words on it were *Nate is a loser.* No sound came from within. I tried the handle. It was locked.

Jordan's shoulder slumped against the frame. "What now?"

A white board marker was stuck to the top of the white board. Not as good as flogging his shirt, but it would have to do. Short of something fun to write, I glided the pen over the slippery surface, drawing. Then I returned the cap and stepped back to admire my handiwork.

Jordan chuckled. "Nice. What is that? A self-portrait?"

I punched him in the arm. "It is clearly a male and obviously Nate, being lame. Nothing at all like me."

Sighing, I walked away. We trudged down the stairs, through the courtyard and back up to our floor, where I stopped off in my room to pour a fresh drink. The fridge swooshed open and slapped closed, and by the time I reached Jordan's room he walked in right behind me, holding a bottle of water. No that was more like him.

Collapsing into the desk chair, I said, "Well, that was a fail."

He plopped onto the bed. "I dare you to—"

"No," I said, taking a long sip from my glass and eying off that fine chest I'd seen earlier. "It's my turn. I dare you to streak around the courtyard."

A laugh burst from him. "You want me to run around Oxley completely naked?"

I grinned.

Jordan shook his head. "No way. You're insane."

He wasn't going to do it, and this was quite possibly the best dare I'd ever challenged him with. Way better than stealing T-shirts. "I double dare you."

It was out before I had time to think the double part of it through.

"That's a big call. You know what that means, right?" Jordan's grin was entirely too confident. Crap, maybe he'd do this.

"Of course I know what it means. Aren't you game?"

He eyed me up for what felt like forever, no doubt trying to call my bluff. There was no way I'd back down. Him, though ... Jordan wouldn't do it. There was no chance in hell. I raised an eyebrow and he shook his head.

I went to take another drink, but no liquid met my lips. "You have two minutes to think it through."

Ducking out of his room, I returned to mine and splashed some vodka in the bottom on my mug then topped it off with lemonade. If he did this I wasn't sure I'd be able to hold myself together. It was bad enough when he went shirtless. A naked Jordan ... my cheeks heated. My tummy flipped.

I had a pretty good buzz going as I returned to the room three doors down from mine. Jordan met me with a wide grin. He tipped his bottle up, finishing off the water, then slammed it on the desk. "Let's get this over with then."

Holy cow. He was for real. Laughing, I followed Jordan

out of the room and downstairs. The cool evening air hit my face, and good god, he was right—this was insane. If Jordan did this, then as a double dare, I had to do it too. What the hell was I thinking? I couldn't back out now, though.

He strode into Back Courtyard and straight to the far corner, ignoring the people standing out front of block K. Jordan set his drink on the ground and reached over his shoulders, grabbing a handful of shirt, which he tugged over his head. My heart sped up. Quick as a flash the shirt fell to the ground and he toed off his flip-flops, his hand moving to the zip of his jeans.

Someone wolf whistled.

The jeans pooled around Jordan's feet, leaving him standing there in nothing but boxer briefs. Glorious boxer briefs he filled out rather well.

"Come on, Hex, your turn."

I threw off the stunned daze and stripped down to nothing but my unsexy-cotton undies, my arm covering my bare chest.

"Ready?" Jordan yelled.

"I can't believe we're doing this," I whisper-hissed.

"Get it all off!" The voice came from a window across the courtyard. *OMG; a freaking audience.*

Jordan's hand slid beneath the band of his boxer briefs and they fell to join his jeans. My breath caught. Squealing, I dropped my underwear too and he ran, his stark-white rear moving with each step up ahead. My tummy spun with a mixture of heat, nerves, and just plain crazy. Letting out a whoop, I ran after him.

My hair blew back in the wind. The sound of Jordan's

footsteps pounding the pavement in front of me was almost as loud as my pulse rushing in my ears.

I felt as if it took an hour to run around the four walkways that made up the edges of Back Courtyard. Yet, Amber later told me it was over in a flash.

Chapter 13
Jordan

THREE DAYS later, I still couldn't believe she actually did a nudie run. I only did it to call her bluff, but boy was I floored. Pity it was near impossible to catch a glimpse of her skin. For five whole minutes we were both naked and I couldn't even turn around. I was so pumped; I just had to run. Especially once people began hanging out their windows, cheering.

Hex's had such a fun-loving nature. The way she took each moment by the horns and made it hers drew me to her. I snuck a sideways peek at her as we walked down the path from the sports centre to Oxley. Chatting to Amber, she looked at ease with a towel wrapped around her waist and the smooth skin of her back on display. They'd both tagged along with me to the pool, completely distracting me from swimming laps.

As we strolled through the car park, I interrupted their animated discussion. "I've got to run. I need to be at work in an hour."

"Someone picking you up?" Amber asked.

"Nope. I'll walk."

"Hmm ... " She tapped her finger against her thigh. "What're we doing tonight, Hex?"

"Whatever you want."

"I've got to run into town, so I'll give you a ride to work," Amber said.

"That'd be great," I told her.

We walked down the path toward Oxley's gate. The side doors to the common room stood open and a few people spilled out onto the lawn. They were all dudes and inside were even more, about a dozen all up. They weren't rowdy, but as we walked past someone wolf whistled. I tossed a dirty look that way and dropped my arm over Hex's shoulder.

Ignoring me, she yelled to them, "What are you all doing?"

Cade Matthew's raised a seven-ounce glass. "Appreciating the smooth perfection that is whiskey."

"So you're drinking?" Hex asked.

"No we're connoisseuring."

She laughed. "That's not even a word."

He didn't seem to care about his poor grasp of English; he was more concerned with eying off Hex's bikini. *Yeah, not gonna happen.* With my arm still around her, I guided Hex toward the courtyard.

"Dibs on first shower," I said and she harrumphed. "Fine. We could always both—"

She wacked me in the stomach, but it was worth it. The look on her face was priceless.

126

"Because I am kind and considerate and you have someplace to be ..." She paused until I looked her in the eye. "You may go first."

"You know we're on water restrictions here. There's no better conservation than sharing."

She spun out from under my arm. "Don't push the friendship, Jordan."

I chuckled. There was something about tormenting her that made me happy in a way similar to her crazy stunts. Maybe it was how well she reacted.

By the time I'd washed the pool's chlorine from my body and hair, it was a good fifteen minutes later. I climbed out of the shower, wrapped a towel around myself, and walked into the hall. Hex caught my eye as I strolled past, fiddling with her laptop and looking sexy as hell, thanks to her post swimming messy hair. She said, "Don't leave without me. I want to go to town with Amber."

"Sure." My attention slipped to her smooth stomach, and the tiny bar of silver glinting in her belly button. Hot damn, that thing was sexy in a way that made my whole body pay attention.

She pushed her way past me and into the hall.

Back in my room, I slid my ring back onto my pinkie, and pulled on my last clean Mozzarellas polo and black work pants. I wasn't listening for the shower to turn off, but the second the water stopped rushing through the pipes I froze. She'd be standing in there towelling herself dry, maybe wrapping the towel around her sweet body to make the trek back to her room. My head felt a little light as everything else heated up. Yeah, I needed another shower. A cold one.

I picked up my phone and flicked yet another message to Logan to keep my mind out of the gutter. My brother had been pretty quiet lately which was unlike him, but tomorrow was Sunday, and that meant Liv's weekly family dinner.

Twenty minutes before I was due to start, Hex stuck her head into my room. Her hair was wet again, but now it hung in a perfectly straight curtain around her head, the blue ends dulled by dampness. My mind immediately wandered back to its previous vision of her standing naked under the steaming water. In the exact same shower I was in right before her.

"Amber wants to know if you're ready." Good thing she spoke or my mind would have gone somewhere x-rated.

"Yep." I pushed my phone and keys into my pocket.

She walked a few steps ahead as we went down the stairs. An arc of fabric clung to her back where her hair had dripped. That skin was like honey underneath, all smooth and golden. I'd know. I'd spent long enough staring at it every second I got the chance.

Amber was already waiting at the bottom of the stairs when we emerged, twirling her keys around her finger. She asked Hex, "Where do you want to go?"

"To get something to drink that isn't see-through."

My foot fell against the ground with a thud. "I still owe you a dare, remember?"

"What dare?" Amber asked, curiosity written all over her face.

Hex squinted as she met my eyes. Yeah, she had my number. Time to try harder. "Fun, crazy stuff you don't do every day. When I get back from work, you're doing it."

Amber jabbed Hex with an elbow. "You could always do him. That'd be pretty crazy."

"He wishes."

I kind of did. We rounded the corner out of Oxley toward the car park, and my shoulders immediately tensed at the sight of those tools still hanging by the open doors of the common room, swigging down their liquor in a way that most definitely wasn't the savouring they'd claimed.

Hex stopped halfway along the path and yelled to them, "Watch out, boys, we're coming back to join your little club."

They exchanged incredulous looks then one guy broke out in a grin that said there was anything but drinking involved in what he wanted to do. Another swallowed the rest of his drink and declared, "You can't, sweetheart."

"Why not?" Hex took a challenging step forward.

"Girl's aren't invited." He grinned. "Not to participate in the Whisky Lovers Club."

"What? Do you mean just because I'm not a guy I can't drink? Or is it because girls don't like whisky?"

"Hex," I warned.

She glared at me.

"It's a boys club," the dick said, "You couldn't keep up with us, sweetheart."

"Yeah, well, we'll see about that," Hex mumbled as we walked away.

It was so damn hard to hold my tongue as we drove into town, but I was certain if I suggested she stay away from that stupid group, she'd do the bloody opposite. Hex never backed down from a challenge.

NEVER BEFORE had I wished I was somewhere other than at Mozzarellas earning cash. The hours ticked by slower than ever, despite us being fairly busy. It didn't help that Penny ignored me all night, staying up front, even in the customer-less lulls. Nor that the two fresh starters we had didn't argue like they'd done last shift, or that Carlos went home earlier than usual after giving me strange looks all night. And to top it off, I'd checked my phone at least a dozen times and still hadn't heard from Logan, which was weirder than Carlos's glares. My older brother never dropped off the radar. But none of those things caused the clock to move slower more than Hex playing on my mind all night. Despite typing a text out to her at least half a dozen times, I'd deleted every one without hitting send and ended up texting Liv instead.

What's happening?

As I leaned back against the stainless-steel bench, catching a break between rushes, my phone buzzed in my pocket. I fished it out and read the incoming text.

You done yet? I've planned the dare.

Colour me surprised. It was Hex.

Working on it. You staying away from the whiskey?

130

Working on it.

It buzzed again, and this time Liv's name flashed across the screen.

What's up, little bro?

Why is Logan ignoring my texts?

The silence after my text sent spanned on and that was even more concerning. Whatever was going on, Liv was in on it too, which meant I needed to be there. Hopefully our mother hadn't sucked Logan in with some sob story. I slid my thumb over the keypad, typing out one last message since it looked like Liv had gone silent now too.

Family dinner tomorrow. Neither of you can avoid me then.

I muted the volume. The last two hours dragged even longer than the first four, knowing that Hex *was* hanging with those losers. A bad feeling clenched my chest; whether it was because of the way that one guy had looked at her or something else I wasn't sure, but I couldn't stand the thought of her drinking with their little club. It wasn't good news.

Lock-up time finally rolled around and Penny and I were the only two still in the shop. Even though my shift technically finished half an hour ago, I wasn't about to leave her to lock up alone. At last, she showed her face out back for the first time all night. She didn't offer a hello, merely ground out, "We're leaving in ten."

131

I saved us both the hassle by replying, "I don't need a lift."

She made eye contact for the first time since our chat the other night. "Don't be an idiot, Jordan. I'm not going to make you walk home."

I sighed. I wanted to get back to Oxley as quickly as possible and if that meant spending ten uncomfortable minutes in the Focus with Penny then I'd suck that shit up. We both climbed into the car. She switched the stereo on and pumped up the volume. Obviously, I wasn't the only one who didn't feel like talking.

When she indicated to turn into the front car park my heart began hammering against my chest, and it wasn't because of the awkward silence. It was almost midnight; I'd been gone for six hours. And to admit I was slightly worried about what might have happened would be an understatement.

Feeling the need to get inside, I flung the car door open and swung around to step out.

"Shit!" The tyres screeched. "What the hell, Jordan? Are you in so much of a hurry you can't wait until the car stops before bolting out? I had hoped we could still be friends, but if you find me that repulsive—"

"Damn it. We are friends, Penny. We were friends first and we'll always be friends. Shit. I've just ... I've got a lot on my mind." I looked back at her. "Friends?"

She closed her eyes and visibly drew breath. "So long as you don't kamikaze from my moving car again we're all good."

I shot her a smile and climbed out. "See you on Thursday."

"Keep your head screwed on. I'd hate to lose my carpool buddy."

At that I smiled and pushed the door closed. As the Focus drove off, the illuminated pizza box up top flicked off then back on.

I came into Oxley via the front entrance and didn't bother getting changed before heading to the place I knew Hex would be—out back. Front Courtyard was abandoned and in Back a couple of smokers hung around the bench seat. Music from the common room met my ears before I reached it. I walked inside to find a group watching movies in the top room. Hex wasn't amongst them, but that wasn't surprising. Quiet nights weren't exactly her thing. I pushed open the door that led to the bottom half of the common room and the music increased to a heart-thumping volume. Some dude had passed out on the floor, sprawled out as if he slept where he'd dropped. Another guy was slumped on one of the lounges, drink still in hand while he slept. Two more didn't look much better off; they weren't passed out like their buddies, but both were propped up against the wall, butts firmly on the floor and talking to each other in slurred gibberish—something about trees and religion.

Hex wasn't there. After her challenge this afternoon I'd thought she'd be partying with these losers for sure.

Long green curtains billowed through the open floor-to-ceiling doors, reminding me there had been people outside earlier. I left the 'connoisseurs' to themselves and waded through the fabric partition to head back to my room the long way, in case she was outside. Someone had pulled the couches out onto the lawn, and at least a dozen empty spirit bottles piled up against the edge of the rose garden complimented the glasses scattered all over the grass. The next thing to grab my attention was Amber's mousy head barely visible behind a two-seater chair thats high back was to me. My stomach clenched as I sped up, dreading what I was about to find. Sure enough, the gut feeling I'd had all night wasn't wrong.

Hex lay sprawled on the lounge, her arm hanging over the side and her legs, bent at the knees, draped over the end. Her eyes were open, thank god, and she scary-grinned when she saw me. It was that stupid I-have-no-control-of-my-facial-muscles grin that was as much frown as it was smile. She was absolutely trashed, and Amber was only marginally better.

"They're a bunch of sexist pigs." Hex looked up at me, though her attention kept slipping off my face. "But I showed them. Girls can drink too."

"Yeah." I gave her a weak smile. "You sure showed them."

"You got her?" Amber asked. "I'm so tired."

"Yeah. I've got her."

"Good." Amber stumbled to her feet and staggered into the back courtyard while I watched until she disappeared into the stairwell of block K. She'd make it to her bottom floor room fine. Hex, on the other hand, wasn't going anywhere fast.

"I drank them all under the table." She sat up. "Every single last one of them" —she paused, her eyes rolling back— "and I could keep going."

"Not a good idea, doll."

She tried to slap me on the arm, but her aim was two

foot off and her hand sailed through thin air, throwing her off-balance. I plunged my arms underneath her as Hex toppled off the lounge. She giggled and I hefted her up into my arms. "Bedtime."

"You always wanna take me to bed. Maybe tonight I'll let you ... if you stay."

I didn't bother responding, just started the process of getting us both home. I wasn't sure what to do with this girl who'd crept into my life. I'd never wanted to be in this situation again, but despite my instincts telling me to run a mile, I couldn't. Underneath the partying Hex was a great girl who I really liked.

She was a dead weight in my arms, and as I climbed the three flights of stairs to our floor my calves ached. I peeked down at her to check she hadn't fallen asleep, but her hooded eyes looked back at me.

"You smell like pizza," she announced. Then out of nowhere, "I think I'm gonna puke."

Ah crap. I carried her right to the bathroom where she crawled to the toilet and hung her head over the porcelain bowl. For a second nothing happened and I thought it must have been a false alarm, but boy was I mistaken. As she started heaving, I grabbed either side of her hair and held it back as best I could.

Drinking was such a huge part of life. Turning eighteen, moving into college, hitting the grog every weekend—it was all normal, and maybe there was something wrong with me, but since Kayla, I didn't enjoy getting trashed. I loved a few beers as much as the next guy, but this ... I hated seeing Hex like this ... like she didn't give a damn who saw her hurl her guts up or collapse in a communal bathroom half asleep. Sure, when she was sober she never gave a crap what other people thought, but this was different. This was her at her weakest, and Hex was always strong.

She finally stopped heaving and slumped against the bowl. I tucked a few strands of wayward hair behind her ear then ducked out to grab a washcloth from my room. I filled a glass with water on the way back in so she could rinse her mouth and I was only gone for a few seconds, but when I got back she was well into round two. I lost track of how long we sat on the cold tiles, but when Hex finally stopped hurling she collapsed onto her back, breathing hard. A few minutes passed then she said, "Sooo cold. S'good."

After flushing the toilet and cleaning up, I mopped off her forehead and lay on the cool tiles beside her. "What am I gonna do with you?"

Her fingers brushed my hand.

The damp bathroom mixed with the smell of puke reminded me of another place, another time, a situation so similar, only worse.

Much, much worse.

"You remind me of her so much, Hex, and in so many different ways. You love life almost too much. It's just one huge party and you're at centre stage, pulling everyone else into the fun." I sighed. "She was the same. She had this bigger-than-life personality … everyone adored her." I curled my hand around hers. "Well, if you don't include our shitty parents. She was always doing some stupid stunt to make me laugh, and when I was a dick she pulled me into line. I loved that she could have fun, and make me have fun too. But she ... she drank like this, too, and that wasn't fun at all. In the end—"

"Jordan?"

I startled, broken from my memories of Kayla. What I said was all true, and as the words tumbled out, I realised that Hex? She was more than just a girl who lived on my floor. She'd made the Kayla-shaped hole in my heart a little less empty. It would always be there, but Hex had filled part of it.

Her fingers wriggled into mine, and sleepily, she said, "Bedtime?"

It wasn't only Hex's personality that was so much like my lost sister; it was this constant drinking. It was more than confusing how I could love and hate everything about her at the same time. The drinking made me wonder if, like Kayla, Hex was running away from something. If that was the case, I couldn't stand by and let her keep doing this when my gut said there was something not right. The girl was goddamn beautiful inside and out, but as attracted to her as I was, I was pretty sure Hex needed help, and I wouldn't become part of the problem. I'd be there to look after her, but I couldn't get more involved just to lose her.

It was official. I hated my damn conscience.

I climbed to my feet, my back half-numb thanks to the freezing tiles. As I reached down, Hex grabbed my hands, pulling herself up. She was a little wobbly on her feet, so I tucked her under my arm and moved us both into the hall. She leaned heavily against me, her arm wrapped around my waist and clinging on for sweet life.

"Where's your key?" I asked.

She jerked to a stop, shoved her hand down her shirt and I should've looked away, but I wasn't a gentleman so I stole an eyeful of delicious honeyed flesh. She tugged her hand out of the loose T-shirt and brandished the metal in the air, dangling by its red ribbon like a gold medal. She stupid-grinned as if it were, too. We reached her door, second on the right, and I took the key from her, guiding it into the lock. I barely had the thing open before she wrapped herself around me again and shoved us both forward.

Hex's arms locked around my middle as she swung herself onto the bed and pulled me down with her. It took some quick work with my elbows to prevent myself falling on top of her. Skilfully, I managed to land with one elbow above each of her shoulders, propping myself up. My knees did the same thing on either side of her narrow hips, holding my body above hers. I balanced dangerously close as her green eyes stared into mine. Her full lips puckered a little as she swallowed, then Hex caught the bottom one in her teeth. It was so goddamn sexy I almost forgot myself. Damn it, if she wasn't drunk I would have kissed her right then and there.

But things were what they were.

Even if sometimes thinking it through sucked.

I pushed up off my hands and made short work of her shoes. Those boots looked all kinds of good with her short shorts, but damn they were a pain in the arse to get off. The laces went on forever. Hex rolled onto her side and I pulled the blankets over her since the nights were getting colder. As I placed a fresh glass of water on her desk, muted music came from somewhere to my left. Sure enough, her phone glowed through the pocket of her shorts. She didn't stir. It kept ringing, lighting her upper thigh. I took a steadying breath and slid my fingers into the tight space at her hip. They brushed the smooth surface of her phone and I fished it out, forcing myself to ignore the warmth of her leg on my hand. A heat that echoed in my groin.

Who was ringing her at one a.m.?

It finally slid free from her tight pocket, still singing. The screen read *Mum*. That couldn't be good—even if mine didn't, most parents reserved middle-of-the-night calls for emergencies. But there was no point in waking Hex now as she wasn't in a state to talk. I could answer it for her, but ... nope. Terrible idea, it was one a.m. and I *wasn't* Amber. A phone conversation at this time was not a good way to meet her mother. It stopped ringing so I laid it on the desk for her to deal with in the morning. An incoming text made the darn thing buzz again. A message I couldn't miss illuminated the screen.

I miss you, Alexi. Almost as much ...

Alexi? What the actual hell? Hex, Alexi ... her name was Alexi? Then where the hell did Hex come from? I'd always guessed it wasn't her real name, but she never did answer that question. I was so damn tempted to click through to see the rest of the message. Pity I didn't have time to decide before another one buzzed in.

Don't waste your life like I ...

Hell no. This time I did pick the damn thing up and my

139

thumb hovered over the screen. What sort of mother sent shit like this in the middle of the night? Not that I was an expert on mothers. Mine was an asshole. The phone buzzed with another text.

Call me, sweetie.

Like hell Hex was calling anyone right now. Mother or not, Hex needed to sleep it off, and this sure didn't look like an emergency, so it could wait. I flicked the volume to silent and laid the phone on the desk. As I walked to the door, I looked down at Hex's sleeping form. With each inhale her breath shuddered in then back out with a tiny snore.

My head buzzed. My ears rang with the echo of music from the party. Twenty to two we'd flogged them by, and the team all went back to Ben's house to celebrate. His dad had built a massive bonfire on their property and the boys had partied hard. Someone even brought a case of beer.

Haysie, Haysie, Haysie; the chant of the night sounded in my memory. It felt pretty darn good too. I smiled as I recalled that last play; how I'd dodged at least four opponents to score a try mere seconds before the buzzer sounded.

I walked into the house, careful not to make a sound lest I wake him. With any luck Kayla would still be awake and I could tell her all about the win. She hadn't shown at the game today, but he had. She used to be at every one ... once.

The TV droned from the living room, all the lights off. I didn't dare look in there. Best to let sleeping beasts lie.

140

I felt lighter than air as I walked the hall, the feel of Jess Bryan's lips fresh on my own. Yeah, being the half-back came with its perks.

Something slimy crept down my spine. A feeling that stole elation and left a putrid heaviness in my gut. The night was deathly still. Not a sound, not a breath of fresh air. I could hear my heart beating. Faster. Louder. Harder.

I stopped outside the bathroom, a cold sweat prickling the back of my neck as I peeked inside.

Moonlight shone through the bathroom window, casting an eerie shadow on the tiles. The darkened lump of my sister's form lay slumped on floor. Seemed she'd had a party of her own. I leant beside her, my stomach still trying to constrict in on itself.

"Kays ... it's time for bed."

I pushed a wayward long curl from her face. Her skin felt somehow different, too cool. My throat felt just as weird ... tight.

I slid my arms underneath her. Kayla's head flopped back.

Something was wrong.

I shook her.

She didn't move.

Heart racing, I pressed my cheek to her pulse.

Nothing.

Chapter 14
Hex

THE SECOND I came to I knew I was in for a horrid morning. The sun shone through my curtains with a wicked intensity. Those things needed to be upgraded to total blackout, or at least something thicker than my underwear. My tummy churned in a way that was entirely unpleasant and I wasn't sure I could move, and not only because my abs ached as if I'd spent all night doing sit-ups. It was more the feeling on the inside: a nauseous gurgling that said I needed to get something in there, pronto. I pulled myself out of bed and went for the glass of water on my desk. A couple of painkillers sat beside it, which was weird. I usually didn't think ahead like that. Oh well, thanks, me, that was really thoughtful. I popped the tablets and dropped them into my mouth with a sip of water then swallowed. And that took every last iota of my energy, so I collapsed back onto the bed and thought about a shower for a good ten minutes before I actually summoned the willpower to stand.

Showering was a feat, but by the time I finished I felt so much better. My hair had been disgusting, even though I had washed it after swimming yesterday, and my teeth were all kinds of feral. By the look of my nails I'd been at it again. They weren't long and beautiful anymore, hadn't been in quite a few years, but this morning they were worse than normal. All ragged, as if I'd been picking at them in my sleep.

Back in my room, I fished out the box of Fruit Loops from under my bed and munched on a handful as I scooped my phone off the desk and woke it from hibernation. One missed call and several new messages from Mum. It wasn't anything worth responding to immediately, but since the new month had ticked over I'd better sort out our money. I switched on my computer and opened up Internet banking. Last week when I'd checked, my monthly allowance wasn't there, but today it was. I set a transfer up to Bronwyn Penton—$2,500. It was a little less than I'd passed off the last few times, but it should be enough without the extra mouth to feed.

Without my contribution, Mum would lose the house. Her unreliable income wasn't enough to keep us afloat, but the 'child support' agreement made a huge difference. It wasn't that she didn't work. When you were a casual there was no such thing as sick pay, and there were many days when she couldn't function. That meant her income wasn't enough to cover the mortgage. She wasn't entirely good with money either.

I moved back into the Word document I'd been working on yesterday. Chemistry sucked arse, but I needed to somehow complete this assignment. My head hurt just looking at the long names and periodic symbols. It didn't make any sense ... how was protein structure dependent on peptide links, whatever the hell that meant?

I pushed splayed fingers through my damp hair, slamming my forehead into my palms. This was so goddamn stupid. Pity we needed the money. There was no way around it.

My headed pounded so I slammed the laptop closed and braved opening the curtains. As I tied them back, I peered down into the courtyard. There were quite a few people about, but I honed in my friends. Outside block B, Amber lounged on the chain that lined the edge of the walkway. McKenzie balanced on it, too, both of them facing Jordan and Nate, who was probably waiting on me to drag myself down there so we could start phase one of Operation Amber, a plan we'd devised last night. It wasn't exactly a dare, but whatever.

I flicked the residual water out of my hair, and smoothed a little foundation on my puffy face then ducked into the kitchen for a coffee, which I took one sip of and left on the counter because it made my churning tummy worse. I switched it out for a plastic bottle full of water, which I proceeded to take down to the courtyard. McKenzie gave an enthusiastic wave when she saw me, and Nate grinned from under his cap. Amber and Jordan, though, were noticeably subdued. I slid my sunnies on, and took a sip of my drink. "Morning."

Nate made a point of glancing at his watch. "Afternoon."

"It's all the same."

Jordan didn't look my way, didn't even acknowledge my presence, merely fidgeted with his flip-flops, his toes shifting in and out of them. He wasn't wearing his sunnies this morning, and his eyes looked somehow different. Maybe it was because they were uncharacteristically focused on his feet. His hands were shoved in the pockets of his shorts, and damn the guy had nice legs. Pity it would soon be too cold for anything but jeans or sweats. His legs were almost as perfectly curved as his arms, which looked mighty fine in a T-shirt that sported tiny sleeves, a wee bit shorter than short. In fact it showed off that arm vein beautifully.

I broke the brooding silence. "How was work?"

"All right," he answered.

They all stood there acting awkward as hell until Nate winked at me, spun his hat around, then spoke to my friend. "So Amber, I need to go to town and grab some stuff for this assessment I'm working on today. Think you can spot me a ride ... then maybe we can clean up your car, since it got covered in dust last weekend?"

Her face brightened immediately. "Sounds like fair payment to me."

I tried to grab Jordan's attention, but he didn't glance my way. He was too busy staring at the brickwork.

"You free now?" Nate asked.

"Yeah, why not?" Amber jumped off the chain. "I'll grab my purse."

She was obviously keen to get Nate alone, which was probably why she hadn't offered for anyone else to tag along. Suited me fine; she was playing right into our plan, and once Nate started washing her car wild horses wouldn't drag her away, especially if he lost the shirt. That should buy Jordan and me at least two hours.

Once she was out of earshot, Nate said, "Have fun. I'll keep her away as long as I can."

Jordan looked my way. "What's that all about?"

Finally! Eye contact, and now I had it I wasn't losing his attention. "Are you ready to have some fun? Childish fun, I'll admit, but fun nonetheless."

His lips quirked, as if he fought to keep a serious expression. "And here I thought you hurling was the crazy activity."

Nate choked on a laugh.

"What?" I said, "I did not hurl."

Jordan raised a brow.

I raised one right back. He rose a second. I broke our connection by turning to McKenzie. "Have you got the stuff?"

"Sure do. I'll bring it all down after they've gone."

Jordan fingered the ring that never left his pinkie while that smirk still tried to break free. "Amber's not going to like your plan, is she?"

"She'll love it, but shh, here she comes."

Amber bounded up to Nate's side. "All ready?"

"Yep." He swivelled his cap back around and pulled it down, shading his eyes. "Let's go, kiddo."

Amber punched him on the arm. "See you guys later." As she turned around Nate winked again then they walked away, Amber chatting up a storm. McKenzie hopped off the chain and disappeared into Back Courtyard, leaving Jordan and I alone.

He didn't speak. Didn't even look at me.

Well, whatever was up his goat wasn't my problem. He'd snap out of it soon enough, when Operation Amber moved into phase two. We stood there in silence for several minutes while the air between us grew thick with tension, but I wasn't going to be the one to break it.

Finally McKenzie appeared, swinging a shopping bag, which she handed to me. I peered inside. "That's perfect."

"I want to see it, so call me," McKenzie said.

"Sure thing." I tilted my head toward Back Courtyard. "Let's do this."

Jordan shrugged and boy, I'd just about had enough of his attitude. If he didn't want in on this, he could rack off. I strode out toward Amber's block, not caring if he kept up or if he didn't follow at all. Everyone I passed was pleasant and a guy from Science class called my name from amongst a bunch of people lying on the grass. I didn't stop though, just raised my hand in greeting and kept marching. Two hours would go pretty fast, so I needed to hop to it if I wanted to get this job done.

I hit the corridor and the sound of footfall a few steps behind me made my shoulders drop, but only a little. I wouldn't be relieved he'd come. No guy would get under my skin like that; I wouldn't allow it. I stopped outside Amber's door, grinning at the frangipanis taped around her room number. By the time we'd finished it would look way different. I shoved against the door and sure enough, my party trick had worked. It opened with only a little force.

"Huh." Jordan's arm brushed against me as he examined the side of the door. Yep, I definitely refused to feel those goose bumps breaking out along the nape of my neck. Pity I was hopeless at ignoring anything to do with Jordan. His fingers grazed over the latch and he peeled off a thick piece of clear packaging tape, letting the latch spring free.

"Nate's handiwork," I said. "She was prattling on last night about it being her birthday. Had us both feeling like shitty friends because neither of us knew and we'd practically missed it. Then ... and wait for this ... hours later, peeing herself laughing, she told us it was her half birthday. A half birthday! Who the hell celebrates birthdays every six months? So ... joke's on Amber when we actually celebrate it." I raised a brow. "In Jordan and Hex fashion."

I dumped the contents of the shopping bag onto the bed, ignoring how good our names sounded paired together. Jordan laughed and somehow my anger became impossible to hold onto.

"How many balloons are there?"

"Enough." I grinned.

He tore the packet open and plopped into Amber's chair. As he started blowing, the pink rubber expanded. We inflated in silence. Two balloons. Four, six, eight, almost twenty, and Jordan's brooding look faded. Twenty-six, thirty ... they fully covered the carpeted floor. He rested his hand on his knee. I was well out of breath, but we still had miles to go to fill the room.

"This isn't as much fun as I'd imagined."

He stretched out his next balloon. "Ah, but it will be when she opens that door."

I adjusted the one I was midway through inflating and

let it go. As planned, it flew through the air full-pelt and shot right into Jordan's chest where it fizzled, limp and empty.

"You wanna start?" he said, that same gleam back in his eye as there had been that day at the swimming hole. "Huh, Hex? You do?"

In answer I grabbed two of the long rolls of dollar gift-wrap from Amber's bed and thwacked both of his arms at once then went to pull them back for a second go, but Jordan's reflexes were way quicker than mine. He shot forward and clamped his hands around my wrists, then used one hand puppet-like to make me playfully slap my own face.

"That's playing dirty," I said, hooking a leg behind his knee. A little tug forward and his leg buckled, sending him falling back onto the bed. Jordan laughed that laugh I loved then used his hands that were still firmly clamped around my wrists to force me off balance. As I crashed onto the bed, barely missing him, he shot up and took to me with lithe fingers, tickling my sides. Now I was the one laughing while he looked down at me with that goddamn twinkle of mischief in his eyes. My heart zinged, and my belly was on fire. Jordan's blue eyes peered into mine, and something changed. His expression was still predatory but in an entirely different way. Those gorgeous eyes were now dark and his lips had slightly parted, as if he were about to wet them. My heart did that funny flip thing again. I wanted him to kiss me, more than I'd ever wanted anything before. My entire body ached to close the miniscule distance between our mouths.

It wasn't me who did it, though. I lay there watching

149

helplessly, frozen with desire and the remnants of laughter still on my lips as Jordan edged toward me. He crawled over me, his entire body not touching mine in a single goddamn spot. His face dropped until it was so close that each breath he expelled seared my lips. It was pure agony. I might have groaned, but I couldn't be sure because it took every last ounce of my focus to stop myself pulling him down on top of me. I inhaled a deep breath, filling myself with his musky scent, and my chest brushed against his. Tingles shot all the way to my toes from that brief touch.

It wasn't enough.

I needed to touch him again, for longer. I took another breath, this one even deeper, and held it. Our chests touched, burned, scorched against each other and the desire that evoked within me drew another groan.

Jordan's mouth dropped to mine, hitting with a fierce pressure. The burn spread through my entire body as if he'd set my veins afire. Neither of us moved; didn't even draw breath. It was as if this moment had paused. Jordan's lips were soft, supple and finally, finally, his mouth moved, pushing against mine. Our lips discovered an urgent rhythm, matching rushed movements in sync. As if we'd both been holding back from this since the moment we first met. I didn't even draw breath as we kissed with a fierce passion. Kissing Jordan was both a relief and an increase in tension, because this wasn't enough. Each kiss was stronger than the last, but I still needed more. Jordan moved off my mouth, trailing urgent kisses along my jaw while my hands fisted in the back of his shirt, pulling him closer to feel that same relief against the rest of my body that I now felt at the contact of our lips. Jordan crashed on top of me, his chest crushing into mine, and his knees locked either side of my thighs. I turned my head to claim his lips again and this time Jordan's tongue edged my mouth open and swept inside, exploring, tasting, *demanding* every inch of my mouth.

It was a sweet relief to the tension that had been building since that very first night in the courtyard. Our kisses grew more heated, more urgent, until all of a sudden Jordan pulled back, his eyes even darker than before.

"Alexi."

It wasn't a question or a statement, merely an acknowledgement of my real name, and it felt like a slap to the face. I froze. So did the fire inside me.

Where the hell had he heard that?

"Jordan."

I must have said something last night, but did I even see him? I'd assumed I was in bed by the time he got home, but maybe I wasn't. Maybe I'd spilled my guts to him and not realised. He said I'd been sick, so he'd at least heard me. Humiliation curled inside me, replacing the heat low in my belly.

"Why Hex?"

"What's your tattoo stand for?"

"Tell me about the name and I'll tell you about the tattoo."

His question took me by surprise, and when I met his eyes it was clear that this time he wouldn't let up until I gave him something. "I like it." I slid out from underneath him and off the bed, grabbing a balloon from the bags that were now strewn on the floor.

"But it's not your real name."

Good God, would he not let up? Suddenly full of breath again, I filled my mouth with air and brought the purple balloon to my kiss-tender lips while Jordan stared at me as if he knew all my secrets. As if he could reach into my soul with those steady eyes and read the word stamped on my heart: *cursed.*

"No, it's not," I said, "it's a nickname and I like it a hell of a lot better than my real name. It's got character."

He swung himself off the bed and leaned on the wall beside me, careful not to stand on any of our inflation work that almost covered the floor in a single layer. "Where did it come from?"

So he didn't know everything. I shrugged as I tied off the balloon. "Just something my dad called me once. Guess I liked it enough to own it."

I closed my eyes and licked my lips, which did nothing to expel the bitter taste of rubber. A taste similar to the one my own name left in my mouth.

"Alexi is beautiful. You should be proud to use it."

"Yeah ... well ..." The rest of my sentence vanished when Jordan's fingers pushed my chin up, forcing my attention back to his face.

"Last night ..." Now it was his turn to stop midsentence.

"You never showed up."

"Does your mum always text you in the middle of the night?"

"What the hell?" I pulled away, a state of great disturbance coursing through my mind. "How the hell do you know who texts me when?"

152

"Because I was in your room when the phone rang." He sounded angry. "If you weren't so damn wasted I wouldn't have been there and wouldn't have seen the texts. What did you want me to do? Leave you passed out on the lawn all night?"

"Heeeex." The voice came from outside Amber's room. I spun around and one of the guys from last night ... be damned if I could remember his name stood on the doorway. "If it ain't the girl with a cast-iron stomach." He looked to Jordan. "Drank us all under the bloody table last night, she did. I wouldn't have believed it if I wasn't there."

I gritted my teeth to stop from lashing out. "Yeah, well, maybe next time you'll think twice about saying a girl can't keep up with your little club."

He chuckled. "Yeah, maybe. What the hell are you doing in here anyway?"

"Celebrating," I snapped.

He leaned against the door as if he intended to stay, and Jordan's gaze bored into my back, but I wouldn't go there. I wouldn't give him the satisfaction of admitting I drank a shit-load last night. Like I needed a goddamn babysitter when I'd been looking after myself my entire life.

"If you're going to hang around, make yourself useful." I tossed a bag of balloons at the whiskey lover and he caught it out of the air.

I never looked back at Jordan and even though I expected him to leave, he never did. But the air in that room was so heavy with anger you could have carved right through it and removed a slice without the rest tumbling into the gap.

By the time all the balloons were inflated, my head felt dizzy and my temples pounded. I still had an empty stomach, but it had finally settled down. Now, the only thing left was the finishing touch. I grabbed a sheet of print paper and a pink highlighter from Amber's desk and in big block letters wrote:

HAPPY HALF-BIRTHDAY.

Then I secured it onto her gift wrap-covered window with tape. As I thanked Mr Whiskey for his help, he cast a sympathetic look toward Jordan, mumbling something about girls with PMS. I almost took my gracious thanks back. Guys were tools, and these two needed to mind their own business.

Chapter 15
Jordan

THE WALK home was never long enough. My mind churned the whole way, playing back all the shit I'd said to Hex. Shit I shouldn't have uttered, but I swear that girl brought out the worst in me. She made me as goddamn protective as Logan. Even so, I had no right to tell her what to do. And what the hell had I been thinking when I'd kissed her? I hadn't been thinking; that was the problem. I swear whenever we got wrapped up in all the stupid, I lost control and forgot Hex needed help, not another complication.

When I reached the apartment I used to share with my brother, I kicked my shoes off and burst through the front door. The smell of roast dinner hit my senses and my mouth immediately watered as if I hadn't eaten all week. No one sat on the couch or at the dining table. Neither Logan or Liv were in sight. They were probably shagging.

"Yo," I yelled. "Anyone home, or is this food all mine?"

Logan appeared from the hall, not looking rumpled enough to have been doing the horizontal tango. Damn, it was good to see him after the last two weeks' radio silence. I took two strides toward my brother and landed a punch to his arm that was a little too hard for play. "Bro, you think now you've graduated you're king shit? You don't need to answer my calls?"

He shoved me back, pushing me into the wall, then walked around me. "Some of us have to work for a living."

"Returning a text takes two minutes, shithead."

He didn't sound right. His voice was too tight. I took another mock swing at his shoulder and Logan spun around, catching my wrist and twisting my arm behind my back. Asswipe. He always used his height against me.

"Yeah, well—"

"Guys!" Liv peeked out of the kitchen, and I had to angle my head to toss her a smile. She wore an apron that almost wrapped around her tiny frame twice over, something only she could make look hot. One hand on her hip, she shook her head. "Why can't you two just hug, like normal people?"

Logan released his hold on me so instantly I almost kissed the floor.

"Dick-wad."

He grunted.

I strode across to Liv and swept her off the ground in a hug, wrapping my arms all the way around her and then some, spinning us both on the spot. She giggled like a twelve-year-old girl and I smacked a kiss on her cheek. He'd hate that.

"That's enough," Logan said, but I held on to her for

another minute, raising an eyebrow at his glower. Yeah, I knew how to get under his skin.

"We miss you." Liv squeezed me as I set her back on her feet.

"You miss the free pizza." I walked into the kitchen and took a can of Pepsi from the fridge.

Liv had cooked up a storm in here. Not only did the entire place smell like chicken, a saucepan sat on the cook top and roast vegetables cooled to its left. I stole a crispy potato and popped it in my mouth. Fake frowning at my thievery, Liv grabbed the saucepan and held it under the faucet, then returned it to the cook top and stirred with a fork.

I leaned against the fridge and watched Logan sneak up behind her, slipping his arms around her waist and resting his chin on her shoulder. "How's college?" he asked. "You playing footy yet?"

"How's work?" I chugged down my Pepsi. "You using that degree yet?"

"Jordan," Liv chided. Logan kissed her neck and I studied my drink. Sometimes those two could be so full on, they shouldn't be allowed out in public. Still, it wasn't their usual sappy style. Logan seemed somehow distracted, as if he were kissing her out of habit.

"What gives with ignoring me?"

He continued laying kisses on Liv. "Sorry, I should have replied ... I've been busy."

"You're always busy and you always respond." I raised my voice in a piss-poor imitation of his. "We're family, Jordan, and that matters."

Logan avoided my gaze as he moved away from Liv.

"It's just stuff, all right? Stuff you don't need to be worried about while you're studying."

"I don't care, Logan, so spill it."

Liv continued stirring the gravy, studiously ignoring us arguing right behind her. This wasn't my brother and I. It wasn't how we rolled. After Kayla we didn't avoid the important shit.

Logan shoved me off the fridge. "You've barely called me since Easter either, little bro, or been around. What gives?"

Of course Liv chose that moment to speak up. "I bet he's met a girl."

I slammed a hand against the door to prevent him opening it. "Stop changing the topic, Logan."

"Told you it was a girl." Liv spun around, waving her wooden spoon in my direction.

"I think you're right." Logan winked at his girlfriend. "Someone *has* caught his attention."

"Answer my goddamn question." They exchanged a glance and Liv gave a small nod. "Am I the only bloody one not in on whatever the hell is going down? It's our mother isn't it?"

Logan sighed, looking away. "It's just crap with Dad. Nothing new."

"Then ignore the son of a bitch. He's not worth your energy."

"Yeah ..." Logan strode out of the tiny kitchen, leaving me staring at Liv who watched the door through which he'd disappeared.

"He's stressed," she said by way of explanation.

"He should have told me. I asked him about it directly

when I was here, Liv, and he flat out lied."

"Just leave it, Jordan, for tonight. Please?"

I sucked in a hard breath. Whatever was going on with my brother was shit he needed to back away from and me 'just leaving it' went against the grain. "Logan and I stick together. It's always been that way." *Even before we lost Kayla.*

"I know." She patted my shoulder. "He thinks he's doing the right thing by you. Just give it some time, okay?"

Liv turned back to the stove and shoved the saucepan aside, then set three plates on the counter. She threw an oven mitt at me. "Make yourself useful and carve up the chicken."

While I broke up the bird, sliding generous servings onto each plate, she dished up the veggies and finally poured the gravy into a little jug. Two plates fit in her tiny hands and she was off, so I took the third to the table. Logan had slumped on the couch. A game was on the TV, but his head was tipped back and his eyes closed. I flicked his ear on my way past. "Dinner."

He climbed up, pinning me with a stare. "About rugby."

"I'm not playing, so get that stupid thought out of your head."

The truth was I'd played a year longer than I wanted to already. I was done playing ball to make other people happy. I didn't love the game like I once had, because in the hours after I came in off the field all I could think about was failing my sister, and that was too much to bear.

The all-consuming lifestyle that went with the game wasn't me. Not anymore.

Logan and Liv took their usual seats on the kitchen side of the four-seater table and I dropped into mine, opposite my brother. This apartment was small, but it'd been our home for three years, and I kinda missed it now that I'd moved out.

Logan picked up the jug of gravy and looked to Olivia, who gave a small nod. Taking her cue, he dribbled the brown sauce over her chicken and potatoes. God, they were extra sickly.

I groaned as they exchanged kisses and whispers. Liv dropped her hand in a spot I suspected was dangerously north of his knee. The seat beside me had never felt emptier, and I wondered when I'd become the third wheel to their perfectly synced duo. This blew.

"Can't you guys wait until I'm not here to make out?" It wasn't that I hated seeing my brother happy. I just felt more alone than ever, aching to have Hex in my arms the way Logan had Liv, but it wasn't that simple. Wanting something didn't mean it was a good idea.

"So who's the girl?" Logan asked, his voice still monotone.

"You're like a damned dog with a bone. There. Is. No. Girl."

"There so is," Liv said. "You're smiling while denying it."

Damn it she was right, and it wasn't a small smirk. My whole goddamn face was angled up like the Joker. I took a deep breath and dropped the bomb I knew would level the room. Logan was already acting weird anyway. "It's not like that. She reminds me of Kayla."

My brother looked up, deadly serious, and suddenly

Liv thought her dinner was more appealing than our conversation. I shovelled a forkful of chicken into my mouth.

"How so?" Logan asked.

"In lots of ways."

He stared at me for an eternity while I continued eating, as if he wasn't being weird as shit. Stupid psychology graduate was probably analysing everything I had and hadn't said. I wasn't one of his future patients. Trying my best to ignore him, I mopped up the last of the gravy on my plate with a roast potato.

He was still staring. "Is she okay?"

"I don't know. How's the new degree?" I asked Liv.

A huge smile lit up her face. "I'm loving it. We've got this assignment ..."

Finally, the scrape of cutlery on crockery announced Logan had joined us in consuming dinner.

IT WAS almost ten p.m. when Logan pulled into Oxley's car park. I swung the door of his ancient Corolla open, more than ready to head to bed. Mondays were an early start with a Bio prac at eight. My brother cleared his throat, so I shifted around to meet his stare.

"If the chick makes you happy, she's worth it."

I patted his shoulder. "Don't take his shit, okay?"

"I mean it. Olivia's the best thing that ever happened to me and I want that for you too. A lot of bad shit goes down in life, so if you see something good make sure you grab hold of it."

I suppressed a groan and said, "I mean it, too."

Logan's blue-eyed stare pinned me to the spot. "Don't ignore me, dickwad. But if she's got issues like Kayla, then make sure she sorts them out."

I climbed out of the car. "Good night, bro."

Walking back into Oxley I couldn't help but smile. Logan was right about Hex. Just the sight of these brick walls brought warmth to my chest. This was mutual ground; the place Hex and I both belonged. My attention flicked to Amber's room, the glow of light behind her green curtain. The place where we'd kissed. I should fight to save Hex, but not for me. Not because I wanted her. I should do it for her, to make her life better.

God knew she wasn't fighting for herself.

The entire dorm was quiet as I walked through and up to our block. Everyone must have settled down since tomorrow was the start of another week and end of semester assessments loomed. I had two major assignments worth more than fifty per cent of the total grade and another smaller task. It would be a huge week.

The second I hit our floor my focus shifted to Hex's door. The damn thing was closed. I slowed as I walked past anyway, trying to hear if she was still up. My earlier anger had now faded, but the feel of her lips against mine hadn't. Had hers? I raised my hand, ready to knock, then sighed and continued on to my room. What the hell would I say anyway? Wanting to fight for her was one thing, barging in without a game plan was another. I needed to think this through.

I emptied out my pockets, tossing my wallet and keys

on the desk, then toed off my shoes. A sudden burst of laughter echoed down the hall. Perfect. I scooped up the empty water glass from my desk and yanked my door open, clicking it into the open position. That throaty laugh wasn't hard to place: Amber. Which meant Hex was still awake. I readjusted my shirt, spun my ring around so the plaque faced out and sauntered down the hall as if I hadn't been hovering there waiting to see her. I swaggered right past Hex's open door then stopped, rocking back on my heels to peer in, as if I hadn't noticed she was home. I smiled, the half-mouthed one that seemed to get the best results.

"Hey."

Hex looked up from where she was pouring vodka into a glass of something clear, probably lemonade. I swallowed the sour taste in my mouth while Amber looked from Hex to me, to the empty glass in my hand—an excuse for passing by—then back again. She rose from her position on the bed. "It's late. I ... ah ... better get going."

Hex gave her friend a tight smile and said, "Night."

Amber bustled around me mumbling, "Thanks for the balloons."

She shot out the door quicker than I could step out of her way, leaving me facing down Hex's intense glare. Once again the air felt too thick for the room. Anger simmered in my belly like a foul brew and the longer I stared at her the worse it got. She was beautiful, smart, fun, and I'd enjoyed every second I'd spent with her. I didn't have any right to say it, but damn it, I cared. And when you cared about someone it was so bloody hard to sit by and ignore all the shit.

"Don't you think it's time for a break?"

She scoffed. "Excuse me?"

"We've got classes tomorrow. You should be ... I dunno... studying, or some shit like that."

"Who the hell do you think you are, Jordan? You kiss me once and you think that gives you the right to tell me what's good for me and what's not? Get the hell out of my room." She slammed the glass down, then stalked across the room and peered up into my face.

I glared back at her. Anger throbbed in my temples.

"I said get out."

No way was I leaving. Instead I took her face in my hands, forcing her eyes to stay on mine. "Stop partying. Spend the next week hanging with me—doing the fun stuff we normally do."

Her green-brown eyes bore into mine, the anger slowly fading to something else. Her breath washed over my lips and damn it, the urge to kiss her tugged me closer.

"I dare you, Alexi."

If it were possible to see someone's breath catch, I swear that's what happened. She'd never turned down one of my dares and we both knew it. Every iota of her attention focused on me: her hands now clasped my forearms, her face tilted toward mine, and those eyes were like pools that reflected what she felt. That connection returned, reeling me in, closer to the edge of something great. I wasn't sure I could stop it from overwhelming my plan to help her. Hex blinked slowly and said, "Okay."

Chapter 16
Hex

HE GUY was crazy. Overbearing. Controlling. Sexy as all get up, but what the hell? I took a deep breath and snuck a peek at him across the books sprawled on my floor. A wave of almost black hair fell in front of his face, and if he wasn't leaning forward it would have been in his eyes. Eyes that looked down at a Human Bio text, giving me a close up view of the darkest, longest lashes I'd ever seen on a man. He looked a little scruffy tonight, the stubble across his jaw and cheeks as dark as his hair. I remembered what it felt like—not soft, nor prickly either.

He acted as if he thought I had problem, which clearly I didn't. 'Cause here I was sticking to his stupid dare. Hanging out with him wasn't hard work—unless he got all preachy again, then I might just kick him in the shins. It boggled my mind how someone who was so unbelievable one minute could turn holier-than-thou the next. Who didn't like partying anyway? Was this guy seriously eighteen? Sometimes it sure didn't seem so. Either way, there we were, smack bang at the beginning of an alcohol-free week.

Meh; no big deal.

Jordan had rocked up to my room right before dinner declaring night one study night. And this was a far cry from how we usually spent our time together. It was almost too normal, too natural, too intimate in the wake of yesterday's kiss. Which neither of us had acknowledged, nor had we let it happen again. Not that I was sure it would. It was one of those spur of the moment things that didn't mean anything. That didn't mean it wasn't hanging in the air between us, though. Our usual easy banter was off, and everything felt a little awkward. Not because I wanted more—I didn't. Truly, I didn't.

Gah, who was I trying to kid? Of course I did, but that was beside the point.

Jordan's lips were harder than they looked ... the way he pinched the plump bottom one between his teeth while he studied made it look soft. Not so. His lips were as strong as the rest of him. Cripes. I shook my head to expel those thoughts and forced myself to focus. This essay on *Pride and Prejudice* wasn't happening with Mr Distraction sitting opposite me. I pushed my notes and bare-as-bones essay plan away then picked up my battered copy of Austen's best work, shuffled around so my back leant against the bed and opened to chapter one. A refresher wouldn't hurt, and maybe reading would be easier to concentrate on.

Overbearing. Controlling. Thinks I party too hard. Those

thoughts should have helped, but my attention wandered off the page before I'd even reached the end of the first paragraph. Strange ... he wasn't using a computer, but rather Jordan scrawled across a lecture pad, the muscles in his forearms flexing with his rapid writing. A vein snaked from his elbow all the way up under the sleeve of his white T-shirt. Where did it go after that? His perfectly formed chest, maybe. I sighed.

"Trying to study here," he said.

"Like you're the only one." I held up my book.

"Your staring is making it kind of hard."

"I am not staring."

I lifted Austen higher than my eye level, so I couldn't see him. But he shuffled, rumpling paper like no man's business. I didn't trust him one iota; he was probably about to start a spitball fight, or worse. I peeked over the top of my book. His mouth tugged at the corner as his eyes met mine. "We both know that's a lie."

"I do not lie, Jordan Hays."

"Ooh, she's pulling out the fighting names." His eyes had that damn mischievous sparkle, which only meant bad news. "Prove it," he said, with a challenging smile.

I lowered my book. "Prove what?"

He tapped his pen against his chin several times while he narrowed his eyes. Whatever plan he was thinking up better not include the words 'I dare you' when I was still in the midst of his last dare. The next one was mine.

"I've got it," he said. "Prove to me you don't lie by answering my questions with nothing but the truth. No dodging, no evading, no lying. If you do, I'll know. That little twitch, right by your eye ..."

167

My hand shot to my eye, which I was sure never twitched. "Fine, but only if your game of truth or dare goes both ways. You have to answer my questions truthfully too." This could be interesting.

He extended his hand over the pile of textbooks and I placed mine inside it, ignoring the heat the contact caused in my belly. We shook. Up, down. It was done, but his hand remained in mine, his grip firm, our thumbs interlocked. My lips went dry. My whole mouth was like the Sahara Desert. "Deal," I croaked out.

Jordan grinned. "Deal."

I dropped his hand before I did something stupid, like used it to pull him to me.

"I'm going first because you already owe me an answer from the balloon day."

"I do?" He scratched his chin.

"Yep. About your tattoo."

"And you owe me a straight answer about your name."

"I gave you a straight answer." *Sort of.* "It's a nickname bestowed from my father. Tattoo?" I gave him a questioning look.

He lifted his shirt and traced the black symbol with a finger. "This is the symbol for infinity, and see right here ..."

I leaned forward. I could see all right—see the nicest set of pecs in Oxley, all toned and tanned. Jordan cleared his throat. "Can you see the words in the infinity symbol?"

"Yeah." I almost breathed the acknowledgement. A part of the sideways eight, the font was so tiny I could barely make it out. Reading the actual words was near impossible.

"Here it says dare and over there"—he pointed to the opposite side—"to remember."

I frowned.

"It's a reference to my past. And even though it's damn hard to remember, doing so makes me a better person."

He dropped his shirt and sat back, his fingers twisting the tiny silver ring on his pinkie. "Why English Lit?"

Feeling a little flushed, I placed Austen on the ground beside me. "I like analysing what I read. Taking a good book and figuring out why it works. Plus it was the only subject I actually enjoyed at high school. Why Nursing?"

"I want to save lives. Help people who need it."

"Why not Medicine then?"

"Hey. That's two questions, you skipped my turn." Jordan scowled—only it didn't look brooding or cranky, just funny, as if he were taking the mickey. I chuckled and he said, "Why Oxley?"

"Why not Oxley?"

He raised his eyebrow and I sighed. "It was as good a choice as any. All the dorms here looked good, but I liked the feel of this one best. It felt right. Speaking of ... why live in a dorm when you have a place in town?"

He over-exaggerated an eye roll. "Once you meet my brother, Logan, and his girlfriend, you'll understand the need to escape."

Silence claimed the tiny room. Did he invite me to meet his brother? I wasn't sure if that was a slip-up or the real deal. By the way he started doodling on his leg with the pen, he probably wanted to take it back. "They can't be that bad."

"Okay, you got me. They're great, but according to my

ex-roomies you can't make friends if you don't live in." He continued swirling the pen around his calf. I reached across and snatched it right out of his hand. He tried to claim it back, but the books got in the way, and I was too fast.

"Why not Alexi?"

Boom, boom, boom. My heart took up residence in my throat, forming a fist-sized lump. I took the pen to the inside of my knee.

"Why won't you play footy?"

Jordan's brows pulled down.

"I overheard Cade moaning about you refusing to join the team," I explained.

"No you don't. Answer my question first."

I concentrated on drawing lines, curves, more lines. Jordan watched me, his stare burning through the walls I'd carefully constructed over the years. "Hex is more fun."

"That's a lame answer, and also isn't the truth you promised. Try again."

I filled in the shape on my knee. A solid blue heart—unbroken.

"It's not a matter of choosing not to go by my real name, but rather deciding I liked Hex better. It reminds me of who I am."

Jordan continued regarding me, clearly waiting for more explanation, and how he knew that wasn't the end of the story was creepily in tune with me. Surely he didn't know me that well. I focused my attention on the pen again, moving it in time with my thoughts while I told him, "I've stuffed up a lot of things, and reminding myself of that curse helps to keep it simple."

His knee bumped against mine. I wasn't sure when he'd moved to sit beside me, back against the bed, but he was right there all up in my personal space. His closeness made my heart think this was a party, and beat to the rhythm of a dance mix. Dumbass heart, didn't know what was good for it.

"Hex as in an evil spell?" He tugged my hand with the pen away from my skin, revealing the two sappy hearts I'd drawn. "That's bullshit. You are not a hex."

He was so wrong. He also knew nothing. That didn't stop him spouting crap though. "It doesn't matter what you've stuffed up or how badly. We've all made mistakes in life. Hell, I doubt anything you've done is that bad. And even if it was ... so what? You're not a bad person, Alexi. No matter what anyone says."

My heart turned to mush, melted into a pile of goo because of his sweet words. The way he emphasised my name was like a weight lifting off my soul. One that stopped the constant crush and that was the nicest thing anyone had ever said to me. He rested his hand against my thigh, with the tip of the pen right near the hearts I'd drawn.

A few seconds of silence passed.

"I don't want to play footy because I hate what it stands for. It's so easy to get wrapped up in the game and forget about everything that matters. Sure I love playing ball, but I want more out of life and I know if I start playing again, footy will consume me. I'll train every spare moment, I'll hang out with my teammates ... everything else will slip into the 'when I have time' basket. I won't do that again." Passion flared in his dark eyes and I didn't doubt the truth of his words, even if they were a gross stereotype.

I held his fired-up glower as I said, "Not all teams are like that. The inter-college comp is hardly pro ball, it's for fun."

With each stroke of the pen, his curled pinkie rubbed against the skin of my thigh. I was more aware of that tiny touch than I was of anything else. The ring I'd never really looked closely at before caught my eye. The flat shield sat off-centre, hidden between his fingers.

"It's not the team I'm worried about."

"If you don't want to be that person then don't be. Surely you can play without letting it take over your life."

Jordan's shorts buzzed and he dived into his pocket without moving his hand from its artwork at my leg. After a quick look at the screen, he said, "Sorry, I gotta take this." The pen continued to move as he answered, "Ye-ello."

There was a moment of silence, while he sat there with the phone pressed to his ear. The pen stopped moving; his hand didn't shift. "Cut?"

Silence again.

"Why would he cut my damn shift?"

I studied his face for some clue as to what was going down. Work, obviously.

"That's bullshit, Penny."

Something nasty slithered into my tummy at the fact it was a girl. Excluding a few texts here and there, I'd never called his phone, but now I suddenly wanted to, so that I had this part of him too. Penny must be one of his workmates, but if it was about shifts why did she call and not the boss who they were clearly talking about? I bet she was some six-foot tall, blonde bombshell. *Yup, pretty sure I hate Penny.*

"Yeah, well ... we both know that's a lie. He needs me there for the full shift."

His hand still hadn't moved, but completely covered whatever he'd drawn. I stayed statue-still, breathing shallowly as if I wasn't there.

"All right. See you then."

Jordan tossed his phone across the room. "Suppose we'd better call it a night."

I wasn't ready for him to leave. "Suppose."

He drew in an angry breath and let it go. Then he tossed his pen to the floor right next to his phone and gathered up all his books. He must have had second thoughts about the evil-doing phone, because he retrieved it as well. I climbed to my feet as he stood, and said, "Night, Jordan."

His expression softened as he stepped around me. "Fun dreams."

I closed the door behind him and dropped onto my bed. Right under the hearts on my inner knee, in block letters was the word *Lexi.*

Chapter 17
Jordan

CARLOS DIDN'T have the gall to show his face on Thursday night. Four years I'd been here. Loyal as all get-up, I'd always dropped everything for work. No matter when he called or how short the notice, I'd been there. And now here I was, one hour into a stingy three-hour shift. A shift that had always been a close, at least five hours long, and this blew.

I stalked the store, watching the juniors work. Kev sliced and diced onion while Joe scowled, as if something had crawled up his arse. The cranky son-of-a-gun slammed a fist on the counter, growling, "Your sister sucks faster than this. I need that damn onion yesterday."

Kev plunged across and tugged the redhead against the metal bench until his face was right up in the other guy's. Screw this shit. This wasn't a bloody bar, and I wasn't paid enough to be a frigging bouncer. Pushing myself into the middle, I shoved each of them in the chest so there was more space between them. "If you two shits keep this up, one or both of you will find yourselves out of a job. We can't have staff that would rather slice off each other's heads than make a fucking pizza. So whatever your beef with each other is, get the hell over it or you're gone."

Neither of them looked me in the eye. Kev kept his focus downcast while Joe sported a gloating smirk, his eyes resting on the other dude. I got right up in his face and said, "Capiche?"

The jerk-off didn't even nod, merely slid his gaze to mine and pulled a plastic smile. I'd seen his kind before.

"I know a troublemaker when I see one," I ground out. "Now get back to work." I stared him down until he did just that. This guy clearly didn't want a job.

I stalked back to the oven and slid a few pizzas through, listening for the juniors the whole time, but neither so much as sneezed. After ten minutes the orders ran dry, and satisfied that they'd stick to the job at hand, I ducked out the front. It wasn't that busy tonight, and up front was no different. Penny slouched against the counter, her hair hanging loosely about her shoulders rather than the way she generally wore it. Something about the way she looked and even stood felt off. She peeked my way, but before I could ask her about tonight's roster change the front door chimed, indicating we had a customer.

Penny dagged herself into an upright position and waited for the older guy to reach the counter. She heaved an audible sigh and looked at him. The man blinked a few times and stared back at her, but Penny just tapped her nails against the counter. The dude looked to me, and we were both as confused as each other. Penny was at the counter; she ought to be serving. The man cleared his throat.

"Yes," Penny said, her tone flat. "What can I get you?"

The man frowned and looked up at the menu. "Two Supreme, a ..."

Well, that was weird. I headed back out to the work area, glancing around as I did. The roster hung on the back wall. We'd been too busy for me to check it out earlier, so I took a look while I waited for the order to come through. I wanted to see who had the rest of my shift.

What the hell?

Not only had today's shift been halved, but Saturday's was crossed out, as if it had been a last-minute choice. I quickly scanned the other names and heat crawled up the back of my neck. Not only had I lost shifts, but those two jerk-offs had picked up my hours and Penny was on close alone. Alone, on a goddamn Saturday night. Whatever the hell was going down, I needed to talk to Carlos and sort this shit out. I was a good bloody worker and he knew it, so why the hell had he cut my hours? I needed that shift more than anyone. I snatched the phone off the charger that sat on Carlos's desk and jabbed at his number on speed dial. It took three rings for him to answer.

"Carlos," I said. "What gives with the roster?"

"Jordan?"

I grunted.

"Nothing gives. It's a quiet week."

"Like hell it is. Penny can't do close alone on a Saturday."

"Don't question me, boy."

I slammed the phone onto its charger. How the hell did he know Saturday would be quiet? And regardless of how busy it was, there needed to be two senior staff here until late. It was insane. Kicking the cool room door on my way past, I returned to the front counter where Penny had a few customers waiting for their orders. I really should get out back, but she wasn't with anyone right now, so I walked up beside her. "He cut my Saturday shift completely. What's going on?"

Penny shrugged and made a noise somewhere between 'dunno' and 'huh' while keeping her focus on the coins she flicked around the inside of the till. This was bullshit.

I returned to my post on the oven, and those damn idiots were at it again. I got right up in Joe's face and said, "Can it. Now."

He raised a mocking brow. "You're hardly the boss around here, asshole."

I pointed toward the back door. "I'm the boss when Carlos isn't here. You're done for the night. Go home."

He laughed.

I drew in a deep breath and set my jaw. "Do I have to call Carlos?"

He undid his apron and tossed it onto the bench. "I'm done," he said. "But not because you say so. I don't need your shit tonight."

Two minutes later Kev and I were flat out. A heap of orders came from nowhere and we struggled to get them out on time. Penny stood at the oven, tapping her foot, and spirited the cooked pizzas away quicker than we could put the next one in. We hardly had time to breathe, which is probably why I didn't notice it was nine until I felt the tap on my shoulder. When I spun around, Carlos's dark eyes bore into mine. "You're off."

It took me a moment to register that he meant my shift was done. I stared right back and he didn't waver. Apparently our words from earlier still stood.

"Why's my shift cut?"

Carlos stared back at me without answering. Whatever. I was too pissed off to say anything more.

By the time I'd reached the halfway mark on the walk back to my dorm, my feet ached from pounding the pavement, my lungs seared from sucking back the evening air, and my throbbing temple was the worst. I rounded the corner and Oxley came into view. I was in no mood to socialize, so I stormed into the courtyard and right upstairs.

Carlos knew I needed the money, and that I'd work damn hard to earn it. So what was his frigging problem? I strode down the hall and slammed my door closed behind me. Tugging my silver ring over my knuckle, I let it clatter onto the desk then turned to my wardrobe, still angry. Everything reeked of pizza shop; even digging into the depths of my cupboard didn't help. It must have clung to me. I yanked out some clothes anyway and tugged the door open, going straight to the shower. Bloody Carlos—built up people's trust only to remind them he had all the power and that we were no more than dirt under his feet. Seemed like I was in the market for a new job, because I couldn't survive on three hours of work a week. I might be on a residential scholarship, but I still had to live. I needed that money, damn it.

The hot water pounding my back didn't make me feel any better. The headache from hell still throbbed through my skull when I stepped out and dried off. As I came out of the bathroom, Hex called my name. I doubled back and shot a glance into her room where she was sprawled out on her bed. Books, pens, and papers covered the entire surface. They looked like the same old books she'd been working with all week, no doubt for that English essay. She grinned up at me. "You want to hang for a bit?"

Staring into her eyes, I sighed. This girl was the picture of happy, yet if the other night was any indication there was more shit in her life than in mine. Her dark hair was pulled up in a way that was cute as hell, with all the short bits coming loose to fall against her ears and the blue ends sticking out of a hair-tie like a mini faucet. She looked up at me hopefully and I couldn't say no. I gave Hex a weak smile and said, "Sure." Then I dumped my stuff in my own room and came back, plonking on the far end of her bed.

"Day four," she said, "of just hanging with you. Got a fun plan?"

I sighed again. With all the crap at work, I'd forgotten that I was supposed to be hanging with her. Unfortunately, this week had only made me more attached to her. Hex had a soft side that made me like her even more, made me want to take all her worries away and wrap her in my arms forever. She wasn't only fun and crazy; she was sweet and caring too.

Hex looked at me as if she knew I'd had a shitty night. She shoved her books away and got up from her spot leaning against the wall's corner. Walking right past me, I was certain she was going for that bottle of vodka, so I closed my eyes and drew a deep breath. But then ... a soft pressure landed on my shoulders.

"Scoot over," she said.

I did. She moved in behind me, her knees pressed against my butt and she loomed over me while her hands moved over my shoulders. Hex's hands were like Houdini working their magic on muscles I hadn't realised were tense. Her thumbs dug into the flesh and smoothed over lumps until there was nothing but supple muscle left. A slow, deep breath in through my nose relaxed everything but my mind, which concentrated on the feel of her fingers against my bare skin. She was sent to this earth for me, I was sure of it, because this ... this was heaven. I probably couldn't stand if I tried; my entire body felt like melted ice. I let my eyes slide closed and enjoyed the way she made me feel, made my shoulders like putty in her hands. Finally those hands slowed and their movement became more caress than massage. My body caught onto the change quick smart. Tingles spread from her touch, heating my neck, shoulders, down into my chest, lower ... I readjusted my position. This girl was my undoing. Her hands warmed my entire back, making me let it all go, and even though we didn't speak I felt like she knew. She knew what it was like to feel pain, knew what it was like to lose love, and above all else, she knew me. I wasn't sure when it happened or even how, but Hex had become far more than I'd ever wanted her to be.

I swung my arm behind me, hooking her around the waist, and in a movement I didn't realise was possible landed on my back with her pulled flush against me while our lips met. I kissed that girl with everything I had: all the anger, all the frustration, all the desire I'd suppressed for the past few weeks and then some. Her tongue met mine without me even asking for entry, and it was like neither of us could hold back any longer. We'd been fighting this for so long that now it felt as if we battled each other to give more than either of us could take. My hands slid up her sides and Hex's moan vibrated against my mouth. If that wasn't permission then I'd be damned. She pushed her hand under my shirt and fuck, the after-effects of the shiver that rippled across my chest could be felt through my entire body. Her door still stood wide open, and as much as my foot itched to kick it closed, it was probably the only way to keep us clothed.

I swept my tongue over the roof of her mouth and Hex arched her back under my hand. This needed to end right now, or I'd be in her bed all night and I wasn't sure how she'd react to that. She might run. I dragged my mouth to her cheek and kissed the soft flesh. "You're ..." I kissed her temple "... gonna be the death of me."

Hex chuckled and pressed her forehead against mine. "I don't know what we're doing, Jordan Hays."

I needed Hex like I'd never needed anything else before. Being with her felt too right to be wrong; we'd work this out somehow. We had to, because I was pretty sure she'd stolen my fucking heart.

Chapter 18
Hex

IT WAS day five and I felt pretty darn accomplished. The essay on *Pride and Prejudice* was done, I'd finished all the required readings for Economics and now, making sense of the first three chapters in this Science text spread out before me was all I had left to get caught up. The only issue being I was three weeks behind and the words on the page made no sense. I jammed the pencil into my ponytail and squinted at the page. Freaking peptides. I'd never understand them, that was for sure.

Once again Jordan sat across from me on the floor, his back against my wooden cupboard door, his legs up and notebook perched on his knee. He scrawled across the page, stopping every once in a while to peruse the—I twisted my head to the side to read the title—Human Anatomy and Physiology text.

Now that was a science I could get into: studying

human anatomy with the fine specimen of a male sitting opposite me.

Focus, Hex. Forcing my attention back to my own work, I grabbed a highlighter and dragged it across the page. *Peptides are naturally occurring biological molecules.* And that means? My head swam in a sea of strange words. Yanking the pencil out of my hair, I drew a giant question mark by the bright yellow passage. This science subject was so hard. Curse my stupid father and his stupid keep-your-options-open subject-choice rules. I shoved the pencil back in place. The lead scraped my scalp and I swore. I didn't get it. No matter how hard I tried this stupid class was impossible.

"What is it?" Jordan asked.

"Nothing." I slammed the book shut. "Let's take a break."

"We only just started."

"So? I'm hungry."

Jordan levelled a flat stare my way then returned his attention to his studies. Yeah, he knew what I was up to. I shoved the pesky book aside and grabbed my pillow, which I swung around from the side, my sights set firmly on breaking up his little study party. Oblivious to my intentions, Jordan's notebook remained his sole focus.

I felt the smile tug at my mouth a second before projected impact.

Jordan's arm shot up, snatching my pillow from the air and reefing it right out of my hands. Leaning forward, he shoved it behind him, sandwiching my precious pillow between his back and the cupboard door. Without even cracking a smile, he kept jotting down notes.

"Kill joy."

"Procrastinator."

"Square."

He looked up, his eyes sparkling under the fluorescent light. The smirk that spread across his face was near intoxicating. In fact, my head felt kind of woozy.

Keeping my eyes on him, I climbed up on the bed, before I could crawl into his arms. Jordan never dropped his gaze. I cleared my throat.

"Damn Hex, you're making it hard to work tonight and I really gotta get this assessment done."

I graced him with a half-manufactured smile and reached for my long-time best friend, Jo March. I hadn't found time to finish *Little Women* again with the huge reading list for English Lit, so poor Jo and her sisters had been waiting for my return since O-week.

I WASN'T falling for Jordan Hays. I wasn't. No matter which way I looked at it, this was just ... something. Something that would be over before it started, and he was only a friend anyway. Nothing more. It didn't matter that today marked night six and my heart fluttered like a freaking hummingbird on steroids just waiting for him to show. It wasn't like he had kissed me a third time, but last night after studying when we'd watched a movie on the television that sat in the corner of my desk, he *had* pulled me up against him and wrapped his arms around me. My stomach did a crazy dance the entire time and I wasn't sure what it was about this guy, but I definitely *wasn't* falling for him.

No sir-ee.

My ducks were all lined up perfectly and they didn't include Jordan Hays or any other guy. No permanent fixtures, because permanent fixtures were never permanent. Yet here I was, sitting at my desk, facing the door, and it wasn't even five p.m. But it was Saturday and Amber had already been on my case about going out tonight. I took a small swig from my water bottle and set it aside, then peeked at the door again. Maybe I should go to his room. A second gulp of the sweet liquid was enough to push that thought away. I wouldn't be controlled.

But he knew how to see inside me in a way no one else had even tried. I sighed. We hadn't pulled any stupid stunts since before Amber's half birthday. And that was a hit; she thought the balloons were sweet, so now I had to think up something even better for her actual birthday before September.

Stupid stunts aside, hanging with Jordan was great. Too great. Somehow he managed to take the lamest things and turn them into fun, like last night's movie. Who would've thought being held while staring at a screen could ... *argh*. I needed to stop thinking about him. I glanced at the empty doorway. Dares ... technically we were still on my dare, but I had one lined up for him anyway.

Amber appeared in the space I wasn't watching intently, because I *wasn't* looking for Jordan. I breathed a sigh of relief.

"What's the plan?" she said, plopping herself onto my

185

bed.

"Hadn't really put any thought into it. I promised Jordan ..."

Her eyes flashed to mine, full of questions—or rather, accusations. I hadn't exactly been honest about what wasn't happening between Oxley's hottest nurse and me. She raised a brow, daring me to continue. I sighed. Again. My lungs were like an old balloon that couldn't hold their air.

"It's not like that ..." *it totally was* "... we're just friends, hanging out."

Amber's eyes lit with excitement. "Jordan and Hex sitting in a tree ... K-I-S-S-I-N—"

"G." Jordan leaned against my doorframe.

"You"—I pointed at him—"are incorrigible."

"You love it." He winked at me, then continued down the hall.

My stomach absolutely did. Not. Flip.

"It's not like what now?" Amber asked, raising a brow like she had a moment ago, clearly not believing a word I said.

"So about tonight ..."

She straightened up. "I heard curry's on the menu. We should eat out."

Half an hour later, I was in the stairwell, making my way to the courtyard to meet Nate and Amber. McKenzie didn't want in on the pizza run, since she'd stocked up on snacks and was writing a paper with a tight deadline.

"Hex." I stopped mid stride at the bottom of the stairs, looking to Dono standing in the door of his room. "You got a minute?"

"For you, Dono, I've got a whole hour."

I didn't really. He stepped back, holding the door wide for me to enter. He looked flushed today, pink spots marking his cheeks, probably due to the warmer weather. It'd been cool now we were moving toward mid May, but today was like a flashback to summer.

"How are your studies going?" Dono asked once I was inside.

My defences shot up. "Fine."

"No, really. How are you coping?"

"Fine."

"Hex, I'm your resident senior. You can talk to me. That's why I'm here."

Heaving a sigh, I dropped onto the beanbag, sinking into the squeaky balls until my butt hit the hard floor. He needed to refill the darn thing.

Dono flipped open the mini fridge that sat in the corner of his room and extracted a can of soda, which he passed my way. I snapped off the ring pull and took a swig. "Why are you asking?"

"I keep an eye on everyone in this block."

Phew. I hadn't been singled out as failing. "It's all right."

He looked at me for a long moment. I fidgeted in the beanbag. "Sheesh. Do they give you guys training in spotting struggling students or something?"

He continued to stare as he leaned against the wall. "It's my job to look out for everyone who lives in this block. You can talk to me, and what you say stays in the room. It's completely confidential."

"I'm not sure I really have what it takes for Science."

"What do you mean?"

I tapped my head.

"Sure you do. If you didn't you wouldn't have got into the course. You just need a little focus, maybe. Can I get you some help? Perhaps another student in your course to study with?"

How did I tell him the problem was my motivation? That I was struggling because I didn't want to be here, I didn't want to take Drama, or Economics, or Science, or any other stupid subject. I had no idea what I wanted to do with my life, and as yet ... I hadn't found anything I enjoyed. Other than English, but what the hell did one do with a degree majoring in English Lit? Become an editor or a journo, maybe?

Dono looked at me expectantly. Right; he expected an answer. I drew in a long breath. "I don't know."

"Hex, you've got to do something if you think might fail. Because if you fail too many classes, they'll put you on probation, and no one wants that."

"Really?"

"Really. How about I set something up?"

If I got put on probation that'd be it; my father would cut off the money, tell me to get a job. And there was no way I'd be able to snag something that would bring in the kind of money we needed to keep the house.

"Sure. Why not?" I climbed up out of the beanbag. I'd kept my friends waiting long enough.

"Great. I'll let you know when I have something sorted."

"See you later," I told Dono and ducked out of his room into the courtyard. Sure enough, my friends were all waiting by the picnic table, Jordan included.

Amber gave me a concerned look. "Everything all right?"

"Yep, let's grab some food!" My response was probably too upbeat, but Amber passed me a grin and twirled her keys around a finger. Jordan however, wasn't as easily fooled. His gaze rested on me as we walked to Amber's car and stayed there all the way to town. By the time we pulled up outside the pizza shop where he worked, I was convinced he'd never look away.

We strolled into Mozzarellas and it looked like this was the most popular cheese-covered-dough place in town. There was barely room to move. I only could because the girl beside me was thinner than a beanpole. She sure didn't look as if she ate a lot of take-out.

"Wow this place is packed," Amber said, shouldering her way to the front counter. Jordan growled something behind me, but I couldn't hear him over the buzz in the room. When we made it to the front, without looking up the blonde cashier said, "What can I get you?"

Poor girl looked like crap with smudged mascara and tangled hair; maybe it was because she was so flat out. Surely there wasn't only one cashier working on a night like this. I felt a hand on my shoulder, but before I could turn around, Jordan spoke in my ear, "They're slammed. I'm gonna see if they need me to stay."

I would rather he came home with us than worked on a Saturday night, but I wasn't about to say that. Especially with ... I spotted the blonde's 'Penny' name badge as she looked up. Her attention caught on me. Her mouth parted then her jaw set, her eyes hardening. But her icy stare didn't stay on me. It moved to my left, even though Amber rattled off our order. And it wasn't until he disappeared through the staff-only door that I realised Jordan was at the receiving end of her dirty look. I kind of liked that she seemed not to like him. I guess he wasn't supposed to be here, but I was certain Penny wasn't the boss, so what did she care? Whatever the heck her problem was, she snapped her attention back to Amber, but her gaze kept sliding to me then Nate.

"You get that?" Amber asked.

"Sure." Penny focused on the screen. "Two pan bases. One Supreme, one Meat Lovers. What name's that for?"

Amber giggled, totally ignoring the poor girl. Probably had something to do with Nate's fingers tickling her side. Her head tipped back as if she were trying to look at him upside down. Their flirting was getting ridiculous. Even I could feel the sexual tension between them.

"Name?" Penny prompted.

"Hex," I said.

Penny's eyes narrowed on me, as if this were some kind of prank.

"My name's Hex."

She dragged her teeth over her bottom lip and gave a sharp nod. I grabbed Amber's arm and tugged her toward the biggest gap in the waiting area, right by the staff door Jordan had disappeared into. Leaning against the red door, I jolted when someone shouted angrily from the other side.

"What's her problem?" Amber said. I could feel Penny watching me. I shrugged.

A few moments passed, then Amber nudged my arm. "Are we getting wild tonight?"

"Doubt it," I said. "Jordan—"

"Screw Jordan. He's ditching us anyway." Amber rolled her eyes toward the counter where Jordan was speaking to Penny, so close his mouth practically touched her ear. The girl had a tiny smile as she punched at the touch screen in front of her and my belly burst into fire. My throat ached and damn it, Amber was right; he'd ditch us for sure. I dragged my attention away and looked my friend square in the eye.

"The Central?"

She gave me a grin so huge I felt kind of bad for neglecting her this week. She said, "That's my girl."

The cow behind the till called my name and Jordan was right by her again, pizza boxes in hand. He placed them by the till as I strode up to the counter.

"It's crazy busy. I have to stay, sorry."

"Sure," I said, looking right at her. Penny slid the two pizza boxes toward my edge of the counter and even though Jordan slipped out back again where I couldn't see him, I said, "Thanks. Make sure he gets home."

"Right," Penny said, her eyes holding mine.

I spun around to my friends. "Let's go rock this town!"

Amber cheered and Nate looked toward the staff door then back at me. I gave him the biggest grin I could dredge up.

I didn't care that Jordan chose to stay here, or that Penny was still casting me filthy looks. I didn't care that my bottle of vodka was near empty. I didn't care that night six was no longer. And I sure as hell didn't care about Jordan Hays. I always knew he wouldn't hang around.

So why was I so pissed?

Chapter 19
Jordan

I SLAMMED ANOTHER pizza into the oven, waited the full two minutes and shoved in a second. The line of waiting bases was longer than the Sydney to Armidale express train. Carlos's glare cut into my back, but I didn't give a damn. The work needed to be done and he was short-staffed. I shouldn't have given a shit, but after being here for over two years I wasn't about to walk out the door and leave them in this crappy mess. It was bullshit. He knew we got slammed on Saturday nights, so why he'd thought Penny could do it with only a couple of juniors was beyond me, even he was on the floor too, instead of flicking through supplier orders at his desk.

I dunno when the oven became my place, but the minute I came back here Kev stepped aside, returning to the topping bench as if he were keeping my spot warm. I stood there like it was, pushing them through one after another, even though I'd rather be back at Oxley. My thumb landed too close to the edge, copping a nail full of tomato paste, so I swiped it on my leg. Not like my jeans weren't already covered in grime from dirty fingers.

A soft touch brushed my shoulder. "We need to talk," Penny whispered. "Meet me out back."

"Okay." I popped another plain cheese pizza through. Penny nodded and headed toward the back door. After giving her a few minutes head start, I approached Kev. "Watch the oven for five while I take a leak?"

"Sure." He moved right over and I slipped out the back door. Penny stood by a pile of crushed cardboard, dragging on her cigarette. Her eyes were downcast; her usual smile absent.

"Jordan, I'm sorry things between us got messy."

"No, I'm sorry. If I hurt you that was never my intention—"

She flicked her cigarette butt to the ground and toed it out. "Don't say it. I'm glad we had what we did, and you aren't the bad guy here, okay? I broke my word. I was the one who stuffed up. Who let my stupid feelings get in the way."

I was an asshole, an absolute and utter dick. I should have realised that things had changed; hell, I probably shouldn't have gotten involved in the first place. Sex never came without strings; it might seem like it, but it turned out those strings were hidden.

"I'm sorry, Penny." I pulled her in for a hug. Her arms snapped around me tightly for a few seconds, then she pushed back.

"It's all good." She gave a tiny smile. "Better get back to

work."

It took hours before things started to slow down. Honestly some nights it was like the entire town got lazy and decided not to cook. Backhanding my forehead to swipe off the sweat, I looked around. I'd be damned; every single staff member was still here. Even Carlos. Only now he hunched over his desk with the phone to his ear.

He glanced up and his gaze hardened.

"What the hell is his problem?" I muttered.

"He was fine before you showed up," Kev said. "I mean ... he was all right, still in a shit mood. But—"

I slid the last pizza through. There weren't any more in the line, so I decided to duck out front to see if Penny had much else to come in. I took two steps forward and hit a solid wall of Carlos barring my way with his huge barrel of a chest right up in my space.

It took every last scap of restraint I had not to lose my shit. "What's the problem, Carlos?"

He dropped his voice to a growl. "You're a good worker, but stay the hell away from my family, you hear me?"

He what? "You dropped my shifts because of your family?"

Carlos crossed his arms over his chest.

"Why the hell did you cut my shifts? If this is because of some stupid bloody thing I said about Marcy, I'm sorry." Honestly, the only person this could be about was Penny, but I didn't want to say that aloud in case I was wrong.

Carlos shook his head. "Go home, kid. You're done."

I slammed my fist on the counter. "Like hell I'm done. I saved your arses tonight. Without me, you would've been giving every bloody order away free."

Carlos's glare was like ice. "I said you're done here. For good."

I tossed the towel I'd been using as a heat glove onto the floor and pushed through the side door. As I reached the front entry to the shop Penny called my name. I spun around and the look on her face said it all. So did my boss standing right behind her with his chest puffed out like a bloody peacock.

This *was* about her.

He had to know about our hook-ups. That time we'd kissed in the middle of the store ... the CCTV. Shit.

"You need a lift?" she asked.

"No," I growled.

She scooped the keys from the hook under the counter anyway, frowning at me as if I'd spoken another language.

"Don't be a jerk," she said.

Carlos shook his head from behind her, warning me to stick to my negative answer.

I pushed through the door. And screw me, if I didn't need a good reference so badly I would have punched him in the nose. There was no going back from that though and I wasn't a fucking idiot. God knows what he thought, what Penny had told him, if anything. She didn't seem to realise he had her back. The guy was an arse.

I fished out my wallet, but I should have known without looking that I didn't have the cash for a cab. I had two choices; call Logan or walk home. There was no way I wanted to 'talk it through' with my brother. If I called him, he'd pull his psycho shit out and tell me I was out of line, that I needed the job so I ought to apologise. Like hell.

"At a guess," Kev said, "he saw the two of you go into the cool room together last week and now she's all mopey, so ..."

I didn't even bother glancing over my shoulder.

"Apparently we got a late delivery and since all the drivers have gone home, I've got to run it. To one of the dorms ... Oxley, I think Penny said."

I shook my head. Un-fucking-believable. She couldn't care less that I was just fired from the job I needed more than anything, yet she was worried about me getting home.

I climbed into the Focus and didn't say a word to Kev for the entire trip, even when he dropped me back at Oxley. I climbed out of the car and slammed the door. He pulled off right away.

There was no goddamn delivery.

At nearly one a.m. Oxley should be quiet. I peeked up to Hex's window anyway. And for some reason, the fact her light wasn't on made me feel like punching the wall. I shouldn't be angry, but I couldn't rein it in, even though it was a good thing she must have turned in already. She'd been going to bed earlier this week than she usually did so I wasn't all that surprised, but geez it would've been nice to see her face before I went to bed. I was a dick ... I should have stayed here with her tonight instead of wasting my time at Mozzarellas.

Disappointment weighed down my feet as I trudged up the stairs. Even taking a shower didn't help me wind down. I returned to my room and tossed my jeans in the corner. As I flopped onto the bed, guilt became my anchor. I really shouldn't have skipped out on Hex for an entire night, especially when it was the second last night of my dare. I would've been so much better off hanging with her rather than run off my arse, unappreciated. I hoped that this week had been enough to make her realise that what we had going was worthwhile. Hell, it was worth more than being spat out by the asshole bosses of this world.

SIRENS: POLICE. Ambulance. Fire.

I jolted upright in bed. Something was wrong. Fire … *fire.* The fire alarms were going off and through the pitch darkness of my room I couldn't even make out the time. My clock wasn't on. I yanked on my jeans, and jammed on my flip-flops. Screaming filled the hall. "Arses out of bed, it's a fire alarm. Go! Go! Go!"

I reefed my door open and stepped out into the hall, avoiding the manic path of a girl running along, bashing on doors.

"Get down to the car park," she ordered before spinning around and shouting down the hall, "Wake up!"

People spewed into the corridor and down the stairs. Most of the doors along my floor were tightly closed.

I thumped my fist on Hex's door, but there was no answer. She was probably already downstairs. By the fogginess in my head and that chick bashing every door down, I got the feeling I hadn't exactly woken quickly. Probably an effect of how hard I'd worked my arse off tonight.

Giving one last knock on her door, I decided she must

have beat me out, so I hauled my butt downstairs and joined the mass of pissed-off students standing in the front car park. Most were in various states of undress; boxers, skimpy little pyjamas and for shit's sake, I was pretty sure Cade only wore a sheet. Scanning the crowd proved difficult. Even though I was tall enough to see over most heads, there were so many people I couldn't really make individuals out in the darkness. Sure, floodlights lit up the space, but people sat on gardens or propped against cars as if they were still asleep. Then there were the ones who obviously hadn't been to bed yet, still fully clothed and ... Amber stood by Nate, shifting from foot to foot, her hand on her hip while she wore his favourite Mambo shirt. Well, I'd be damned. They'd actually hooked up.

The moment he saw me Nate gave me a wide grin and pointed my way. "Sis, good night?"

"Not as good as yours."

"It's not what you think."

Amber's elbow dove toward Nate, tipping her off balance. He caught her in an arm. "Where's Hex?"

"I was hoping you'd know," I said.

The sirens continued blaring and I hoped to god it wasn't a real fire. I didn't drag anything out here with me. Not even Kayla's ring. I'd slipped it off before my shower and forgotten to put it back on. I didn't give a rat's about any other possession, they were all replaceable ... but that was the only part of my sister I had left.

I stood on tiptoe and swept a look through the crowd again, but couldn't see Hex. Amber giggled, wrapping her arms around my waist and tugging me down onto my heels. "I'm still planning to get you back for all those balloons, bug-a-lugs. Ooooh ..." She ran her fingers over my chest, tracing the lines of my tat. "... what's this?"

"A tattoo."

"Funny."

I held myself still, but Amber didn't seem to notice, merely continued her caress like the guy whose bed she'd clearly rolled out of wasn't standing right beside us. That's when it made sense. "You're drunk, Amber."

I pried her off me and she made a show of falling backward right into Nate's arms, giggling again. "Am not ... I'm ... sobering."

Nate patted her on the head. "Sure you are."

A fire truck hooned around the corner and into the car park, lights flashing. I couldn't smell any smoke. In fact, all I could smell was someone's cigarette. Where the hell was Hex?

Moving through the crowd, I couldn't find her and my pulse pounded faster. Surely she was here somewhere. She had to be; there was no other place she could be. Unless she'd gone out partying with Amber. Even so, surely she'd be home by now. I brushed by Cade again who had his phone out, snapping selfies with some leggy blonde. "You got the time?" I asked them.

"Three-ten."

She'd definitely be home by now, unless she hadn't come back to Oxley. That thought twisted a nasty feeling in my gut.

"All clear!" Dono called from atop the arched bridge that led into our dorm. "False alarm."

A groan reverberated through the throng of people.

Somewhere near the back of the crowd, I had no choice but to wait while the bottleneck going into Oxley thinned. When I finally made it back up to our floor, I bashed on her door again for good measure.

No answer.

Clearly Hex wasn't in.

I turned away. A groan came from within, muffled by the thick timber. She was in there and she sounded ... wrong. I spun back around and bashed the crap out of her door. Down the hall someone yelled, "Shut the hell up."

"Open up, Hex."

The door rattled from the inside for what felt like a lifetime, then finally swung open. Her room was pitch black, but the light from the hall fell across her bed where she lay sprawled on her back fully clothed, shoes and all, as if she'd slept where she fell. I shifted her up on her side, in the recovery position. Listening for regular breathing, I then flipped on the light to make sure her lips looked pink. Once she was sorted I flicked the lock on her door to open, and slammed the thing closed. Then I did what I should have done in the first place: turned my back and walked away. I couldn't go through this again.

To say I went back to sleep would be an exaggeration. I tossed, turned, thrashed, and thought about nothing but Hex and the goddamn mess she was in. I even got up three times to check she hadn't choked on her own vomit.

By morning I knew.

I needed to take a huge step back because she held such a massive part of my heart, and losing Hex would be as bad as losing Kayla had been. I'd tried to help her, but Hex couldn't even last the agreed week without booze.

What hope was there?

I collapsed on the bathroom floor, my sister's limp body in my arms. As I pulled her up against me my attention landed on the bottle of pills spilled by the base of the toilet. Panic climbing up my throat, I dug the phone Coach had loaned me from my pocket and dialled the only number I knew by heart.

"Hello?" my brother's groggy voice answered.

A sob tore from my throat, the panic finally breaking loose. "Loges, I can't wake her. She won't wake up. Something's wrong."

"Did he hit her?" He instantly sounded more awake.

"I don't think so. There are pills."

"Shit. Get the fuck off the phone and call an ambulance."

I held Kayla to my chest, and with shaking fingers dialled 000.

Chapter 20
Hex

EVERYTHING AROUND me rattled and shook with the violent earthquake that made even my head crash against itself. I tried to scream, but no noise came from my hoarse throat, probably because it was caked in a dryness that tasted foul. Breathing deeply didn't slow my racing heart, and even through scrunched eyes I could tell this was bad.

Dragging open those very same sandy eyes, I realised I wasn't in the middle of a disaster after all, but rather someone was trying to ram open my door. I groaned and reached up to turn the knob without climbing out of bed, but the door flew open before my fingers even touched the handle. The whirlwind that blew in shot straight to my window and drew open the curtains. Good god, the light.

"Are you trying to blind me?" I croaked out.

I blinked again, but it was no use, so I buried my head under the pillow.

Clank. Clank. Whatever the heck it was clanked again and it was worse than the imagined earthquake. Whoever the hell let him or herself into my room needed to get out before I killed them. Slowly. And painfully.

"Did you know ..."

Jordan.

"Yes, I know that when you wake the dead, they kill you. So I suggest letting me go back to sleep."

He thunked whatever the hell it was against the desk again.

"Did you know that when someone overdoses on painkillers they don't pass out, they don't vomit—they just drift off to sleep and never wake up?"

Clank.

"Did you know that alcohol poisoning is the opposite and just as fatal? The drunk person might pass out. They might find it hard to breathe. They sure as hell won't know what's going on, even when they're chucking their guts up and gasping for breath. But if they passed out on their back the spew falls down their throat and chokes them. If they're lucky."

Clank.

"My sister is dead, Hex."

Clank.

"Fucking dead. And I saw her in both those states, one multiple times. Kayla had the world ... god, she had hell too ... but she had the world to live for, and she threw her life away like it was an empty bottle. Like the people she left behind wouldn't give a rat's she was gone. She might not have died from drinking, but it was the goddamn alcohol that took her away from me."

I dragged myself into a sitting position, crossing my legs and staring down the angry guy sitting at my desk, his hand fisted around the neck of my vodka. Jordan looked like fury personified and it wasn't attractive.

"I'm sorry you lost your sister. But gee, Jordan, loosen up. I'm not an alcoholic and I've never drunk so much that I got alcohol poisoning. Whatever the hell gave you that idea give it up, because it's wrong. Just because I like a drink doesn't mean I've got a freaking problem. It's not like I roll out of bed and reach for the bottle, even if right now I feel like grabbing that bottle and tossing it at your freaking head." I drew in a deep breath to refill my aching lungs.

"None of that defines alcoholics."

"Is this what that last dare was about? You thought I couldn't go a week without drinking?"

He didn't answer, just sat in my chair, dropping the bottle against the desk only to pick it up and let it slide through his fingers again.

"Answer me."

"Last night, Hex, you were so ... she never drank in the mornings either."

I let out a frustrated growl. I was not his sister. I had no idea how she died, but alcohol was not about to off me.

"Look, Jordan, I don't know what the hell you think you're doing here, but I'm not a puppy that needs saving. There's nothing wrong with me, all right? Nothing. So go bark up another tree. Find yourself another damsel, because I don't need a father. Hell knows, I've got one and that's enough."

Calm as a freaking cucumber, Jordan stood, placed the

bottle right in the centre of my desk, pushed the chair back into place then walked out my door. Somehow the calmness of his movements spoke louder than his words.

Well, I was pissed too, so I raised my voice and shouted down the hall, "I'm not Kayla." I shoved the door closed and flopped back on my bed. What the hell was that all about anyway?

I pulled the quilt over my head to hide from the blinding sunlight and must have drifted back to sleep eventually, because I woke slowly, blinking against the light. My door rattled with a soft knock.

"Just a second." I threw my covers off and smoothed down my hair. Rubbing at my eyes, I pulled the door open.

"Late night?" With a big smile, Dono looked entirely too chipper as he took in my crumpled clothes. I must have fallen asleep in what I was wearing.

"Just napping" I lied, sneaking a glance at my digital clock, which read 2:04 p.m. "What's up?"

"I've hooked you up with a study partner. One of the second year students who's done that class before, and passed with high grades. I think you two might be friends already?"

"Yeah," I asked. "Who is it?" *Not Jordan, thank God.*

"Luca Brown."

I nodded. "That's awesome. Thanks for helping me out."

"No worries. Make sure you talk to him to figure out the details. And Hex ..." He took a step further back into the hall, waving to someone down the other end then turned back to me with a smirk. "Try and get out of bed before dinner, okay."

206

"Shut up." I grumbled, watching Dono walk away. I was lucky to have a resident senior who cared about his block.

Closing the door, I flopped back on the bed and lay there stewing in my own thoughts. Hopefully Luca would help me understand Science. For a second there I was worried Dono was going to say Jordan, since he had science subjects. I sighed. *Jordan.* I'd thought Jordan was different, that maybe we meant something to each other, but I was wrong. He was just like Aunt Susan, another saint out to make himself feel better by fixing a goddamn sinner.

This was exactly why I didn't need anyone but Mum in my life.

Chapter 21
Jordan

I HADN'T TALKED about Kayla like that in years, not even to Logan. Thinking about the night I'd found her wasn't easy and being around Hex dragged up all those old feelings, as if they'd never faded. Now they were back, I wasn't sure how to deal with them. I threw myself into study and swimming laps, but the pent-up anger wouldn't fade. That was probably how I wound up on the footy field out behind the dorms, kicking the shit out of an old ball Liv had passed me earlier at the pool. It had been a long day of classes in which I couldn't concentrate. For the past week my head had been overflowing with thoughts of Hex, and not the kind I should have been having. More like the kind that belonged in a bloody chick flick; the smell of her blueberry shampoo, her smile after we'd done something stupid, the way it felt to hold her in my arms while we watched TV.

The way she looked in those short shorts and Dr. Martens boots.

"Sis!"

Cade's voice booming across the field pulled me from my thoughts. I dropped the ball and kicked it toward him. Like a pro, he released the pile of books in his hand and caught it on the full, tucked it under his arm and ran for me.

I squared myself off and rushed him, easily swiping his feet out from under him in a tackle and stealing the ball then bolting back the other way.

"Game on!" Luca's backpack fell to the ground and ran toward me, as did a third guy out to my right. I tossed the ball to the dude on the wing who continued my play, taking the ball all the way to the end goal and slamming it into the ground.

"Try!" I shouted.

"First to five," Cade called.

Blood pumped through my veins with a renewed vigour I hadn't felt in days. If that first play was anything to go by, I could whoop Cade's arrogant arse.

"Sure," I said. "I'll play."

"You and Baker against me and Brown."

I indicated I understood with a nod and Baker clicked his fingers to grab my attention. I jogged over to where he stood, ball balanced on his hip. "We've got this," I said. "Looks like Cade underestimates anyone he thinks can't pull him down, so if we run hard and fast we should have this in no time, regardless of Luca Brown's brawn."

Baker eyeballed me. "How'd you know that from two minutes of play?"

I shrugged. "Seen Cade's type before."

He slapped me on the back and yelled, "Game on!"

Being on the field took all my thoughts away. For the thirty minutes we played I managed to forget about Hex and Logan and even school, everything except the ball and getting it to the try line. We made some dumb moves, but all in all, Baker and I played hard and thrashed Cade and Luca, five to none. They were both big guys, but every time either of them made a dive, I dodged and ran like hell. We were too fast.

The sweat dripped out of me as we trudged back to Oxley together, laughing and recalling ace moves. I felt better. Like maybe life wasn't so shit after all. Maybe it was playing the game, or maybe it was letting all the tension out through sport. Either way, as I climbed the stairs I was finally relaxed for the first time since the fire drill.

Until I saw her door.

Then I slipped back into the goddamn chick flick and my heart felt as if it were trying to squeeze itself out of my chest through my throat. If I listened really hard I could probably hear saxophone blues in the background. It was fucking ridiculous, and it needed to stop before I kicked the useless damn organ right out of my chest. I didn't need this shit. I needed to man the hell up and do what I was here to do: learn how to be a good nurse, and how to save lives.

I twisted the ring off my finger, then took a quick shower, letting the cold water wash everything away. And afterward I plonked myself at my desk with the notes I'd scrawled in Human Bio today. Exams were looming, so I needed to get a grip and pull my head into the right place. Focus was key.

After ten minutes of failing to find that focus I got up and inched open the door. Not all the way, only enough to hear the comings and goings in the hall because I was an idiot who couldn't stop wondering what was happening three feet away.

Despite studying with my door open, I didn't hear any movement from her end of the hall. The other half dozen students on our floor came in and out, talking loudly, some saying g'day on the way past. But I made it clear I was busy with the books, so they all moved on pretty quickly. No matter how hard I tried to focus on Human Bio I still heard every noise. Even one that sounded suspiciously like the guy who lived in the room next door had his girlfriend over for a bit of nookie. But from Hex, nothing other than seeing her in passing a few times; a flash of blue hair as she dashed down the stars, a slammed door as I rounded the corner. As much as I'd decided I needed to cut her off, I still wanted to talk to her. So I knew she was okay. It was like an ache in my chest that wouldn't go away.

When I collapsed into bed, it was through sheer exhaustion. Well after midnight, I couldn't keep my eyes open any longer.

Moonlight shone through the bathroom window, casting an eerie shadow about the room. The darkened lump of my sister's form lay slumped on floor. Seemed she'd had a party of her own. I leant beside her, my stomach still trying to constrict in on itself with a feeling of wrongness.

"Kays ... bedtime."

I pushed a wayward long curl from her face. Her skin felt somehow different. My throat felt just as weird ... tight.

I studied her face again. Her straight hair had flopped back over her eye, the blue tips brushing her full lips. Her cheeks weren't the same alabaster they had been; they were beautifully tanned.

I slid my arms underneath her small frame. Hex's head flopped back so far her neck arched, her hands dangled, brushing my knees.

Something was innately wrong.

I shook her.

She didn't wake.

Heart racing, I pressed my cheek to her pulse.

"Hex!"

I woke covered in sweat, my twisted sheets clinging to my legs. My heart thundered and I bolted upright in bed, dread curling in my gut so tightly I thought I might hurl.

Chapter 22
Hex

OR THREE weeks Jordan never showed for our standing date. Well, not a date really, since we weren't dating, but rather our standing Wednesday afternoon coffee upstairs at the bar. We hadn't organised it as such, but previously every Wednesday when I'd climbed the stairs he'd been there. Today, he wasn't again, and I couldn't say that surprised me. It was amazing how you could live two doors down from someone, share a bathroom and kitchen, and not see them for three weeks and three days running. It wasn't like I'd been avoiding him—truth be told I was still pissed about that Sunday morning. Where did he get off, thinking he could treat people like projects?

Good thing it was almost the end of the semester, because I was well and truly ready for a break. In the past week Amber had dropped off the radar, I wasn't talking to Jordan and that left me with no actual close friends. Sure

I'd met lots of people and partied with the best of them, but after Jordan's rant I didn't feel like hanging out with anyone, not even McKenzie. He'd ruined me. The guy had single-handedly killed my mojo, so even hanging in the courtyard felt dirty. I wanted to hate him for that, but as the days wore on I found myself looking for him. Glancing toward the places he usually appeared. Like the stairs that led up here to our secret café bar. They were still empty.

Yep, it was official. I hated myself for caring.

Staring at my ragged nails, peeled back to the pink skin, I picked up my phone and dialled Mum's number. It rang, and rang, and when I was certain it was about to hit her voice mail, she answered.

"I miss you," I said.

"Alexi, honey." She sounded with it. "You'll be home in a few weeks."

"I can't wait to see you."

"Is it school?"

"It's nothing ... I just miss my mum."

"I miss you too, honey."

"I'm not sure I can do this."

"We can talk about it when you get home, okay?"

I hung up, feeling worse than I had before I called. I'd wrongly thought hearing her voice would make me feel better. I was here for her. This life I was living on campus was a lie and I was surrounded by judgmental people that had no idea who I truly was. Maybe I was the fraud ... I didn't even know what career I was working toward, when every other single person had his or her entire lives mapped out. I picked up my phone again, this time opening the browser, and flicked to the state rail website.

214

Booking a ticket took all of ten minutes. Tomorrow, I'd be on my way home. Maybe a reminder of why I was studying would help get me through the rest of this semester.

I sent a text to Amber.

Going home for a long weekend.

FARMLAND ZOOMED past my window and *Jane Eyre* rested against my lap, while I pulled my thoughts together. I'd read it before, but never seen this kind of depth. Who would have thought that it was all about love versus autonomy? That Jane was scared of losing her sense of independence to a man? Previously I'd enjoyed it for the unconventional romance, but after last week's lectures and the discussion in the follow-up tutorial, I was looking at the classic story in a whole new light. I grinned as all the pieces clicked into place, excitement coursing through me. I didn't really need to be reading this right now, as the exam wasn't for another two weeks. Science was first up, on Monday. The thought alone made me shudder.

Bringing the second-hand copy of *Jane Eyre* to face height, I inhaled its old book smell. There was something about it you couldn't replicate. I brought my attention back to the page and continued reading.

It felt like no time at all before the automated voice announced the next stop would be mine.

215

The train pulled into the station and before it even stopped I spotted my mother standing on the platform, her skirt and blouse perfectly in place. I grabbed my bag and stepped off the train, making a beeline right for her, and despite all the people crowding the station, she saw me straight away. Rushing toward me as if we were in one of those slow-motion movie moments, she caught me in a hug and god it felt good, even if she had pushed me away by urging me into choosing university.

I felt as if her hug instantly lifted the weight of Jordan's accusation from my chest. Even so, there was one worry no hug could ever consume: the worry I had for her. That was why I pushed her back to arm's length and took in everything about her. Sure the work clothes were on, but on closer inspection her blouse was rumpled and the navy pencil pleat skirt had a splotch of something that looked like suspiciously like old ice cream on it. Scratch that, it had two splotches, and a watermark. The polish on her nails was chipped, and when I met her gaze again the bags under her eyes stood out through the layer of makeup. And worse, although her eyes crinkled in a smile, they held no sheen. Yep, my worries for her were wedged too far below the surface for a simple hug to make them fade. Or perhaps I just didn't want her to find them. Someone had to worry about her, after all. She sure as hell didn't give two hoots about herself. Depression was like that.

"I missed you so much." I pulled her in for another hug.

"Me too," she said, picking up my duffel bag.

We only lived a short drive from the station, but I must have peeked at her at least a dozen times on the way there. I'd only been gone for a few months, but it suddenly felt like forever. It was impossible to tell if she was doing better or worse without me. The fact she'd been at work was a plus, but those bags ... they were the real concern. It meant she wasn't getting a lot of sleep and she was still feeling bad. She was probably drinking way too much as well. I guess I'd known that already. There'd been enough middle-of-the-night phone calls. Jordan's words reappeared and I found myself looking at her in a different light. Was suicide what I was worried about?

"Home sweet home," Mum said, breaking my sombre thoughts.

Grass so tall it tickled the bottom of the front window filled the flowerbed, but that was nothing new. Cobwebs hid under the eaves, yet it wasn't anything I wouldn't expect at the average house inhabited by a single, working lady.

Mum was already hoisting my bag out of the backseat, so I climbed out of the car and followed her inside. Noise droned from the television but I ignored it, taking my bag from her hands and dumping it in my room, which looked exactly as I'd left it.

I poked my head into my brother's room and Riley hadn't been to visit in my absence. My heart sank. It wasn't as if I expected he would, but that didn't mean I didn't hold out hope. It was as if my brother ceased to exist when he left with Dad. She could have fought for custody, since Riles was only twelve, but she'd been too heartbroken to pull it together. I could count on one finger the number of times he'd seen us since that night. My father was an asshole.

I walked back into the kitchen where Mum had poured

us each a glass of wine. Heaviness slammed into my tummy at the sight of the amber liquid.

"So," she said, "tell me about the boy."

I pulled myself up onto the bench, drumming my feet against the cupboard doors. "It's not about a *boy* boy. It's just everything." I sighed. "I'm not sure I'm cut out for university. More school seems kind of pointless when I could be out there doing something else."

"Like what? What do you want to do?"

I shrugged. There was no job I could do that would pull in the same money my father gave me for studying and we both knew it. She passed me a glass of wine.

"It's a great opportunity to make a good life for yourself. Aren't you enjoying the course?" Mum asked.

"It's all right. Drama is boring as all buggery, and Science is impossible, but English Lit is kind of fun."

She leaned against the counter, sipping on her wine. "So if you left, what would you do?"

I shrugged again. "That's the thing. I have no idea."

"Then what's it hurt to keep up the study until you do know?"

I sighed. Why was she always right?

"So, now tell me about the boy."

"Do you never give up? It's not a boy like a B-O-Y. He's just a friend ..."

"I see." She took a sip of her wine, which reminded me I had one in my hand too. I swished the amber liquid around the glass. How could I drink when he thought I had a drinking problem? Taking a sip would prove him right: here I was about to have another drink.

He'd royally played with my head. *Screw you, Jordan.*

I brought the glass to my lips and downed the entire contents, then swiped the back of my hand across my lips. He had no freaking idea what it was like to walk in someone else's footprints. And having a quiet drink with my mum didn't mean I had a problem. It meant I wanted to kick back and relax with her. Share a nice evening, have a few drinks. It wasn't like I was mixing vodka with my morning coffee. I held the glass out and Mum refilled it, then turned back to me with a cocked eyebrow.

"A friend, hey?"

"Not anymore. He lost that privilege when he started trying to control my life."

"Oh."

"Yeah ... apparently I party too hard."

Mum looked at me for entirely too long.

"I'm young, right? And college is about partying. Just because he's a teetotalling nancy boy who thinks everyone who isn't needs saving ..."

"How'd you two get to be friends?"

I paused, thinking back to the first time we'd met. "You know, I should have steered clear of him right from the start. His first sentence to me sure was a tell-tale sign of *exactly* the type of person he is." A quick sip of my wine revealed the sweet taste of Moscato on my lips. I sighed again. God, it was good to be home.

"What'd he say?"

"He told me to slow down."

Mum spat out her drink, almost choking on her laughter.

"Oh, honey. I'm sorry ... Tomorrow, you call Sally and go out. Spend the night meeting other boys."

"Yeah." I wasn't entirely sure I felt like meeting any boys ever again. I had a no-dating policy for good reason. "What's been happening here?"

"Oh, you know, same as always."

This time I cocked a brow while Mum concentrated on smoothing out her work skirt. She could pretend all she wanted. I knew she was still broken. My father had smashed her heart the day he walked out to start a new life without us. I held up my glass. "Cheers."

She raised hers as well. "To having my baby girl home."

"Indeed." I clinked my glass against hers.

The next few hours passed in a blur of conversation, takeout pizza—which absolutely did not make me think of Jordan or that Penny chick—and plenty of hugs. Sometime around midnight, lying on Mum's bed, talk turned to my father, as it tended to do.

"I often wonder where I went wrong. We had one of those epic loves that should have lasted a lifetime, but something must have happened to dull it. Maybe I wasn't—"

"Shut up, Mum. Men are bastards. We don't need that poison in our lives, right?"

"Love isn't poison, Alexi. People are poison, and sometimes they poison what is good."

"Jordan's good." I sighed, and threw my arm over Mum's side, then snuggled up against her.

She combed her fingers through my hair. "If that's the case then, you've got to hold onto the good, honey." That was funny; a few hours ago she'd thought he was ridiculous. I laughed as I gave her a squeeze. "I mean it," she said.

"Whatever." I pulled her against me and picked at the cuticle on my thumbnail. We fell into silence. Jordan was good. It was me who wasn't ... he didn't need my curse poisoning his life, as it had my parents'. God knew he'd had enough already.

I fell asleep curled against my mother's back.

ACROSS THE dance floor, Mum rocked six-inch heels and a little black dress that had been wedged so far into the back of her closet I was certain it hadn't seen daylight in ten years. Still, she looked good, if too thin. Probably because she didn't eat, just like I didn't call. Fake-calling old school friends had backfired when I'd announced no one was free. Then Mum had insisted on coming with me to the bar. So there we were, dancing to the sounds of a DJ who'd stepped right out of the seventies.

I motioned that I wanted a drink, because hell was I parched. Dancing sure was thirsty work. We left the dance floor, and plopping onto a bar stool, I pushed sweaty hair off my forehead. It was funny how time away from a place could change your perspective. I hadn't gone out here much before I'd left for college, but when I had I'd always thought it was the most rocking place in town. Yet now, it felt kind of lame, and on a Saturday night to boot. It wasn't crowded, but it wasn't dead either. There was no one I knew in sight. Nothing like hanging out at the bars around Armidale; those were always packed to the rafters, and so loud you had to shout to be heard over all the other voices.

"What about that one?" Mum tipped her head toward a guy. "He's pretty spunky."

"Spunky? Are you even speaking English?"

She slid a vodka and OJ onto the round table in front of me. Picking it up, I snuck a look at the guy in question. Sun-bleached hair sat in a perfect dishevelled mess, the tips made even blonder by his awesome tan, which also made his teeth look super white and his eyes—

Crap. He flirty-smiled at me. I looked away quicker than a stray cat in a dog-fight.

"I already told you I'm not hitting on a random guy." Even if he was pretty cute.

"Why not? Isn't this what you girls do?" she said.

I groaned. "You're trying too hard, Mum."

Regardless of this bordering-on-embarrassing conversation, it was good to see her out enjoying herself, or rather, trying to force me to have fun. Shame it was Saturday already; I only got here two days ago, and I really wasn't ready to leave her yet. If I stayed here with her things might be different. Better than what they were before. She seemed to be in control, but she still needed me. Just in a different way now, but I couldn't stay. Dad would cut me off, and we needed that money.

I downed the rest of my vodka and dropped the glass on the table. Mum did the same.

"Now let's have a good time." She pulled me back out to the dance floor as if she wasn't nearing forty-five and hadn't spent the past five years, since my father left, barely leaving the house.

As we danced the room grew fuzzy, my legs tired, and I

couldn't help but think of my studies. Exams were less than a week away and I felt pretty confident about English Lit, but Science was a worry. I'd left in such a state I didn't bring any work home expect *Jane Eyre*. Everything else sat in neat piles on my desk at Oxley. Where Jordan lived. I heaved out a sigh. Jordan was only one person. One insignificant little person and I was a big girl. I could cope with his judgemental arse. Didn't mean we had to slide back into being best friends ... his opinion of me didn't matter.

Really, it didn't.

It didn't make my throat feel too tight or my temples pound. It didn't make my heart ache so much I wanted to kick the wall.

One. Measly. Person. That's all he was.

Mum and I danced and drank and drank and danced. Mum's 'spunky' guy somehow ended up on the dance floor with us. His hands found my hips and I backed up, dancing against his firm chest. It wasn't as nice as Jordan's. Even through two layers of clothing and with the insensitive skin of my back, I could tell he held nothing to Jordan's impressive muscles.

Drinks. Dancing. Laughter. More drinks. Then somehow through the haze the night became, I blinked and we were walking home.

"What happened to Spunky?" I asked Mum.

She shook her head. "You've got it bad for that Jordan, sweet girl."

Mum grinned at me and it was so good to see her happy, I smiled back and shouted, "I love you!"

And like that I felt like me again. No one judging. No

one expecting anything from me. Just me. Mum, and I laughed, watching her stroll along the bitumen like it was a footpath. "Get off the road."

Her heels hung from two fingers and she grinned at me. "It feels nice on my feet. They're aching from all that dancing."

"That wasn't dancing." I laughed. "That was you swaying like a tree in the wind." I swished my arms from side to side to show what I meant. "I was dancing."

She threw her head, laughing, and spun around.

This—hanging with Mum—was fun, but not the same type of fun I'd grown used to. This used to be enough, but now a hole swelled inside me, as if something were missing. And that niggled in the back of my chest, as if my heart didn't fill the space anymore.

The vibration of an incoming text tingled against my boob. I wasn't sure I wanted to look at the screen in case it was Jordan, or in case it wasn't.

The nausea of not knowing clenched my stomach.

I had to know.

I fished the phone out of my bra.

Tyres screeched on the bitumen.

Twin beams of light blinded me.

"Mum!" I dove for her.

Chapter 23
Jordan

I ROLLED MY foot across the ball then back. Across and back. The clavicle was connected to the manubriums, which was part of the sternum.

Footsteps in the hall.

First rib through twelfth rib were all connected via the—

Knocking on a door down the hall.

... spinal vertebrae. Which was made up of—

Could've been Hex's door, I wasn't certain. Not like I was listening for movement from her room.

A series of disks labelled L—

Knocking on my door.

I dropped my pen and swivelled the chair around. God knows why, but my heart jumped into my throat at the sight of McKenzie standing in my doorway. Although I'd seen her visit Hex a few times, she never came to my room. She was frowning, her cheeks slightly flushed. I'd never seen her look so ... unhappy.

"Do you know where Hex is?"

Like I'd know. The girl had avoided me for three weeks. I hadn't even seen a glimpse of blue hair making a quick exit in the past few days. "Nope."

McKenzie's frown deepened. "She's not answering her door."

"So? She's probably studying up at the library with Luca."

"Why the hell would she do that?"

Was this chick for real? "Because it's almost exam time."

"We're talking about Hex here."

I sighed. "Have you asked Amber? I have no idea where she is."

I kind of wished I did. Avoiding me was understandable after our fight, but ditching one of her joined-at-the-hip party buddies ... I pushed myself off my chair and strode down the corridor. I made a fist and dropped it onto the timber in a series of raps. "Hex, open up. McKenzie's looking for you."

I watched the handle, but nothing happened. Not even a sound from inside. "You studied yourself into a coma?"

"Come on, honey," McKenzie said. "We're worried about you."

I knocked again. "Correction. McKenzie's worried about you."

"Jerk," she whispered. "Jordan's more worried. Open up."

At least a full minute passed.

McKenzie shifted, like she was uncomfortable. "I couldn't get a hold of her last night either."

There was still no answer and my heart picked up a crazy beat. Like an offbeat echo against my chest. Something was wrong. I could feel it, like I'd felt weird right before walking into the bathroom the night I found Kayla.

"Go ask Amber," I said. "She'll know where Hex is."

Mckenzie turned for the stairs while I strode back to my room and snatched my phone off the desk. I typed out a text and press send.

Where are you?

Shit, we hadn't checked the bathroom. I pushed open the door, but the only thing inside was a dirty towel piled on the tile floor. I had no idea where she could be. Hex was usually in her room, in the courtyard, or up top. Almost always with Amber or McKenzie. The fact that her friend had no idea where she went was more than a little concerning. Surely, McKenzie had checked all the usual places.

I went back to my desk, but returning to study was even more useless than it had been before. My gaze slid to the window, watching the odd person walk in and out of Oxley. Amber's RAV4 sat in its usual park, so wherever Hex was it wasn't out with her.

My mind spiralled into all the scenarios of where she could be.

I flicked out my phone again and woke it up. The last message was sent, but I had no idea if she'd seen it or not. Honestly, I wasn't certain she'd respond to me anyway.

That weird feeling still lingered in my gut. I didn't care if she didn't want to hear from me. I typed out a second message.

Hello ...

It wasn't like Hex was one to tell the world her every move, but I checked her social media anyway, just in case. No new activity since the night we'd trashed Amber's room, almost a month ago. I drummed my fingers on my desk, glancing at the skeletal system in my open textbook. After a good three minutes of alternating between staring at the image and my phone, I gave up and typed out yet another message then hit send.

Wondering if you're still alive.

Frig. I of all people knew exactly how not funny that was. I tried again straight away.

You don't want to talk to me. Fine. I get that. But no one's seen you in days, so please, give me an 'I'm okay'.

I hovered over the words, reading them back. Deleting and rewriting. But screw it ... I needed to know she was okay. Placing the phone on my desk, I forced my attention back to the books.

The femur was the bone that ran through the top of the leg. Tibia and fibula made up the bottom half, but both were connected to ...

She could have hit the town and gone home with some

other guy, but surely if she went out, Amber would have been with her. And hitting the hay with a random man for three days? I hoovered cool air into my burning lungs. Total stranger, three days—nope. She wouldn't do it. No matter how peeved she was at me she wasn't like that. She could have walked home from the library in the dark and—

Damn, my focus was shot. I picked up the football and grabbed my phone off the desk. If I couldn't study I'd at least burn some of the thoughts away in a run. It was still early and the air felt cooler than it had been a few weeks ago. Perfect weather to let off some steam.

I jogged down the stairs and through Back Courtyard, then made my way to the oval behind the dorms. There wasn't a soul in sight, thankfully. The second my foot hit the open space I dropped the ball and kicked it with as much force as I could. It didn't make me feel any better. Nor did sprinting after it so fast my lungs burned, or kicking it again so hard my foot cracked. I played hard anyway, running the length of the field over and over until my legs felt like jelly. I could have gone on like that until I dropped.

My phone buzzed in my pocket, pulling me to an instant stop. I fished it out faster than a winger in the second half of a tied match. Her name illuminated the screen. Thank bloody god. I clicked into the message.

Jordan, is it? She's not answering because she was involved in an accident.

If it were possible for a heart to explode, mine did just

229

that. It stopped beating entirely, and everything around me faded into white noise. I couldn't even hear my own breath. That was the calm before the epic storm, because all of a sudden everything came back; my heart exploded in a beat ten times too fast, my pulse rushed through my ears, and my throat split in half.

An accident.

Reality

Chapter 24
Jordan

DESPITE WANTING to rush to Hex's side, with an early morning Monday exam Amber couldn't. She'd offered her car, but Logan insisted on coming with me. I had exams this week too, but I couldn't care less if I missed them. Hex was hurt, and being with her was more important than anything else, even my studies. We'd been driving for almost an hour and if I'd thought I couldn't concentrate before, now I could barely make sense of whatever it was Logan talked about. My chest was still too tight, my stomach too empty, my head too full. Why the hell did she go home right before exams without telling anyone? Hopefully, everything was all right with her mother, because after those middle-of-the-night texts who knew what Hex had run home to face.

And now she'd been hurt.

Apparently she was in surgery after being hit by a freaking car. How the hell that happened needed to be investigated. The driver bloody well better have been sober. I knew nothing about the surgery as I'd only received a handful of texts before the responses stopped.

I couldn't lose her, too.

I was pretty sure I cared about her more than I'd ever cared about anyone else. Hex was special.

The ringtone blared from my phone and both Logan and I jumped. I picked up, wondering what the hell Carlos wanted. He'd made it damn clear I was fired.

"Hello."

"Jordan."

"Carlos."

Logan glanced across at me and raised a questioning brow.

"Look, I might have overreacted to the thing between you and Penny. I need you tonight. I'll send a driver your way in thirty."

"Overreacted?"

Shop sounds echoed in the background: voices, phones, clanging pans. "She tells me it was a misunderstanding, so about tonight ..."

Anger curled in my gut. So he'd assumed whatever damn rumour going around was true. I clenched my free hand into a tight ball while Logan drove one-handed, as if he didn't have a care in the world. "I'm out of town tonight, sorry."

"You're what? We're going to be slammed. I need you here to supervise the team."

"I can't, Carlos."

He sighed. "How far out of town?"

"Too far."

Logan's attention rested on the road ahead, and even though he pretended not to listen I could tell he soaked in every word.

"Well, you're on the roster. Please, come in on Thursday."

"I'll see what I can do." I should've jumped at the offer, but I was still pissed and he owed me a goddamn sorry. I knew I wouldn't get it though; it was Carlos, after all.

"You're a good worker, Jordan. I need you around."

"And ..." *I'm sorry, Jordan.*

"And?"

Figured. "All right. I'll be there."

"That a boy."

I hit *end call.*

Logan tapped his fingers on the wheel. "He found out about Penny, didn't he?"

I grunted.

"I told you last year: screwing around with her was a dumbass idea."

"I don't need your lectures, Logan." I resumed staring out the window, my teeth worrying the inside of my cheek. I didn't know much about Hex's state, but surgery was serious. A damn car against her fragile body was bad news. Everything inside me constricted at the visual of her laid out on a hospital gurney. A gurney like the one they'd wheeled Kayla away on. It was too much to imagine. She had to be all right. There was no way I could lose her.

"She drinks," I said, looking out the window. "Like Kayla used to. It scares the shit out of me, Loges."

He didn't shift his focus off the road, but ran a hand

235

through his too-long hair. "Why does it scare you?"

"Because there has to be something she's hiding from, and what if I can't figure it out? What if I can't help her?"

"Most people drink because they like drinking, not to escape from some horrid past. Not everyone's like Kayla."

"I think she might be."

He tapped his thumbs on the wheel. "Is this why you think she's like Kayla?"

I glanced out the window. Was being attracted to a girl who reminded you of your sister weird? "It's not her look, or the fact that she needs saving, but the way she seizes the day, lives life to the fullest. She does all that without drinking, Loges, it's who she is. Hex brings joy to every situation and I love that about her."

He studied the road for a long while. "Are you two together?"

I laughed, bitterly. "It's complicated."

"Because you think she's going down the same path?"

"Maybe. I dunno, bro, it just is. I guess we're too different."

This time Logan actually looked at me, but I pulled my attention away, focusing on the trees zooming past. He sighed. "You can't fix her, mate. It's clear as mud that you love her, but you won't let yourself. Figure your shit out. Let Kayla go. I couldn't be happy with Liv until I did, and you're the same."

Did I love her? I'd never allowed myself to be in love before, but this consuming feeling inside of me ... the need to see her, to be with her right now, the desire to wrap my arms around her and make sure she was protected, maybe that *was* love. I stared out the window for the next hour, wondering if it really was about me. If I'd been projecting my fears onto her.

Logan had a way of getting in my head and shifting the way I thought.

IT WASN'T hard to the find the hospital once we reached the centre of town; conspicuous blue signs pointed the way. Logan swung the Corolla into the car park and I practically jumped out before the hand brake clicked on. The hospital's front entrance spanned almost as wide as footy goals. A massive neon light lit up the emergency department, but she should be out of there by now. I needed the front desk. I raced that way, my sights set on the check-in station dominating the length of an entire wall. Running up to it, I slammed my hands down on the counter and looked at the nurse typing.

"Alexi Penton. She was brought in overnight and had surgery this morning."

The nurse focused on the screen in front of her, running her finger along it as if searching for Hex's name. "Hmm," she said, as if she had all the goddamn time in the world. "She should be in recovery soon."

"Recovery? The surgery was successful? She's okay?"

The nurse's lips pressed together. "And you are?"

I floundered for a second, knowing full well that this woman wouldn't give non-family any details. "Where's recovery?"

"You can't go in there, sir," she said, as if talking to an

237

imbecile.

"Where's the fucking recovery waiting room then?"

Her lips puckered into a tight knot. "If you can't be respectful I will call security."

A hand landed on my shoulder. "I'm sorry ... Alice ... if you can direct us to the appropriate waiting area, we'd appreciate it."

Her stare moved from me to my brother. Her lips remained tight as raisins. "Level one. Follow the corridor around to the right when you come off the elevator, and you'll see it down a little ways on the left."

Logan squeezed my shoulder too hard as he steered me away from the desk. I didn't care. My heart thudded as we rode the elevator, hammered as we walked the corridor, thrashed as we entered a waiting room crowded with people. Surely they weren't all here for Hex.

There was no nurse's station nearby, nor even any signs indicating where the staff responsible for this area could be found. I spun Kayla's signet ring around my finger. With no idea what Hex's family even looked like, I weighed up each person in the room. A middle-aged woman looked the right age to be Hex's mum, but there wasn't really any resemblance. She sat with a harrowed-looking man, which struck her out as a relative since I was pretty sure Hex's parents were divorced. Another woman sat in the far corner, her frizzy hair bright orange against the cream wall. The hair made me pretty sure she wasn't here for Hex either. Same deal with the woman in a sari.

With nothing left to do, I had no choice but to sit. Only sitting made me feel anxious, so I stood. Running my fingers over the painted brickwork, I traced the lines and divots while I tried my best to ignore the smell of anti-septic. Hospitals had a smell that was theirs alone and I hated it. It smelled like death.

Chapter 25
Hex

INHALE.
Beat.
Exhale.

Beat.

Inhale.

"Alexi ..."

Exhale.

Inhale.

"Alexi, honey, you need to wake up."

I was asleep? *I am asleep?*

"Come on now. Open your eyes."

My eyes were closed? It was dark. My eyes *were* closed.

But how could I open them? The lids felt glued together or heavy as lead, I couldn't decide. Either way, opening them proved impossible.

Sounds faded in. They weren't there before? I wasn't sure. But now there was definitely a low-pitched *bleep,*

bleep, bleep. Rustling of fabric; sounded stiff. And footsteps, shuffling. People talked and not quietly—something about upping fluids, checking med dosage, waking someone up. Me?

My heavy eyelids wouldn't lift. It was easier to surrender to whatever was pulling me away.

Blackness.

My chest rose and fell.

Someone shook my shoulder.

"Alexi. Time to wake up." The voice was harder, more forceful.

I'd never had to fight so hard to open my eyes. And my mouth ... so dry, like it was stuffed with cotton wool.

"Drink?" It came out more like a moan.

Finally no longer heavy, my eyelids rose and fuzzy shapes moved around me.

Too much effort.

They fell closed again.

Chapter 26
Jordan

SITTING IN the recovery waiting room that Sunday afternoon, my phone didn't stop. The texts kept rolling in, most of them from Amber.

How is she? Have you seen her?

Still in recovery, so no.

She had surgery? For what?

I don't know. No one will tell me shit
'cause I'm not family.

SO MAKE THEM.

Groaning, I shoved my phone in my pocket and tipped my head back against the wall. Surgery was a good thing, right? It meant there was something to fix. Better than not being able to fix whatever it was, but hell ... sometimes surgery was worse.

Sometime later, my phone vibrated against my leg, so I fished it out. McKenzie.

Heard Hex was in an accident. Hope she's okay. Keep us updated.

Sure.

Another incoming. Amber again.

She out yet?

It's been an half an hour. I'll let you know when she's out.

Resting my phone on my knee, I stared at the huge double doors that led into recovery. She'd been in there an awful long time. We hadn't learned about anaesthetic in class yet, but I was sure it wore off pretty quickly after the gas was turned off.

My phone pinged. Sighing, I peeked at the screen. Nate.

Shit man, I just heard. Let me know if there's anything I can do.

Thanks. Just sitting tight.

Logan sat beside me, playing on his phone. Mine however, was almost dead, due to hours of texting and playing mindless games. He flinched mid lobbing a bird at a pig and his shot missed by a mile. I chuckled, until I saw the name of the incoming caller flash on his screen as it vibrated in his hand.

Mum.

Logan cast me a worried look as picked up. "Hello."

He dropped his foot off his knee onto the floor with a thunk, and planted his elbows on his knees. "He was? What for?"

My heart thudded despite my rising anger. Even though she was a shitty parent, I didn't want to see anything bad happen to her and the look on my brother's face said something wasn't right.

"That's terrible and I'm sorry it happened. Where'd they take him?"

"Okay. Thanks for letting us know. And Mum ..." Logan sunk back in his chair. "Take care of yourself."

The doors flew open and a hospital bed emerged, a warden pushing it from behind. I stood to get a better look and it was Hex. Her eyes were closed, her hair under a cap. A blanket covered the rest of her body. Without stopping, the warden wheeled her down the hall. I jumped up and followed him all the way to the ward.

FEET SHUFFLED; someone cleared his or her throat. Logan sighed. The four of us had been in this private room for what felt like forever and she still lay motionless on the bed. Weren't they supposed to keep patients in recovery until they recovered? It seemed like the logical thing to do.

"Sit down. She's going to be okay."

244

I wouldn't turn to look at the coolest voice in the room. "She's not awake yet. She should be awake."

A heavy sigh came from somewhere behind me, but I couldn't take my eyes off her. A sheet covered the bottom half of her body, so I couldn't see the damage beneath or the work the surgeons had performed. She wore one of those awful white hospital gowns, and her hands rested by her sides. I wanted to pick one up and cradle it in mine, but both were covered in scrapes, dried blood caked on the open skin. A cannula protruded from her hand, attaching her to an IV of fluids and another that would have been morphine, which was where the constant beeping came from. The whole sight was damn wrong. She shouldn't be here like this. It made my gut clench.

Her eyelids fluttered, but didn't open.

Looking at her face, you wouldn't know she'd been in an accident. It was practically unblemished. Her porcelain skin was deathly pale against her long lashes. Her plump lips almost blended with her skin.

"Who's this girl's next of kin?"

We all looked at the man who presumably was her doctor. I stepped forward, but Logan pulled me back with a look, as if he knew that I was considering lying. "Let her family deal with it."

"I am," said that cool voice and the three of them stepped outside the room, leaving Logan and I alone with an unconscious Hex.

Chapter 27
Hex

HE BATTLE with my eyes began anew. This time though, I could hear voices clearly. Whispers, as if they didn't want to disturb the silence. And it wasn't women, like before; it was men.

"Sit down. She's going to be okay."

"She's not awake yet. She should be awake."

I knew the second one ... kind of strained, but familiar. It was impossible to hold onto though. My thoughts floated in and out of existence. I'd never been so tired.

And sleepy ...

"Who's this girl's next of kin?" The new voice jarred me back into the haze of half wakefulness and my leg was on fire, a searing pain from top to bottom.

"I am."

It hurt so much.

"She groaned. She needs more meds." The familiar voice again.

Something was wrong with my leg. And my head ... it felt heavy. But that leg was definitely on fire. I screamed, and even though the sound was more in my head than audible, he must have heard it for he growled, "Get a goddamn nurse in here!"

Jordan? It was Jordan.

I forced my eyes open and he stood right by me, his beautiful face etched with concern. Everything around us glowed white. So strikingly white.

"Leg." I couldn't croak out more than that. "Thirsty."

Jordan stroked my cheek, caressed my forehead. I couldn't see much beyond his pale face and dark hair. "She's awake," he said over his shoulder then turned back to me. "You're awake." Pinched eyebrows, lips slightly parted, his gaze held concern. "You're okay. They'll come to up your morphine, surely. That should help with the pain."

What in heaven's name was he talking about? As if to punctuate his declaration, pain shot through my entire leg, maybe even both of them. It was so severe I couldn't tell.

"Hurts," I said.

"I know, babe. I know ... I'm going to get that under control for you."

The pain was pure agony, as if my skin had been slowly ripped from the flesh. Jordan continued murmuring as his hand brushed my forehead.

Vague images flashed through my mind: fighting with him, riding the train home from Oxley, dancing the night away with Mum, but through all of it, pain, so much pain.

"Mum?"

"Welcome back," said a strange voice. A man dressed in a suit overlayed with a white jacket came into focus. Blinking, I realised it was more than only Jordan and me in the room. A hospital room. Jordan moved to make room for the man I could only assume was a doctor. The man pulled back one eyelid and near blinded me with a pen torch. "What is your name?"

"H—" Better keep it real. "Alexi."

"How are you feeling, Alexi?"

"Sore." Why was my throat so damn dry?

"As I'd expect from a girl who threw herself under a moving car."

I had no idea what he was talking about, but that had to be the cause of this pain. A rotund woman bustled into the room, right up to my side, and lifted my hand. A dull sting shot through the centre and what the hell? A bunch of tubes snaked out of my arm.

"She's in pain. She needs more relief." Jordan moved around near her and started talking, but my focus was on the doctor who told the nurse, "Hold off on upping the dosage for a moment." He moved his attention to me while the nurse strapped a heart-rate monitor around my arm and began pumping. "Do you remember the accident?"

I shook my head imperceptibly. It was as much as I could manage.

"You were hit by a car some hours ago and we had to perform a little surgery." He paused as if waiting for me to catch up. It sure felt as if I'd been hit by a car, or maybe a steamroller. The doctor continued, "Everything checks out internally, but there was severe damage to your right leg.

A compound femoral shaft fracture caused extensive damage to the muscles, ligaments and the tendons in that area. As a result we have pinned the bone in place with a titanium nail, secured on either end with a matching screw. This is a temporary fix to hold the bone in place while it heals. We also repaired the bicep and surrounding tissue. Thankfully, no major blood vessels were damaged."

He paused, studying my reaction, and it was all too much. I hardly understood half of what he'd said. My head was fuzzy as all get-up, but boy, this sure explained the pain. Surgery would do that. The nurse shoved something in my ear and held it in place until it beeped.

I suddenly felt more exhausted than I had before.

"I expect you will make a full recovery, however, we can't be certain until your body begins to mend." The doctor nodded. "You get some rest now. I'll be by to see you again tomorrow."

Thoughts tumbled through my mind as I tried to figure out just when and how this had happened. Jordan was here, but I had come home on the train. And there was a blond guy standing in the corner. Not bad looking, either—god knew who he was though. He didn't look like hospital staff in his casual low-hung jeans, too-tight white tee, and weird plaid cap. I didn't have the energy to figure him out though ... it took everything I had to focus on him. And that focus was already shifting around the room to Aunt Susan perched in a seat on the opposite side to McHottie. Standing beside her was the man I had never wanted to see again.

I let out another groan, this one not because of the pain.

249

"Can't we up that morphine already?" Jordan demanded.

"I'm doing that right now, lovie," the nurse responded from beside me.

I directed a glare toward the statuesque man surveying this situation like it was a boardroom full of his employees, and suddenly I couldn't keep my eyes open any longer. "You cheating bastard. Get—"

Sleep.

Chapter 28
Jordan

THIS MORPHINE shit was the bomb. Hex had drifted off the second the nurse upped her dosage, which was good even if she fell asleep mid-sentence. If the doctor was right then sleeping it off would help her recover and that made me feel more at ease.

"She's asleep, bro. Why don't we go find something to eat?" Logan said.

"I'm not hungry."

Greg shifted, as if to remind me who got me inside this room when the nurse had insisted family only. I think the man could tell I cared about his daughter. He looked me in the eye and said, "It's not like she'll be alone."

Like hell he was staying when I wasn't. "She flipped when she saw you. She obviously didn't want to see you, so I'm not going to leave and have her wake up with only you and Susan here."

I owed the man a favour or two—he did let me know she was hurt—but I wasn't about to leave Hex with him after her reaction. My gratitude didn't extend that far. He sighed and leaned against the wall, shifting his focus to Logan. "Right then, how about you and I go grab a bite to bring back?"

At least the man had a solid head on his shoulders. It made me wonder if calling her a curse was the only thing he'd done to make Hex hate him so strongly. Today hadn't been the first time she'd mentioned her feelings toward him.

Wearing a business suit and bossing the staff around, he looked every bit the caring father. People weren't always what they seemed though. I sure knew that from my own parents.

Logan passed me a long look then he left the room with Hex's father, clearly thinking I'd made the wrong choice. Screw what-my-brother-thought-was-best; he didn't even know her. Just because he was a psychologist didn't mean he could read every damn person and situation. I wasn't budging from this spot, no matter what he thought I should do.

I dragged a chair to the side of her bed and practically fell into it. It'd been one hell of a day. She'd only been awake for a few minutes, but they had felt like hours. Seeing her hurting like that was worse than if I'd actually felt it in my own body. At least she was out of pain for now and it sounded as if the fracture was a clean one. She'd be okay. She had to be.

I reached out tentatively. I didn't want to hurt her, but I couldn't be so close and not touch her, especially after the past six hours, since I got Greg's text. There was a crazy tug inside me that had been pulling since the moment I'd heard she was hurt, and it didn't let up until my fingertips brushed the softness of Hex's inner arm. Other than her face, it was the only place I felt sure wouldn't hurt.

"The doctor said there are several complications that can arise from this condition, the most common and worst being infection."

I'd been so lost in Hex that I forgot her aunt was still in the room.

"The broken bone being exposed is a high risk, but apparently the muscle can get infected too," she continued.

I sighed. "I'd love to get a hold of the bastard who did this."

Susan sighed this time. "I'd hazard a guess that it wasn't entirely the driver's fault. If Bronwyn was as intoxicated as I heard, then ..."

"Bronwyn?"

"Alexi's mother. I've been worried about something like this happening to her. It was only a matter of time really, and I tried to be there for my sister-in-law, but it's impossible to help those who won't help themselves."

"God, ain't that the truth."

I didn't take my focus off the girl lying broken in the bed, but the vinyl chair squeaked with Susan repositioning herself. She'd been in that chair a long time, watching her niece since she'd been back on the ward. "She's a good girl, our Alexi. I hope this changes things. Makes her realise life is precious."

"Me too." I couldn't stand the thought of losing her, and

I'd come too damn close.

It seemed like Susan's floodgates had broken with Greg's exit, because she kept talking. "Bronwyn hasn't exactly been the best role model these last few years. And what Alexi needs to realise is that her mother is not her responsibility, nor can she change the woman's damaging behaviour." She sighed, as if she thought the weight of the world was on Hex's shoulders, which it kind of sounded like it was. "It is good though, to see her making friends and building a life again. It's been far too long."

"She's an amazing person. She's got loads of friends."

"That's wonderful to hear."

We fell into silence then. I was right about Hex; everyone back at college loved her. Amber had texted me every half hour since I'd arrived, to check up. Nate had sent a couple of messages as well, and McKenzie. But it wasn't only her close friends who adored her. Whenever Hex walked through the courtyard, people stopped to say g'day. She had one of those magnetic personalities that drew everyone in. I had no idea what had happened before I met her, but she sure wasn't short of friends now. I guess this was what I'd suspected though—that everything wasn't as it seemed. That she was hiding something that hurt. It churned my gut that I was right, because I'd really wanted to be wrong.

Whatever was up with her mum sounded like Hex thought it was her fault, and she was trying to change that problem. Susan was right, though—you couldn't change someone who didn't want to change his or herself. And Hex was already trying to save someone else.

I had it all wrong. Worried about her well being, I'd

told her to stop partying, but it wasn't my place to do that. Logan was right; that had been all about Kayla. I was so shit-scared of a repeat of what happened with our sister that I kept forgetting Hex wasn't Kayla. She wasn't an alcoholic and she wasn't suicidal, but I was so damn scared of losing her.

Chapter 29
Hex

HERE WAS no noise other than the constant beep, an instant reminder of where I was and what had happened. I opened my eyes easily, waking like I normally would. Not in the drug-addled way I had the last few times. It was day again—the bright light peeking under the closed blinds. A form came into focus: Jordan, sitting right by me with his head resting on my bed.

I swallowed against a throat that was no longer dry, but blessedly moist, albeit sore. My leg still hurt, but not with the searing agony of before. It was far more muted now, almost like a memory of the prior pain. The doctor had said there was an accident and I remembered I hadn't been at Oxley, I'd been home. When I'd asked Jordan about my mother he hadn't answered.

He was asleep, but I needed to know she was all right.

"Jordan." His name came out a loud whisper; apparently that was all my poor throat could manage. "Jordan."

"Alexi ..." That wasn't the name or the voice I wanted to hear.

"What are you doing here?" I demanded of the man I refused to acknowledge as a father. Fathers didn't abandon their daughters, after all.

"I'm here because I care."

"Like hell you do. If you cared you wouldn't have walked out on me when I was fourteen. You wouldn't have taken my only brother away like he was a possession. And you sure as hell wouldn't have tossed Mum and I aside as if we were replaceable, which is apparently what you thought all along."

Jordan's sleepy, azure eyes rested on mine. "You're awake."

I gave him a tight smile, grateful he was here, but pissed as all hell at the man standing tall and proud in the corner, as if he had a right to be in this room. He had no right to be anywhere near me. I was the daughter he didn't want.

"Where's my mother?" I directed the question at Jordan.

He held my gaze. "She was hurt in the accident."

Greg cleared his throat. "Apparently the driver swerved to miss her. That didn't stop her from falling under the wheels though."

I think I stopped breathing, or maybe I was breathing too much at all once, taking in all the air in the room, and my lungs hurt from trying to hold it. "She's okay though?"

He studied the ground. "She's still in the ICU."

"What the hell does that mean?"

257

"Babe." Jordan squeezed my inner elbow. "It means she's not out of the water yet. She's in intensive care, and she's getting the best help available."

The asshole opened his mouth again. "She had a lot of alcohol in her system, and that may have been her saving grace. She's got some internal damage, Alexi, and the doctors aren't sure—"

"No." I sobbed. "No, no, no."

Everything hurt again, only this was different. Like an ache that ran through my very soul. My mother had to be okay. We'd been through so much together; she couldn't give up now. I needed her just like she needed me. We were a team.

"She's a strong woman—"

"No thanks to you." I swung my glare to the man who was responsible for her constant heartache. "Why are you even here? Are you getting some kind of sick enjoyment seeing the woman you two-timed for almost a decade fighting to survive? Or is it that you feel a twisted kind of obligation to be here for me? Because if that's the case, you may as well leave right now. I don't want you here. I never wanted to see you again, and that hasn't changed. You're off the hook."

The look he gave me was one of disappointment, something else he had no right to feel. After trying to burn that look into my soul, my father turned and left the room to go I didn't care where. Good riddance to him. I was used to seeing his back. Hopefully this would be the last time.

Jordan stroked my inner arm. "How are you feeling? Any pain?"

I took inventory of all the places that hurt before and they mostly seemed okay now. Not pain-free, but bearable. It wasn't me I was worried about though. "Do you think she'll be okay? Can I go see her?"

"Hex, you can't get out of this bed. There's no way you can go to her. But I'm sure she'll be fine. Your Aunt Susan says that the internal damage is mostly a single bleed, which they have under wraps. It's a good sign."

"Susan's here?"

"Yep, and Greg, but I guess you got that."

It was hard to summon anything more than a groan. I didn't understand that man's presence here at all.

"So, your dad ..."

"Greg," I snapped. "I hate him."

"I got that." Jordan settled back.

"He should never have been a father. He doesn't know the difference between employees and children. You know, he never wanted kids and he wound up with two of us. But Riley's different ... it's just me he never wanted. Being the first meant I ruined his precious life ... then when Mum wanted Riley I guess he didn't care anymore."

Jordan squeezed my hand.

"You're so lucky to have decent parents."

He gave a cynical laugh. "I've lived with my brother since I was fourteen because my father verbally and emotionally abused us until my sister killed herself."

My throat ached. I'd known about Kayla, but that was deplorable. "What about your mum?"

"She checked out. Most of the time, ignoring or not caring what went on in her house. That's when she was home."

259

I closed my eyes, drifting into the haze that came with almost-sleep.

Jordan's thumb making circles on my palm pulled me back into wakefulness. He'd said before that he hated footy and just now that he hated his father, blamed them both for Kayla. It didn't make a lot of sense. "How's footy fit into all that?"

Jordan sighed. "I played before Kayla died and was state champ for Under Fourteens. It was my father's dream. He played when he was younger, but injured his knee in a bad tackle and couldn't play again. I guess he wanted to relive his lost dreams through me ... since Logan was shit at sports, and I could actually play." He looked away, toward the closed blinds. "I failed her by being so wrapped up in it all that I didn't realise she needed me."

He thought her death was his fault? Just like he thought I had a problem he could fix. He was using me to make up for past errors.

I sucked back a long breath. God, my head felt fuzzy. Almost as if I were floating. Suddenly any train of thought was near impossible to hold onto. Internal bleeding was okay? Greg was here, but he didn't care about me. And Jordan ... I narrowed my eyes on him. "I thought you didn't want anything to do with me."

"I never said that."

"Why are you here, anyway?"

"I think I'm Greg's peace offering to you."

"That doesn't make any sense." Nothing made sense, the pain and drugs had scrambled my thoughts.

He shrugged. "I'm here because I care, Hex."

He might have thought he cared. Maybe it was the painkillers, or maybe it was the truth, but Jordan's words were merely an echo of Greg's reasoning, and that man didn't care at all. No one cared about me; no one ever had. From the moment I'd first realised my father never wanted children to when I discovered Mum and I wouldn't eat if I didn't cook. Her pushing me out of her life, toward college—even the past few months at Oxley with everyone just wanting me for fun, nothing more, were tell-tale signs of people not caring. Whatever favour Jordan thought he was doing me by running to my sick bed would only make it harder when he recalled that I wasn't good enough. He might care now, but it would eventually come back to that. I may as well save us both the trouble and sever a clean break now. It might not hurt so much then.

"Go home, Jordan. Go back to your perfect life, with your perfect blonde at Mozzarellas."

"What?"

My pulse pounded in my temples so hard my head hurt. "You heard me."

"I heard you say something stupid."

"You heard me call it for what it is." My voice rose, face flushed. "I am not the girl for you, Jordan. Not now, not tomorrow, not a year from now. So pack up and go home; there's no point waiting around."

"What the hell, Hex? That's bullshit. Someone once told me to fight for what's good in life, and you? You're what's good."

"You're trying to save me and I don't need saving." And that was the truth, I'd said it before; I was not his sister.

261

"This is just you trying to make up for what happened to Kayla."

He slowly rose from his chair, nodding. "Fine I'll leave. If that's what you want."

"It's exactly what I want," I ground out.

He stopped by the door. His bottom lip caught in his teeth. "You're wrong though. You are the girl."

If I didn't hold onto the anger I'd cry. "Just go."

He nodded again, shoved his hands in his pockets and walked away, calm and collected as anything. And that stung. It would have been easier if he'd yelled and shouted and fought back, but this ... this calmness ... it proved he didn't care.

With a shake of his head, Jordan strode out of my room, closing the door behind him, leaving me alone, which is exactly how it should have been. I didn't need anyone else in my life stuffing everything up. I didn't need people I grew to expect to be there. And I sure as hell didn't need Jordan Hays stealing my heart.

The pain meds sucked me back into sleep.

Chapter 30
Jordan

IT TOOK me ten minutes to find my brother holed up in an empty waiting room that I suspected belonged to the maternity ward. Lying across a row of chairs, he was sleeping. I had no idea how long I'd slept in Hex's room, but Logan looked as if he'd caught a half-decent sleep, too. With a hand on his shoulder, I shook him awake.

"We're leaving."

Yawning, Logan looked at me as if I were full of shit. "You dragged me on a three-hour road trip only to leave a day later?"

"I've got stuff to deal with and an exam tomorrow. It's time to go."

"You didn't care about the exam yesterday." His look morphed into that one where he weighed my words until he found the hidden meaning. Only there was no goddamn hidden meaning. If I wanted to be part of Hex's life, I needed to pull my shit together, like he'd told me on the ride here. What she'd just said proved that. She'd said she wasn't the one for me, because I thought she wasn't good enough. Well, that wasn't true. Maybe I was the one who wasn't good enough for her: Projecting my demons and fears onto her wasn't healthy.

I strode out of the room.

"All right-ee ..." Logan jogged to catch up. He didn't have much choice. Now I'd made up my mind, I couldn't get out of there fast enough. Hex would be okay. She had her aunt and her father—although I wasn't sure what was going on there. And chances were her mum would be all right. She didn't need me there when I was making her angry. And angry wasn't good when you were doped up to your eyeballs on pain meds. She needed to relax and let her body heal.

Outside, chirping birds greeted the new day while the sun inched its way higher in the sky. I sucked in a deep breath, the smell of morning fresh on the air. We reached Logan's piece of crap Corolla, and I held out my hand. He passed the keys over without argument. I jammed them into the ignition and pressed my feet on both the accelerator and brake, revving the guts out of the engine.

"Go easy on the old girl," Logan chided. He gripped the oh-shit handle as I took off out of the parking lot. For an old car, the Corolla sure handled well.

Navigating through town and out to the highway was much easier than it had been on the way here. In no time at all we were on the highway and about ten kilometres out. Logan released his death grip and settled back in the bucket seat. "That call from Mum yesterday ..."

Once I saw Hex, I'd forgotten all about it, but now my heart thudded again like it had when I'd seen the look on Logan's face as he took the call.

"Yeah."

"Dad's been arrested. They were short on money for some debt, so he sold off some of that pot he's always had growing under the house. Turns out he wasn't that smart about who he sold it too."

"Serves the old bastard right. Wait ..." The time she'd called was about money? Figured. "Is this why you lied to me?"

Logan sighed. "They rang begging for cash, again. I was trying to protect you."

"Loges, I don't need protecting. We stick together, all right."

He tapped his fingers on the gearstick. "What happened with your girl?"

"Nothing."

"Don't give me that bullshit."

I wasn't giving him anything. I knew the problem didn't only lie with Hex. It was mine too, which was why I travelled this road now. I needed to let go of my fears.

MORE THAN five hours later we pulled up at the one place I swore I'd never come. I let the car idle, taking in everything this place stood for. Ancient trees lined the perimeter of the huge square block of land. A low-lying stone fence barred the front entrance, but didn't stop any

265

damn person who wanted from entering, and wild grass had overrun the small patch of cracked tar that marked the parking lot. It sure wasn't anything fancy, but it was all my useless parents could afford—or rather, all they'd cared to afford.

I'd tried to visit her once before, not long after they put her here, but the thought of my sister lying in a wooden box, six feet under the ground, was too much. I never even made it past the front gates; just sat on my pushbike, staring at the rows of concrete slabs that were the only thing left of one hundred lives.

I killed the engine and Logan stirred, stretching his arms out front and opening his eyes. He'd been asleep for the past two hours, so wouldn't have noticed when I'd deviated from the route home. His lips thinned, the only indication he'd taken stock of where we were. Then he gave a single nod, as if this made sense. I didn't stop to explain; I needed to get this over with before I lost my nerve. I climbed out of the car and sucked back a breath of fresh country air.

Kayla and I had been close. Born barely a year apart and more similar in looks than Logan and me, she'd been almost like my twin. We were even in the same grade at school. Not sure how our mother managed that one, but I'd bet at four and five she was keen to get the last of her spawn off her hands for six hours a day. That was the kind of slack-arsed parent she was.

Kayla and I had shared the same friends most of our lives, and a shitty home life. We were each other's backbones when things got messy, not so much sticking up for one another as cleaning up the mess, helping each other deal. She would remind me about the grades I'd pulled in Science and Math when Dad called me dumb, and after his rampages, I'd clean up her up and tell her she was pretty. It was the truth, after all.

God, I missed her. Life hadn't been the same since she left me.

After Logan went to college, it was just the two of us, and you'd think we would have stuck together, grown closer, but I'd gotten in with the footy crowd and she'd moved in another direction. A direction I didn't realise she'd gone in until it was too late. Maybe it was me moving into Logan's old room that caused the rift, or maybe it would have happened anyway. If only I hadn't sunk so much time into the game, I might have been a better brother. I might have seen the clues before it was too late. I might have saved her.

I stepped over the stone fence and into the cemetery. There weren't many headstones here, unlike some of the newer, nicer places. A huge angel towered over the plot closest to the gate, casting a shadow over the weed-infested dirt path. It seemed as if the older headstones were closest to the entrance, but I tried not to think about how long they'd been here, or how empty the caskets would be now. I was doing this for Kayla—for Hex.

Winding my way through plots overgrown with grass so long it brushed my knees, I kept my focus on the far-left corner of the cemetery. Flowers grew as wildly as the grass, as if they'd spouted from dying bouquets. When I reached a plain concrete headstone with no border marking the plot, only a layer of dandelion weeds and grass, I stopped. My throat was so tight it could have been

267

used as a vice. My chest ached as if someone had pulled its laces too tight. I read the inscription.

KAYLA LOUISE HAYS
BELOVED DAUGHTER AND SISTER
TAKEN FROM THIS WORLD TOO SOON

Most of that was true. She was a beloved sister, and she did die far too young. I lowered myself onto my haunches and studied the plain font, the even plainer stone. It was only four years old, but already moss grew around the base on the western side. When she'd first been laid to rest, the ground had been open, and I was a little surprised the area was now flat and not a mound. *Yeah, don't think about that, 'cause then you'll think about what's beneath.*

Death sucked.

When someone died people turned up at the funeral, told you they were sorry, that it was such a tragedy. Then a few months later they all acted as if the person you cared about hadn't ceased to exist, even though you carried their memory around every day. You drew in the reminder they were no longer there with each breath you took and they didn't, with each moment you'd normally share. Even moving in with Logan hadn't helped. I still expected cold water to come flying over the shower screen if I took too long, still expected to hear her muffled sobs when I was lying in bed in a dark room. I still expected to see her face every morning across the table at breakfast.

Kayla had been beautiful. I knew that, even if I could

barely remember her features. Her eyes were dark, not brown like our mother's, or blue like Logan's and mine, but I'd be damned if I could recall the exact colour. I'd looked at them often enough when we talked or conspired—I should goddamn remember. It pissed me off that the image that sprung to my mind when I thought of her wasn't the pretty girl I grew up with. It was the alabaster skin of an unresponsive sister as I shook her, begging her to wake up. The sunken cheeks and too prominent bones on her slight frame. The dark marks under closed eyes. The colourless lips and limp body.

My heart hurt. Psychically hurt, as if someone squeezed it in a stud-lined fist, then when I inhaled, they squeezed tighter. Sixteen was too young to die.

She should still be here. I swallowed against the huge lump in my throat and dropped from my haunches onto my arse. She'd taken her own life and it wasn't fair or right, but I was helpless to change that. It was different here than when she crept into my thoughts any other time. Looking at the stone marker, I could almost feel her through my memories, as if she were sitting alongside me.

"I miss you every day, baby girl."

At the sound of Logan's voice, I dropped my forehead onto my knees. He didn't need to see the expression I knew was plastered across my face like a bloody billboard.

"And I think about you all the time. You'd be proud of us … Jordan and I … we don't put up with their bullshit, and your little brother …" Logan paused and I could tell he was fighting back tears, 'cause I was too. "He's a damn good person, but I guess you knew that already. He cares about people more than anyone else I know, which is why he's going to make a great nurse."

I felt his hand on my shoulder. He kept talking, as if being near her resting place made it all spew out of him. Maybe he'd been here before. It wasn't something we talked about.

"I met a girl ... she's beautiful, and kind, and she has this way of making everything perfect, no matter how crappy it is. I wish you could have met her. I'm in love with her, baby girl, and I'm going to ask her to be my wife."

He stepped in front of me and crouched before the headstone, tracing his fingers over Kayla's name. I fought the stinging in my nose, my throat, even in my eyes. Logan whispered something I couldn't make out and dropped his hand to the base of the monument. He paused there for a long moment, then finally rose, leaving a flower behind. Squeezing my shoulder again on his way past, he walked away.

I stared at the words so long they blurred together. I'd still do anything I could to change that day, even switch places with her. There was so much about the proceeding days I didn't know. She'd always called me her rock, but I wasn't there for her that night. Hell, if I was her rock, then Kayla had been my anchor, and for a long time I'd been floating adrift.

I didn't try to force the memories away; I embraced them, thinking every damn thing about her I'd been actively not thinking for years. How she'd stood up to our prick of a father, but he still beat her down with his hateful words. Finding her crying in our room time and again, after he'd called her a useless whore, a fat bitch, a good-for-nothing slut, usually for no more than leaving a dirty dish on the bench or failing to make sure he had cold grog in the fridge. But then there were the good memories, too: the practical jokes we'd played on Logan, the times we'd ditched school to visit him at college, the verbal sparring. That girl sure could argue.

I took a deep breath. Nothing about being here was easy, but I felt ready.

"I didn't meet a girl; I met a damn tornado. She's our type of people, Kays. You'd love her. She doesn't put up with anyone's shit and she's taught me how to have fun again. She's not perfect, or kind, or even beautiful. She's goddamn gorgeous. And she's so wrong it feels right. We fight and we play and do the most ridiculous things together, but if I could choose to only have one other person in my life for the rest of ... well, ever, I'd choose her."

My fingers wound around a long weed by my foot and I tugged it out of the ground.

"I stuffed up though ... I'm so damn scared of losing her the same way I lost you, that I tried to stifle her. That's why ..." I swallowed against that god-awful throat again. "That's why I have to let you go, Kays. I feel like I'm stuck in that August night with you lying in my arms and no matter what I do I can't save you. I can feel your barely-there pulse, I can see your chest struggling to rise with the shallowest breaths and I can't do a goddamn thing to help.

"And when I think about Hex, and how much she drinks, I think of that night and everything I did wrong that led up to it. I'm sorry I wasn't a better brother. I'm sorry I let Dad bully me into taking up rugby. I'm sorry I loved the game and used it to escape our crappy life. More than anything though, I'm so fucking sorry that I didn't take you with me. That I left you there to deal with the crap alone."

I swallowed; the simple movement making my eyes overflow.

"I'm so sorry, Kayla. I love you. I always will. But I can't hold onto the blame any longer. I did a lot of things wrong, but suicide was your decision, and it was a crappy choice, but I understand why you did it. Hell, at times it was so hard, that it could have been me who wound up here in the ground instead of you."

I'm not sure when I made the choice, but as I sat there staring at her name, and finally, allowing myself to feel the relief that she was gone rather than guilt, I slid Kayla's ring off my pinkie finger. Bringing it to my lips, I kissed the warm metal, then placed it on my sister's grave, right next to Logan's lone wild rose.

"The blame isn't either yours or mine." I touched my palm to the warm concrete as if I could actually feel her and choked out one last, "Love you, sis."

Then I turned and walked away.

Chapter 31
Hex

OTHER THAN daily visits from Aunt Susan, my room had been blessedly empty. That was a bad thing; it gave me plenty of time to think. I'd perfected the art of *not* thinking by watching all kinds of rubbish on the TV hanging from the roof of my room, and by listening to the staff gossip. Apparently a Doctor Kostal was the hottest thing about and everyone was trying to feel up his arms, which rumour had it were not only rock hard, but could hoist a girl off her feet. Sure was better brain fodder than worrying about Mum or thinking about things I couldn't have. Like Jordan Hays. Or things I didn't want, like Gregory Penton's attention.

After leaving Mum, he'd visited me exactly once. And I'd told him where to go. So colour me surprised when he'd appeared in the doorway of my room again days later, holding two espresso coffees. If he'd thought me accepting it was a sign of my forgiveness he'd be disappointed. I had no qualms about taking a coffee from anyone, friend or foe.

"Want a decent coffee?"

I focused on the daytime soap grazing my attention. I could feel him looking at me, but this show was more interesting than anything he had to say, even if it was a bunch of Botoxed wannabes in a weird five-way love triangle.

"I thought I'd never pry that boy away from you."

"He left. I told him too." *Even though I hoped he wouldn't.* "You should too."

Greg placed the disposable cup on my moving table.

"Alexi, I'm here because you're my daughter. I know I haven't always been the best father, but things will never improve between us if you don't allow to me try."

He backed out of the room.

No less than a minute later Aunt Susan poked her head around the door, a too-serious scowl filling the place of her usual smile. "Alexi," her voice was firm. "It's time you moved past this hatred."

"And it's time he disappeared again."

"Your father is trying."

I sucked the inside of my cheek into my bite to stop from buying into that conversation. I sure as hell wasn't interested in his efforts when he'd never cared before. She moved fully into the room, her fingers working at her solid gold earring. "Your father loves you. He's always made sure you're taken care of."

"Money doesn't replace love."

"Come on, sweetie, let's talk this out."

Anger curled my toes, soured my mouth. Both Susan

and her brother thought his money forgave his ultimate betrayal and that was bullshit. Money was a thing. It didn't fill empty hearts or mend broken souls. It didn't stop Mum drinking. And it sure as hell didn't excuse his rotten behaviour.

"You want to talk?" I asked her. "Alright, let's talk about him walking out of my life without so much as a goodbye. Let's talk about him missing the past five years of ... of EVERYTHING. Or, I know! Let's talk about him living with another woman while he was married to my mother, cheating on us both with a whole other family. Let's talk about that."

Her jaw worked, but I wasn't done yet.

"Let's freaking talk about me cursing their marriage."

If a person could turn to stone, Susan did just that. Not moving so much as her diaphragm. "Is that what you think?"

"I think," I said, "that he never wanted children, and when I came along, he sure as hell didn't want me. He would have been far happier if Mum had that abortion, right?"

She stared at me. The way her eyes bugged were confirmation that she knew he'd put the pressure on for a termination.

"Right?"

"Sweetheart—"

"Secrets! That's all it ever is."

"Alexi, it wasn't like that."

"Then what was it like, Aunt Susan?"

"It wasn't your fault that he left."

"Yeah, whatever." That was another lie. I was the hex

275

on their marriage. He'd said those exact words—*that child hexed our marriage*—and if they weren't true then I was diced ham. That man didn't give two hoots about me. Never had, never would. He only cared that it looked like he cared.

"He loves you."

I coughed into my hand, muttering bullshit. "Then how come he never visited me afterward? How come he didn't take me with him? Was I not good enough for his new family? Is that it?"

Susan dropped into the stiff-looking chair. "Your mother was fragile, and Riley ... she couldn't handle him, but you, you looked after her."

I almost choked on my own saliva.

"What sort of flawed logic is that?"

Susan sighed, a long drawn-out noise that made me notice just how old she looked. I had never noticed it before, but now, slumped in the visitor's chair, she looked tired. "I don't know why my brother did the things he did. The way he treated your mother was deplorable and I'm not going to make excuses for him, but Alexi ..." She reached out and took my hand. "... it is not your fault their marriage didn't work. So don't you ever think it had anything to do with you."

The walls holding everything inside me at bay must have burst, because in that instant my hatred turned to pain. Aunt Susan grew blurry as I blinked back all the emotion threatening to overwhelm my carefully constructed defences. She didn't understand.

"I heard them. More than once, fighting, and every time he threw the same thing back at her. Everything he did was for her ... it was always for her. You know what he said, Susan? He never wanted children. He had a life mapped out for them, living in the city, travelling the world, but then she fell pregnant with me and having kids was a mistake. The one thing that ruined their marriage. He said I was a mistake. He said I was a hex. So yes, I was the hex on their marriage."

She couldn't defend against his hateful words. They were too true. Susan looked at me like the proverbial cat had her tongue, or maybe it was shock that kept her from speaking. Finally, she said, "Is this why Jordan thinks your name is Hex?"

I dropped my gaze.

"Oh honey." She squeezed my hand, as the tears spilled from my eyes. This conversation was too much. I'd held it inside for so long, letting it out was overwhelming. It felt like releasing the floodgates on a bulging damn. But I didn't want to deal with it anymore—I wanted to push it aside and pretend it wasn't there. Go back to Oxley and forget all this family drama existed.

But once I got there I'd have to face Jordan, and that was almost worse. Whatever we'd had was over because I'd done what I did best: ruin relationships. I wasn't good enough for the likes of him and I never would be. I was broken, and he was whole, despite a past much worse than mine.

Jordan and I could never work. It was stupid of me to ever think I could be different. I had cursed every relationship in my life. This one wouldn't be the exception. If he really loved me he would have fought.

THE DOCTORS said I could move again if I didn't put any weight on my bung leg. Apparently it was healing nicely, and I should be out of here soon. My meds were down to over-the-counter stuff and the pain was more of an ache than the searing burn when I'd first woken. Yet still, I felt miserable.

It had been the longest week.

I thanked the nurse who helped me shift into the wheelchair by my bed. My leg stuck straight out at an angle fit for ramming anyone who got in my path. Unfortunately though, I didn't have control of the wheels. That honour lay with the orderly behind me, because apparently patients weren't fit to control their own movements. "All set?" he asked.

"Ready to roll."

As the older man pushed me through the hospital's corridors, I grew anxious. I hadn't seen her since the accident, and even though Aunt Susan assured me Mum was okay, I was still worried. What if they'd been downplaying her injuries? What if she wasn't out of danger at all?

After we'd rolled along a single corridor, we turned into another and only a few steps along, at the third door on the left, the warden pulled me to a stop. Turned out Mum wasn't very far from my room.

"Alexi can't continue being the parent here. I'm going to clean up. I need to ..."

I held up my hand to the orderly, and shook my head,

whispering, "Just hold off a minute."

My mother was still talking. "They sent a social services officer to talk to me and I know I shouldn't act the way I do. I never should have encouraged my daughter to drink with me when she was younger and I shouldn't be accepting her money or drinking so much now. I've wronged that girl in so many ways, Susan."

"Social services? How they get in touch? And just how often do you drink, Bronwyn?"

It sounded as if Mum were crying. The orderly gave me a should-we-really-be-eavesdropping look, but I didn't care.

"Being brought in with such a high blood alcohol content set off a trigger for counselling."

"I suspected as much," Susan said.

Yeah, I bet you alerted them.

The orderly's shoulder rose and dropped, then he walked around the front of my chair and pushed open a curtain partition that provided next to no privacy from the other three patients in the room. Propped up in an elevated bed, my mum looked haggard. Her tired eyes slid closed, before they made contact with mine. Susan smiled at me from where she sat in the visitor's chair.

He wheeled me right up to Mum's bedside, and tugged down something by the wheel. "There you go."

"Thanks."

The orderly nodded before turning away, his flat expression disapproving.

I sat there watching her pretend to sleep for a long while. She looked so much worse than me. All bruised, so that there was barely an inch of creamy skin on her swollen face. It hurt my heart to see her like that ... after everything we'd been through, everything I'd tried to protect her from. This didn't seem fair.

I wasn't quite close enough to reach her, but I wasn't a total invalid either, so I unhooked the brake on the side of my chair and rolled the massive wheel forward.

The moment my hand touched her leg, Mum's eyes opened.

"Sweetheart."

Once again emotion overwhelmed my stupid eyes. I swiped the excess moisture away.

"Don't cry, honey. I'm okay," she said. "How are you feeling? Susan tells me your leg—"

I replaced my hand on her blanket-covered leg. "Don't worry about me. Is your tummy okay? The doctors told me that you had a ruptured spleen."

"You shouldn't have dived in front of that car, honey."

"Mum! Of course I should have. Now answer my question. How are you, really?"

"I'm okay." She winced midway through a deep breath. "It hurts pretty bad, but the doctors are trying to keep the pain under control. There's a few broken ribs. That's probably the worst thing, since it makes breathing ..." she tried to draw a breath again, this time clutching her side "... a tad challenging at times. But what about you? Are they letting you out soon?"

"I should be out of here any day now. The doc said my leg is coming along nicely. The bone looks like it will knit smoothly, but I'll need to come back in about six weeks for a check up. Maybe, if I'm lucky I'll be ready to come off the crutches then." I tapped the cast on my ramrod leg.

"They've got me up and moving around on them now for short walks. I guess that means I'll be heading back to college soon. I've missed a bunch of exams, but surely I can sort something out so I don't fail."

She pulled her hand out from under the blanket and placed it on mine. By the look on Mum's face she was about to say something serious. Bad news, maybe. My tummy constricted.

"I love you, sweet Alexi, but it's time you put you first."

I swallowed against the huge lump in my throat. Put me first? Did that mean she didn't want me to care about her? Because if that were the case, it was impossible—she was my mother.

Deflection was what I did best, so I made a point of glancing around the room. The curtain partition blocked of this tiny space my mother recovered in. There was no TV, no comfy visitor's chair, only the bed, a straight-backed plastic chair Susan occupied and a sad cupboard that wasn't big enough to hold two brooms. "Didn't they give you a private a suite?"

"Those things are expensive without insurance." Of course we didn't have insurance. I frowned as the pieces came together, but she beat me to it. "Your father made sure you were well cared for."

"Of course he did."

She closed her eyes for a moment then focused on me, looking ten times stronger than she had a moment before. "We've depended on him too long, sweetheart. It has to stop, and it will stop as of now. When I get out of here, I'm going to get that house on the market. I'll find something smaller, better."

281

"Oh Mum, you don't have to do that. I know how much that house means to you. It's ... it's your home." My throat constricted. "It's where we've always lived."

She set her unwavering focus on me. "Alexi, honey, it's just a house. Remember our song?"

The words flooding my mind.

When life kicks you down, bite back the frown.

Just keep it together and all will eventually get better.

Nothing ... nothing ... nothing is worth letting you drown.

She watched me while I mouthed the words and when I'd reached the end, she said, "I've been letting us drown for too long."

Tears welled in my eyes ... and not because I didn't want her to move. I hated that damn house for all its memories. But now ... now, the pressure was off. I didn't need to go back to Oxley. I didn't need to finish off my course. I didn't even need to finish this semester's classes. But things weren't the same as they had been a few months ago. I felt like now I had direction; I actually knew what I wanted to achieve. I may not know what I wanted out of life, but I knew I loved English and I wanted to continue along with it. Without the threat of money hanging over me, maybe I'd find my path.

I placed my other hand over the top of hers. "I love you, Mum."

She closed her eyes, obviously exhausted from the the conversation. She'd never answered about how she felt, but clearly she was further from being released than I was. Broken legs, pins or not, weren't as serious as ruptured spleens and broken ribs, and god only knew what else.

I sighed, not wanting to return to the room my father had paid for. I'd rather stay here with mum, even when she was asleep.

"When are you going back to university?"

I flinched at the voice, although I knew Aunt Susan was in the room.

"Gee, give me a break." I indicated toward my stiff leg and we both smiled, albeit weakly.

"She's a strong lady." Aunt Susan shifted on her chair. "She's going to be fine."

"I know," I said. And in many ways I knew Mum would be all right. She seemed to have pulled herself together. She was holding down a job, getting out of the house, talking about moving forward, which was a darn side better than moping over her unfaithful ex-husband.

Maybe, just maybe, Mum didn't need me like she used to.

Chapter 32
Hex

A WEEK LATER, sitting at my computer and twirling a pen around my fingers, I never would have thought finding the right words would be so hard. I set my fingers on the keys.

Father,

I will no longer require your financial support. I can survive without the excess money.

Alexi.

A response came back almost immediately. That was a first. Usually it took days.

Dear Alexi,

As your father, it is my place to see to your needs. I will continue to pay for your tuition. Unless, of course, you have decided that your education is complete. Regardless of that, I want to be a part of your life. For what happened in the past, I'm sorry. I'm not asking your forgiveness, but it would mean a great deal if we could move forward.

Gregory Penton
CEO
Penton Holdings Pty. Ltd.

Again with the moving forward. I set my fingers over the keys again.

Father,

I don't need your money.

Alexi.

I sat there staring at the screen. The man was such a control freak he wouldn't allow me to cut myself off. I would have thought cutting Mum and I loose would be a relief, but no. My fingers tapped the keys so hard my nails clicked.

I intend to continue my education, but $3,000 a month is excessive and unnecessary. I will not be guided into studying the courses you think are the best fit. I'm an adult, and I will choose my own career path, even if I don't know what that path is yet.

My phone rang, his name flashing across the screen. I flicked the power off, but the man was persistent. My inbox pinged with another new email.

Your dorm fees are paid up until the end of the year. Can I pick you up for lunch on Saturday?

I took a deep breath. He was making an effort; maybe I should be the bigger person.

Okay.

When I went back to college things would be different. I'd get myself a part-time job, like Jordan's. Coupled with student support—if I could get it—it would be enough. I'd be studying the subjects I enjoyed, living on a budget, working harder, and partying less. Life was too short not to get the most out of it. I wasn't sure I could be the straight-laced girl Jordan seemed to want, but the path I'd been on wasn't the right one either.

****

I'd been home for a few days and my phone hadn't stopped buzzing, even though I'd assumed everyone would be too busy with exams to think of me. The constant texts made it hard to sleep, but it was nice to know people cared when I had thought no one did. I scrolled through the messages again, each one bringing a smile to my lips.

AMBER: Sorry I couldn't get away to come see you. But hell girl, I've missed you. You need to get yourself better and

286

come back here ASAP. You wouldn't
believe what's happened while you've been
recovering and I'm not getting into it over
text. Call me when you feel up to it.

NATE: Hope that leg of yours feels better.
Oxley isn't the same without you. See you
soon.

MCKENZIE: Sorry to hear about the
accident. I miss you like crazy, so make
sure you're back after the midyear break.
We need some girl time. <3

LUCA: Get better soon. We miss you.

MAX: Speedy recovery, Hex. Hope to see
you soon.

DONO: Heard about the accident. Don't worry
about anything here, I've got it under
control. Just concentrate on getting better.

And the one text I kept coming back to. The one I'd
read so many times that if it were paper it would have
been worn from overuse, tattered around the edges and
falling apart at the creases.

JORDAN: I accept that you're not Kayla.
I accept who you are and I want you. I
love spending time with you. I love the

dares. I love the way you give as well as
take. Basically,
I love you.
You're the girl I want; you always were.
You know where I am. I'll be waiting.

Chapter 33
Jordan

EXAMS AND semester were over. It was winter break, which meant exposure to the public display that was Logan and Olivia in the same room. Tonight they looked happier than ever, and I wondered if he'd popped the question yet. As sickly as their public displays were, I was kind of glad to be putting up with it for the next two weeks while on break. It was easier than being at Oxley without Hex. I hadn't heard from her since I'd left the hospital, even though I'd left a few messages. I wasn't really expecting her back since it had been exam period anyway, but I'd thought she'd at least respond. She'd have to be out of hospital by now. When I'd asked Amber as she was packing up her room, she'd merely said, "Honey, I don't know what's going on between you guys, but I don't think she's ready to talk to you."

Something thwacked my head. "Jordan!"

I glared at my brother who towered across the table with Olivia's posh napkin hanging from his outstretched hand. The dirt bag had hit me. I reefed it out of his hand and Logan dropped back into his seat. "Liv's asked you three times now how exams were."

"They were all right. Pretty sure I aced Human Bio and Science for Nursing was basic. Guess I must have stuffed that one up; it was too easy. How about yours?"

Liv stabbed her fork into her dinner. "I only had one. Sociology had a major assessment instead of an exam, and that was due a few weeks back. Same with Marketing."

"Right." I resumed eating my spaghetti—food choice number one of poor students everywhere—then thought better of it and tossed the balled-up napkin at my brother. "When you're a rich son-of-bitch I want better food for family dinner ... lobster, salmon, that fancy beef with the marbled fat."

Logan's fork stopped halfway to his mouth. "Sick of spaghetti, dude?"

"And pizza. Never dish either up to me when you're rolling in it and I'm on a nurse's wage. I get enough pizza at Mozzarellas."

My brother pointed his spaghetti-laden fork at me. "Free pizza is Carlos's way of showing he appreciates you."

"None of that fancy stuff for me," Liv said. "I prefer wholesome, normal meals. So while you're dining off the fine china, I'll have burger juice dripping down my arms, thank you very much. That's my ultimate meal; something I can sink my teeth into and enjoy without being ladylike."

Logan looked at her sideways. "Ultimate weekend

away?"

"Camping. In an actual tent. I've always wanted to try it."

The spaghetti lodged in my throat and I spluttered, trying to draw breath while they both looked at me, serious as sin. When I could speak again, I said, "In your dreams, princess. You'd hate camping."

Liv's eyes widened in the way a puppy's might. "I'd love it. Being so close to nature; smelling the trees, feeling the freshness in the morning air, hearing the babbling creek water, and oh my goodness ... waking to bird song." She sighed.

I raised a brow. The girl was delusional. Logan draped an arm around her shoulders and said, "If Liv wants to try camping we'll try it."

"Ten bucks says you'll be home before sunset."

Olivia's hand shot across the table. "Ten bucks and a week's worth of pizza and you've got a deal."

"Done." We shook on it.

WE WERE ten minutes from the end of second half and finishing the game was a mere formality. We'd flogged Evan's Hall before we'd even hit halftime. Sweat dripped between my shoulder blades, trickling down my spine. The other team were in possession of the ball, but on their last tackle, and I thought Cade was gonna let them run it since they couldn't win anyway. But the back rower was in there before I could dash down the side. He grabbed the opposition around the waist and tackled him to the ground. As the other bloke bucked to get him off and Cade held firm, the ref blew the whistle and called held. Both teams took position.

"Hey, Sissy, get back to your nurse's station. You don't belong on here with the real men, girl's game on Tuesday."

Ignoring the bad attempt at a sledge, my eyes locked on Cade's a second before he toed the ball back and our winger picked it up, passing it off toward me. I caught the thing, tucked it under my arm and bolted for all I was worth. Air seared my throat as I pushed myself to run harder. They wouldn't catch me today. This team didn't have a good runner and the try line was only feet away. With my sights set on a try, I didn't even take the time to glance behind me. I'd be home safe in seconds.

And done!

I dove, slamming the ball into the ground.

Vaguely aware of cheers erupting around me, I rolled onto my back and god, I'd missed this. The adrenaline of pushing myself to outrun another player, the competition of being better than the other team, the feeling of winning ... it was as if I'd never left the field. I jumped up and waited for our kicker to reach position, not believing I'd hated playing that first year after Kayla, when I was doing it for Logan. Footy had made me selfish at the cost of my sister, but it wasn't me who had popped those pills and told her to swallow. It wasn't my fault, and now I realised I could play without being consumed by the footy life. It was possible to keep things separate and play for the love the game, nothing more. Hex had been right.

I tossed the ball to Luca. The clock read 79:48, seconds from the game's end. He settled the ball on its tee and the whistle blew. With one swift kick the ball soared through the air, aligned perfectly. The white goal posts pointed, like fingers, toward the heavens and that ball flew smack bang between them.

This time I was fully aware of the cheering crowd. Not that the sidelines were packed, only a handful of spectators from each of the team's dorms, but it was enough to make me feel as if we'd won the NRL grand final.

The ref blew time and that was it.

Feeling like a million bucks, I slapped a few backs, shook a few hands, and jogged off the field to where Logan sat with Nate. They got on well, but then I'd never come across someone Logan couldn't talk to. Everyone liked the guy. They both stood at my approach and Logan's grin made this doubly worthwhile. He tossed me a water bottle. "Great game, little bro."

"Not too shabby, hey?" I squirted liquid over my head then gulped down the remainder.

Nate shuffled on the spot. "You had them in the first ten minutes. Man, no wonder Cade begged you to play."

I dragged a hand through my wet hair. Now I'd stopped moving, the air felt rather cool. The middle of winter was always cold though. All the out-of-towners had been complaining, but I'd been in this place for almost five years and I guess I'd become acclimatised.

Nate looked toward Oxley. "We'd better get out of here, mate. Amber will have a fit if we're late."

"You guys going together tonight?"

293

"Aren't we all? She said she'd drive."

"Right."

The Oxley ball wasn't on my list of priorities, but Amber had made a big deal out of me tagging along, even if I was the perpetual third wheel. Between her and Liv there was no getting out of going. Although she wouldn't be there, Liv had tagged it as an Oxley highlight.

"Have fun," Logan said. "And pick up."

Nate chuckled. "A chick in the sack is exactly what this sucker needs. Nothing like a new ride to forget about the last one."

"Catch you later." I told Logan, ignoring Nate and the dumbass smirk on my brother's face. The dirt bag knew that was exactly what the councillor chick he'd hooked me up with had said. Amrita wasn't your typical shrink, but she'd turned out to be exactly what I needed. She'd told me in no uncertain terms that it was time to move on. I couldn't make Hex reach out unless she was ready, and there was a real possibility that she may never be. Not that we talked about Hex much; the topic mostly stayed on Kayla.

As we walked back to Oxley, Nate kept his mouth shut. Probably a good thing, too, since my thoughts had turned to Hex and that always made me feel angry. I didn't want to admit, even to myself, that I missed her like hell. I'd assumed she'd return when classes resumed, but we were a week into semester two and she wasn't back.

LESS THAN an hour later, showered, dressed in a suit—or as close to one as I owned—I chatted to McKenzie while Nate and I waited for Amber, who was not having a fit for us being late when it was already a good fifteen minutes past time and she was the only one not there.

I had no idea what the brunette beside me droned on about. I was too stuck on not really wanting to be there, but Liv had insisted it was a college experience not to be missed, and who was I to argue with her? A fresher, that was who, she'd told me.

Max snuck up behind McKenzie, sliding his arms around her waist and peppering her neck with kisses. Luca wasn't too far behind, but stood a little back. The dynamics in their trio seemed to have shifted sometime over the winter break.

The click of heels on the tile path drew my attention to Amber, emerging from the block D stairwell. It wasn't where she lived, but she made it halfway around to where we waited then stopped, clutching a small bag in front of herself. The short red dress she wore was pretty; I wasn't sure why she wanted to hide behind the bag when she usually flaunted everything she had.

"We ready to go, boys?" Her stare roamed the full length of Nate then moved through the rest of our group, before settling back on him. "You all sure scrub up well."

Spurred into movement, Nate walked around the path to meet her and snagged her hand. "You don't look half bad yourself, Reynolds."

"See you there," Amber told our friends.

"In time to rock this town! Let's go, boys." McKenzie

extracted herself from Max's embrace only to link her arms through his and Luca's and they were off.

When we reached the RAV4, Nate's arm hung over Amber's bare shoulders as he leaned close and whispered what I suspected by her giggles was something dirty. This was gonna be a long night. Maybe I could bow out early and leave these two to hook up properly. It sure didn't seem like the arrangement I'd had with Penny, so it was about time Nate manned up and made it official. They'd been flirting for more than six months now.

I took the back seat and the ride there wasn't too bad. They managed to keep it kid-friendly.

The Oxley ball was a formal event held off-campus, and this year's social committee had gone to town, booking a room at the local golf club. We walked into the function room and throngs of people made it impossible to see the bar. Oxley wasn't a huge dorm, but we sure filled out the room. Helium balloons and those tiny blue lights were the only decoration, yet it looked a million bucks.

Amber giggled beside me and it was definitely time to work the crowd. I scanned the room, searching for Dono or anyone really. With no results, I moved through the sea of people, seeking an out.

"Hey, Sis! Great game today."

I turned to my left and sure enough it was Cade, surrounded by his footy followers. I shouldered my way past a group of girls to reach my new teammates. The captain passed me a full schooner and Luca said, "To Sis. About time you joined the team."

Everyone raised his or her glass.

"To a team who knows how to win," I said.

296

They all skulled their drinks while I took a sip. These blokes weren't that bad. They weren't the diehard jocks I'd assumed they'd be. It turned out my high school team from back home had been the exception, not the norm.

The music changed and my attention swung to whoever was spinning the beats. Turned out it was one of the Oxley kids I didn't know that well. But this song ... shit, I'd know it anywhere. I was suddenly transported back to the first time I'd stepped into block D and saw the room with an enviable speaker set up. My heart kicked up a beat at the sound of Quite Renegade. But it was ridiculous; Hex wasn't there. She hadn't come back to college since the accident, almost a month ago.

I settled back against the tall table, and the guys talked around me, but my focus stayed on the song's lyrics. They'd never meant much before. Now though, it was as if they spoke directly to me.

You're not who you were meant to be
And I can't be the one that you need
If we only belong together in dreams
That makes life a fallacy
Because you ... you're my normalcy

...

...

...

Wait! Don't look away
Need to live for today
And keep the focus future-bound
For you ... you ... you are the love I've found
Live

Love
Survive

I took another swig of beer. Was there really a normalcy? I doubted it.

As I lowered my glass, my gaze landed on her.

I was wrong, it wasn't bullshit, because she was here and right now everything was more goddamn right than it had been in months.

Hex was better than normalcy, she was what made life great, and I'd be damned if she wasn't going to be my future.

Wearing a dress the colour of sunrise, she looked stunning, despite the crutches. Her hair had been re-dyed to include purple, matching the dress, and somehow it was longer. The tips, alternating between bright blue and light purple, fell about her shoulders in curls that barely covered the exposed skin at her chest. God, she was more beautiful than ever.

Now she was standing in front of me, I wasn't letting her leave. I strode across the room, and stopped less than a foot away.

"Alexi ..."

Her breasts rose with her breath and it was damn hard to keep my eyes on her face until she spoke. "Don't call me that. It doesn't feel right."

"Nor does Hex, because you're not. You're so much more than that, so what can I call you? Because I'm not settling for 'hey, you.'"

Her lips quirked up and my chest filled with warmth, because that was all me. I'd put that gorgeous smile on her face, and damn, I wanted to do it again. Every day.

"Lexi. Call me, Lexi."

"Well, Lexi, I think you should dance with me."

She cast a pointed look at her plaster-covered leg.

"That's no excuse." I extracted the crutches from under her arms and rested them against the nearby chair. Then I slid an arm around her waist, and hers came around mine as she was forced to lean on me for support. My heart kicked up a notch; my mouth flooded. She was a little unsteady on her feet, but I directed her to the edge of the dance floor then steadied her with a solid grip on her hips. Lexi's green eyes shone sadly as they held mine, each of us staring, not dancing, not even moving, probably not so much as blinking.

"I got your message, and I didn't know how to reply. But right now? This is me, coming to you. Jordan, I ..."

"Shut up." I pressed a finger to her lips. "Love isn't about saving or changing a person. It's about loving the person as they are, and I'm pretty damn sure that I love you. So I'm not about to force you to change, because you're fucking wonderful the way you are. God, Lexi, you make me feel alive in a way I haven't felt in years. You make me whole."

Her lips puckered beneath my finger and before I could pull away she kissed it, but I wasn't finished.

"You're wild and crazy and the most fun person I know."

She kissed my finger again and this time I did move it, sliding my hand to the back of her head. Looking into her eyes, which were clearer than I'd ever seen them, was the best feeling because her expression held everything I'd hoped it to and so much more. I wanted to kiss her so badly, but I needed to know how she felt first.

"So, I was wondering … since ahh … you're here and I'm here … and I've stopped being a tool …" I studied my foot, toeing the floor. The grade-school stupidity was so us, I tried not to smirk and failed miserably as I brought my focus back to her. "Do you wanna be my girlfriend?"

She dove forward so fast her lips clashed with mine, the force pushing us both back. If it wasn't for god only knew whose steadying hand on my shoulder we would have both been on the floor. I grabbed each side of her head in my hands and parted her mouth with my tongue, delving inside, feeling every inch of her palate and lips and sweet tongue, tasting all there was of her to taste. God, I'd missed this girl. This crazy, fun, impulsive girl. I held her against me, kissing her with everything I could give. Well, almost everything, if I was being honest. The rest would have to come later, when we didn't have an audience. Her arms circled me, pulling us together until we touched at the chest, thigh, hip. Her breasts pressed against me, her heart beating as widely as mine, and that was my undoing. If I didn't pull away now, I wouldn't be able to, and we'd both get kicked out of this stupid ball for public indecency.

Maybe that wouldn't be a bad thing.

I broke the kiss, sliding my hands from her face, down her shoulders and pulling her into a hug.

"Yes," she said, leaning against me, and I wound my arms all the way around her waist. She laid her cheek against my chest, and god this felt good. I never wanted to let her go.

We weren't dancing, weren't moving—just standing there in the middle of the dance floor. Someone behind me cheered, then someone else joined in. Amber and Nate, I'd bet.

"Really?"

"I thought you'd never ask," Lexi said.

I kissed the top of her head. "I thought you'd tell me to piss off."

"Never."

"Well, actually back at the hospital—"

"Jordan ..."

"Yeah?"

"Don't ruin it."

I wound her long hair through my fingers as we slowly began to move to the music.

All along I'd been telling her to stop, when I should have been saying wait. Wait for me. Wait for me to realise that Kayla's death wasn't my fault; that I didn't need to save her, but to embrace the present.

Hex, knew how to live, how to suck the most out of life, and somewhere along the way I'd forgotten it was even possible. But from now on, I intended to live life as hard as I could with this girl at my side and never stop.

Epilogue
Hex

STANDING OUTSIDE the single-storey, brick apartment, I'd never been this nervous. It was utterly ridiculous, but no matter how many times I told myself that, nothing changed. My tummy still jittered as if it were full of rolling marbles that swished whenever I moved, and my head ached like a bitch. Jordan's hand was the only thing anchoring me, and thank god for that or I might have been lost to the massive nothingness of *what if*. What if they didn't like me? What if they thought I was a loser? What if I wasn't good enough for them? What if I was too childish?

"Relax." Jordan leaned across and kissed my cheek. "Logan and Liv are going to love you."

True to form, he didn't stop at one kiss. Jordan's lips grazed my cheek again, then my jaw. His tongue flicked across the space under my earlobe as he kissed and sucked his way to my shoulder. My tummy tingled and my lips ached for him to reach them, but I backed up, trying to retain a little decorum since we were standing on his brother's doorstep after all. The same brother on whom I wanted to make a good impression.

My back hit the bricks and Jordan advanced, his hands pinning my shoulders to the wall. "And Logan ..." He placed a soft kiss right on the hollow of my throat. "... well, you already met him and ..."

I tipped my head back, relishing in the warmth that spread through my tummy, down my thighs, made *everything* tingle. Next those torturous lips made light work of the soft, sensitive skin beneath my chin, edging ever closer to my mouth. I might have moaned.

"... he's not scary; he likes everyone. You'll love him, too."

Jordan's lips slid over mine, finally claiming the one place I wanted his mouth most. Where I could feel the strongest connection between us. I traced the line of his lips with my tongue and Jordan didn't disappoint. He parted his mouth, letting me taste his salty breath as I deepened our kiss. Jordan matched my kiss with such wanton need that maybe this dinner was a bad idea. We should probably turn around and go home to bed.

His hands slid down the length of my waist, leaving a trail of goose bumps before his fingers inched beneath the band of my jeans. This time I definitely groaned and he leaned into me, pressing his entire body against mine. We most certainly needed a room, and soon.

"Jordan, let the girl come inside."

I tried to pull back as my face burst into a blush so hot it burned at what could only be Jordan's brother, laughing.

But Jordan didn't even seem to notice, just continued brushing his fingers against my lower back as his mouth moved over mine, more urgent now.

Way to make a first impression.

Unable to do anything else, I clamped my lips shut and Jordan groaned. "That's no fun."

"Best save the fun for later." I winked and the grin he gave me almost made me change my mind, but this was important.

"I'll hold you to that." He wound his fingers through mine, smoothing his thumb over my lengthened nails. Jordan pulled me through the front door, which stood open, and was now, thank my lucky stars, empty of his brother.

I blushed again as we entered the apartment and the prettiest, peppiest girl this side of Sydney's inner-city suburbs stood next to the giant hunk that was presumably Logan. Although he'd been at the hospital, I doubted I would have been able to pick him out from a line-up of ten guys. I was too out of it that day, and he didn't look one bit like Jordan. With dirty blond hair that brushed his shoulders, the only thing about it similar to Jordan's was the waves. He wore the same sexy stubble of not shaving for a few days, but his was light where Jordan's was dark, and even his eyes were different in everything but that mischievous sparkle. I could tell this guy loved life, by that twinkle.

The girl extracted herself from Logan's side and extended a slender, bejewelled hand toward me. Her jewellery wasn't just gold; it had real stones. But it was her designer jeans and brand-name heeled boots that made her look preppy; or maybe it was the long auburn hair styled into perfect loose curls. I was as different to her as scrawny ducklings were to swans.

"I'm Olivia. It's so, so great to meet you."

Her grip was firmer than I'd expected and warm, like her gaze. Olivia didn't look at me with judgement or jealousy, or even disgust. Instead she inclined her head toward the kitchen and said, "Come, I'll pour us each a drink and we can chat while I stir the gravy."

I snuck a glance at Jordan, who was busy acting like a total guy with his brother, with one arm locked around Logan's head while the other knuckled his hair. What were they, twelve?

"They're such children," Olivia said on a sigh that made me think she thought it was cute. It kind of was.

I followed her into a kitchen that was so clean I doubted a proper meal had ever been cooked on the hotplates.

"Wine?"

I didn't want to appear rude, but I hadn't had a drink since the accident and the thought of one now didn't sit right. When Jordan had asked me to stop drinking that time, I'd fought the urge with every breath and now here I was, sickened by the thought of sharing a wine with a girl I wanted to like me. Sometimes life was weird. "No thanks."

"How's your mum? I heard she was in hospital recently."

Olivia was the picture of politeness. I was sure she'd heard much more than that.

"I'm going home to visit her soon. Jordan said he'd

come with me to check out the house and make sure everything's fixed, so she can put it up for sale."

Olivia shook her head, a small smile on her rosebud lips. "Those two guys are the sweetest. You wouldn't think they'd practically raised themselves. Logan's taking me camping next weekend, just because I've never been."

"Wow, you guys have fun."

"Oh, we will." She smiled as she watched the spoon swirl the brown liquid. I hoped we'd be good friends. I'd never really had a friendship that wasn't centred around partying, but hopefully Olivia would be the first.

"Jordan tells me you're studying too." It was more a question than a statement ... something to open up conversation.

"Yeah, I'm studying Marketing. Hopefully, I've passed all my courses, then next year should be my last. How about you?"

"I'm doing an Arts degree ... looking to major in English Lit, I think. They gave me special exemption from exams due to the leg, so I have to sit them next week."

"Good luck."

She moved from the stove to the bench where she had four plates laid out and began to serve up. Seemed she'd forgotten about the wine for now, which suited me. After Olivia had piled food—that looked far better than what was on Oxley's menu tonight—onto the plates, I helped her carry them out to the table. Jordan and Logan were already there. Each had a beer in hand, and the way that they sat made them look more like brothers than they had before. Each with an ankle balanced on the opposite knee, they were the image of relaxed.

Jordan looked up, and gave me a grin full of promises for later. I placed our dinner on the table and slid into the seat beside him. It took all of half a second for his hand to find my knee, trail up to my thigh and become dangerously close to inappropriate for company. He leaned in toward me and whispered, "When we get back to Oxley, I'm going to make you wish we never have to leave the bedroom again."

"I dare you to follow that through."

"Game on, baby." He dropped a none-too-chaste kiss at the base of my ear before he settled back in his seat.

Sitting at that table with my love and his family, I felt as if I'd finally found where I belonged. I'd found the one place where I could be me without being fake. I'd found what I never knew was missing. This is what I'd been waiting for all along.

Start the **Oxley College Saga**
with Logan and Olivia in *Shh!*

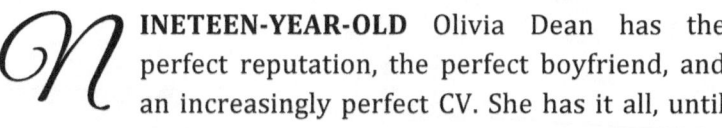

What do you do when you're asleep?

Shh!

Oxley
College
Saga

STACEY NASH

*N*INETEEN-YEAR-OLD Olivia Dean has the perfect reputation, the perfect boyfriend, and an increasingly perfect CV. She has it all, until

Christian breaks up with her in public, calling her out as a self-gratifying sexoholic: the kind that plays solo. But Olivia doesn't masturbate all night — the only thing she does is sleep ... right?

Now all the boys on campus seem to want her attention for the absolutely wrong reason — including resident hottie, Logan Hays. He's pulling out his best moves to gain her attention, so resisting his sexy charm is hard work. With rapidly slipping grades, a disturbingly lurid reputation and demanding parents, Olivia must discover the truth behind her rumoured sleeping problem. If she doesn't, the perfect life she's worked so hard for may slip away, including the one person who has Olivia breaking all her rules — Logan.

What do you do when you're asleep?

Available now

from all major etailers.

Continue the **Oxley College Saga** with book three; coming late 2015.

Stop?

Life's easy when everything's fake.

Two years ago Savannah West had it all: popularity, good grades and a family who loved her, but how quickly things can change. Living half a state away doesn't stop the painful memories of her past ripping her heart in two when she thinks of her family. What's left of it. And sometimes lies are easier than coping with the truth.

The thing she didn't bank on was Dane Beaumont. A blast from her horrendous past, he's the last person she expected to run into at college, and that's not just because he knows the truth. Hot as sin, he's more off-limits than an illegal drug, but damn it, staying away isn't easy when he insists on looking out for her. Dealing with the reality of a lost future, a shattered family, and no idea of her place in the world, Savvy must face the guy who tears down all her carefully placed walls and pull herself together. It's time to grow up.

Acknowledgements

This story was one I wanted to tell right from the first moment Jordan appeared in Shh! calling Logan out for not hooking up with the girl he clearly liked. I probably should have written Savvy first, but Jordan had my heart, even though I knew his story would be difficult and heart-breaking to tell.

It's really hard to write a book like Wait! without it coming across as too preachy or too blasé. Thankfully I have stellar beta readers, who helped me find the fine line to tell Hex and Jordan's story. These ladies are my rocks in the writing world. Thank you to ST Bende, Lauren McKellar, and Anabel Gonzalez. Without the three of you Jordan would never have had his own story, because I never would have kept writing when it got so hard I thought I couldn't salvage it. You three ladies were my constant cheerleaders, telling me that Jordan would turn out just fine and you were right.

To my very talented cover artist Kim of KILA Designs and my equally talented formatter Max of Max Effect, thank you for the beautiful art you both created to make my book beautiful.

Once again Keely Crosbie deserves a special mention for answering all of my questions about life at university. Thank you for always responding to my question filled emails and even tossing me some ideas. You are truly awesome!

The friendship and support from my many writing buddies at Hunter Romance Writers, Story Queens of Aus, and Aussie Owned and Read is always appreciated. You ladies are my tribe.

As always, the biggest thank you goes out to my family. Without their love and support I could never write like I do. I feel like my husband's name should be on the covers too, because I spend so many hours sound boarding ideas off him. Just one of the many reasons why I love him dearly.

To my street team (the Nash-alcoholics), all my blogger friends, and the countless readers that took time out of their day to read about Oxley College, thank you. You guys are what make more books possible. So, thank you for reading my books and for your support!

About the Author

Stacey Nash calls the Hunter Valley of New South Wales, Australia home. An area nestled between mountains and vineyards, its history and culture have always called to her. Stacey has loved reading for as long as she can remember, so it's no wonder she finally opened a word document and wrote chapter one. Stacey made her publishing debut in 2014 with a young adult novel titled *Forget Me Not*. Writing for the young and new adult market, Stacey's books are all adventure filled stories with a lot of adventure, a good dose of danger, a smattering of romance, and plenty of KISSING!

You can connect with Stacey via

FACEBOOK:
www.facebook.com/StaceyLeeNash

TWITTER:
@staceynash

GOODREADS:
www.goodreads.com/author/show/
7150198.Stacey_Nash

To stay up to date with new releases and upcoming titles be sure to sign up for Stacey's newsletter at
www.stacey-nash.com

www.ingramcontent.com/pod-product-compliance
Lightning Source LLC
Chambersburg PA
CBHW020249200626
46816CB00001BA/199